FINN AGAIN

LYNDA MEYERS

HALLWAY
11

DEDICATION

To all the lost boys.

———————

"We're all just walking each other home"

—RAM DASS

finn *again*

1

The Irish are always quick with a story, especially if they've been drinking, which for a lot of us is most of the time. Or maybe for most of us it's a lot of the time. Either way, drinking and storytelling seem to go hand in hand.

I know this better than most. I grew up in the pubs.

My father was a famous footballer in England. He even played for the national team, then met my mum in a pub just outside London when the team came back to celebrate a particularly fine victory.

If you asked him, he would say it was love at first sight. If you ask her, it was mayhem that night, and she simply had too much to drink. At any rate, fall in love they did, and though her father didn't approve, they married, and he whisked her off to a house in Ireland where they had me and my baby sister, Eiran.

My father took his fame and his earnings and began opening restaurants and pubs of his own all across Ireland and a few in England as well. For a long time, we didn't live rich, but we always lived well. Eiran and I spent our summers and breaks from school traveling with our parents all about the countryside, so he could keep an eye on it all.

While Da conducted business, Mum was always carting us off to the nearest city or township to see whatever history may have existed there. We must have visited every museum, art gallery and exhibit known to man, but it was her way of keeping us occupied and instilling a bit of culture in us. It also taught us a fair deal more about history than most of our professors knew in school.

After my granddad died, Mum spent more and more time with my grandmother at their estate outside London, but Da mostly stayed in Ireland. They never stopped loving each other, they just got along better when they weren't living together, and neither one was willing to give up their lifestyle for the other. Mum preferred England. She said it suited her better and that was probably true.

Besides, by the time we were ready for prep, my grandmother insisted on sending us to boarding schools in England. She said it was time we learnt some of the finer points of life, and Grams wasn't someone you argued with. Mum agreed, and Da stayed out of it.

I think Grams was convinced it was all a matter of breeding, and as such you could breed things out of a person. The Irish pub culture had never set well with her, but like a thoroughbred that just knows how to run, I swear it was there, in my blood. So was football. Except for me it was Gaelic football I came to love.

Gaelic football is probably unlike any other sport you've seen. It's a combination of soccer, rugby and basketball - kind of like Quidditch, but without the broomsticks. I played every chance I got–in the schoolyard and on club teams and even at college. Of course, I often wound up at the pubs afterward, even before I was of age, and if my mates and I got kicked out of one place, I'd bring them over to one of Da's pubs and we'd figure out how to get served anyway. As you can imagine, that made me one of the more popular chaps around, especially with the girls.

As it happens, girls don't have much of a tolerance for beer, and almost none for whiskey, but at fifteen, I'd developed quite an appetite for all three. Da would look the other way when I came home langered, or even drive the girl home if it got too late. After all, he'd been a boy once.

Da understood, but Mum was appalled.

If I was staying in England, she never heard me come home. The house was just too big, and her wing was on the opposite side of the courtyard. Most of the time I snuck in through the servant's quarters and made my way through the back kitchens. I'm certain she wasn't oblivious to my habits, but all that good breeding she talked about forced her to pretend I wasn't sick with the Irish flu next morning.

Still, I knew better than to bring girls home to Gram's house. The one time I tried, I was lectured on honor and decency until I thought I might suffocate. We learned the ropes fairly quickly, Eiran and I. When we were in England, we acted like good little Brits, and when we came to Ireland, it was usually to have some fun.

We had it pretty well sorted.

Sort of.

Eiran loved Ireland and embraced the culture. She did well in the English schools, but as soon as she was old enough for university, she headed back to Dublin to attend Trinity College for nursing. Nursing fit Eiran. She was a softhearted sort who was all the time taking in wounded animals and the like. Ended up marrying one of her patients, as a matter of fact, but that's another story.

It's not that I minded English schools. I felt very comfortable in England and could easily switch accents and mannerisms depending on the crowd. When I was at Eton I fit easily with the Brits, but home in Ireland I fell right back into step with all my mates. Clearly, I was half Mum and half Da. Two more different people could not exist, and yet they did. They inhabited the same body.

Never did get over my penchant for women or whiskey. I loved them both in equal measure, and often at the same time, so that worked out famously for a while. Attending an all boys' boarding school can make meeting girls something of a challenge, but we always seemed to manage.

For all my shenanigans I still finished top of my class at Eton and went on to Oxford. That made Mum and Grams very happy, and since Grams was paying, it paid to make her happy. I was studying computer science and business with moderate results and females with great success, the former being a probable result of the latter. Still, girls back home were a lot more fun than most, so while I was at school, I spent more time with my mates and while I was home, I spent a lot more time chasing skirts.

On holiday, my routine went something like this: Get off the train, walk home, change out of my dress blues, walk down to the pub and meet up with my mates, who were almost always there ahead of me. Whoever got in last had to buy a round immediately, so I always made sure I had plenty of money with me.

Walking to the pub assured that I wouldn't have to drive home, of course. Stumbling was the preferred method of transport for intoxicated persons and, as it turns out, is a lot less nauseating than being trapped in a moving vehicle.

One particular break I actually made it first to the pub, so I sat down at our favorite spot at the bar and proceeded to revel in my success. I had just ordered a shot of Jameson's with a pint of Guinness to chase it when the door opened, and in walked the most beautiful girl I had ever laid eyes on. At eighteen I thought I'd seen it all. I thought I knew beauty, but this girl was nothin' like I'd ever known. Blonde hair and gray-green eyes that could peel the paint off a fence.

She sat down next to me, and I swear my stomach flipped over on itself. I offered to buy her a drink, but she refused. In fact, I tried every trick I knew, but she'd have none of it. Eventually she looked straight at me and smiled.

"Do you find this amusing?" I asked, putting my elbows up on the bar.

"Do I find what amusing?" She mirrored my actions.

"Are you going to let me buy you a drink or not?"

"Are you even old enough to drink, young Finn?" She winked at me as if she knew something that I didn't, and yet I couldn't place her.

"Do I know you?"

"Well, I don't know 'bout that but sure I know you Finn McCarthy. I used to watch you get your nappy changed."

My head rocked sideways. "Excuse me?"

She smiled again. "You really don't remember, do you?"

"Believe me, if you were in a memory, I'd have it with me right here." I patted my chest.

"Save it for a girl who's actually going to shag you, will you?" She flagged down the bartender. "I'll have what he's having."

Tom winked at me. "All right, miss."

She turned toward me and crossed her arms over her chest. "He doesn't think I can do it does he?" She inclined her head toward Tom without taking her eyes off me.

"Do what?" I matched her gesture in mock salute.

She was neither impressed nor amused. "Resist your charms, of course."

"I have charms?"

"Don't you?" She smiled as she downed the whiskey, then nodded toward mine, which I hadn't touched yet.

I followed suit, banging it down on the bar to signal Tom for a refill. "That all depends." I wiped my mouth.

"On what?"

"On who the hell you are and why you've seen my mickey, of course." I smiled again and took a long sip of beer.

"Well, don't worry, I'm sure it's grown since then." She sipped her beer and looked straight ahead, leaving me to wonder just what kind of game we were playing. It's not that I disliked this game, I just wasn't sure what the rules were exactly.

I studied her face, which was artfully proportioned. "*Please* tell me we're not related."

"Would that be so awful?"

"Only if I had my heart set on shagging you. Otherwise no." I smirked.

She laughed heartily. At least I could make her laugh. That had to be worth a couple of points.

She let out a long sigh, smiling all the while. "My older sister Maggie used to watch over you and Eiran. I tagged along a few times. Perhaps you don't remember."

I searched my memory banks and found nothing but a lanky, buck-toothed, flat-chested young sprite who couldn't possibly be the girl sitting before me now. She had to have been a few years older than me, but still, this couldn't be the same person.

I just kept staring at her. "Well, braces for sure, but if you're the person I'm thinking of, I'm not the only one whose parts grew in nicely."

She grinned intentionally, revealing straight, white teeth.

"Regan?"

She nodded once with some satisfaction. "Nicely done. I see Eton taught you a bit of deductive reasoning."

As if on cue, the bottle of Jameson's showed up. "Ready for another?"

Tom poured us both a shot and walked away, shaking his head.

She held hers up in salute. "To fully grown parts!"

"I'll drink to that."

Two shots of whiskey in as many minutes and I started to feel the burn, but she looked as if she could match me all night long. I noticed that a few of my mates had come in, but when they saw me with a beautiful girl they knew enough to leave me alone. They settled into a booth in the back to watch the show, and I was determined not to disappoint.

"So, how do you like Oxford?" She asked, still looking straight ahead.

"Better question." I leaned forward on the bar. "How is it you know so much about me?"

She hesitated. "You caught me. I've been stalking you for years now. Got a thing for younger men, you see."

"Oh yea?" I raised one eyebrow. "And yet you refuse to shag me. How tragic. For you, I mean."

Her laugh relaxed into a huge grin. "Maggie saw your da last year at Michaelmas. He said you'd been top of your class at Eton and looking at Oxford."

"Well that does make more sense."

"But besides that, I just saw you on campus the other day."

"What?"

"I'm home on holiday as well."

"You're at Oxford?" I hadn't meant it to sound condescending, but I'm afraid it did. Either that or sexist.

"Is that so hard to believe? Did you think maybe you're the only one with smarts in this town?"

"Well, no of course not I just–how old are you?"

"That's hardly a proper question to ask a lady!" She pretended to look offended and got Tom's attention by tapping her shot glass on the bar a couple of times. After he filled them, she looked at me and said, "Good thing I'm not a proper lady..."

We held our glasses up and toasted before taking the shots in unison.

She wiped her mouth in a decidedly unladylike fashion and continued, "I'm twenty-two, if you must know. I've just started my law courses. Undergraduate in History with a minor in Economics."

"You're attending law school. At Oxford?"

"What can I say? I liked the gowns."

I shook my head, laughing. "So how is it?"

"What's that?"

"Law school."

"It's all right. Why, what are you studying?"

I was tempted to say whiskey and women, but I was pretty sure she already knew that part. I looked her over again. She was unbelievably gorgeous. "Computer science and business."

She nodded. "And don't be lookin' at me like that. I think I've made it clear I don't date underclassmen."

I leaned toward her then, bringing my face close to hers. "If you really knew as much about me as you think you do, you'd understand how much I hate being told no."

She wasn't put off by the proximity of our noses in the slightest. "Perhaps if you heard the word more often, it would help you get used to the feelin'."

I smiled the way a man should smile at a woman–with genuine

compliments and sincere admiration. "You are absolutely breathtaking."

This girl would have none of it. The only reaction that registered on her features was one of disgust bordering on pity. "Aye, but that's just a word, isn't it? And a feeling. And nothin' much else between two strangers. It might get you through the evening, but you'll be just as empty when the daylight hits. I've no desire to be your warm place for the night."

Ouch. "I do like a girl who can speak her mind."

"And I'd like to have some real fun." Her head tipped toward the table where my mates were gathered. "So why don't you introduce me to your friends back there, and we'll have some drinks and play some darts, eh?"

She started to get up, but I put my hand down on hers. I just couldn't go down without a fight. "You really have no desire to sleep with me? Not even once? You know, I might surprise you."

She tipped her head and looked me up and down, then shook it decidedly. "No. Not even a little bit."

A burst of raucous laughter erupted from the table in the back and my face lit up crimson. I couldn't remember the last time I'd been turned down. Regan was already headed toward my friends and I'll be damned if she wasn't even better lookin' from the back. I put some money on the bar for Tom, shrugged, and followed after her.

By the time I got to the table they'd obviously introduced themselves to one another and there were congratulations all around, presumably for her supernatural ability to resist my advances.

"Don't worry love, he needs his pedestal to crash out from under him once in a while. Those Oxford boys can be quite taken with themselves." Daniel assured her.

"Don't I know it." She laughed. "But I've got to give him points for trying, so tell you what – the next round's on me!"

Cheers and glasses went up all around the table and an hour or so later the entire lot of us was inordinately pissed. The boys cleared out one by one, until Regan and I were left talking to Tom. I couldn't for the life of me remember where her family lived, but if I'd known I would have offered to see her home. Truth be told, I was just hoping to have more time with her, whatever that might mean. We walked out of the pub into the cold wind, and she wrapped her jacket tighter.

"Can I walk you home?" I put both hands up in self-defense. "I promise, no advances. Just a gentlemanly offer."

She hooked her arm through mine. "Sure."

I have no idea how long we walked but the conversation was somehow deep below the surface and the laughter came easily. I wanted to kiss her right there on the street, but I couldn't figure out how to do any of it and still maintain her respect, which I felt strangely desperate for. We ended up on the other side of town before she pointed to a door in the middle of two shops. "This is me."

I looked up to see an apartment above one of the shops. "So you don't live at home anymore?"

"Too many brothers."

"Ah yes. Noise can be quite a factor when you're trying to memorize historical data."

"And when you've a scholarship to keep up, that data becomes very important."

"Well" I stuffed my hands in my pockets. "It was very nice... running into you again. After all these years."

"You too." She grinned. "And it's too bad I'm so drunk."

"Why is that?"

"Because normally I'm marvelous at keeping secrets." She giggled.

"Secrets? What am I missing?"

"I've made a bit of money tonight is all." She pulled a small wad of bills out of her coat pocket along with her keys and unlocked the door, stepping into the small vestibule to get out of the wind, and motioning for me to do the same.

"I'm sorry?"

"Your friends." She shut the outer door behind us and started up the stairs. "It wasn't the first time I've met them."

My mouth dropped open and I ran up the stairs after her. "No!" I spun her around. "They did not!"

She doubled over, laughing heartily. "I must say, it was rather convenient that I happened to have a bit of history with you, not that you remembered of course."

Incredulous, I raked my hands through my hair.

"I mean, I actually did used to help mind you and your sister." She looked down at my pants, unashamed. "And I have, in fact, seen your mickey. Granted, it was a very long time ago, and it wasn't very impressive back then." She smirked mercilessly. "But they did pay me to say no to you."

I put my hand against the wall to steady myself. "No wonder no one was about when I got to the pub." It all made so much sense. "There I was, congratulating myself for getting there first when all along they were waiting for the sheep to wander off alone so they could send in the big bad wolf!"

"Aye." She laughed.

"So, wait a minute then" I said, putting my other hand up against the wall, effectively closing her in between my arms. "If that was all a game..."

Her eyes looked up at me from under heavy lashes. "You're still too young for me, Finn McCarthy."

"Says who?" I swept her up in my arms and kissed her solidly. Her words may have said too young, but for a moment there, her mouth said something altogether different. Still, she pushed my shoulders away in a physical reiteration of her earlier comment.

"Hey now! I thought we were doing just fine." I tried to lean back in, but she turned her head just in time.

"I know part of it was a game, but I was serious too, Finn. It's not about your age, not really. I'm just not interested in being someone's *just for tonight*."

She waited to gauge my reaction. I just sat there blinking, so she kept talking.

"Listen, you're very attractive, a surprisingly good kisser, and have...quite obviously grown into your grown-up parts." She pushed me a little farther away. "But I hope you can understand."

"What if I told you I wasn't looking for a *just for tonight*?"

"Then you'd be lying to the both of us. You're eighteen Finn. You don't know what you're lookin' for. I'm twenty-two and I'm barely gettin' the hang of it. Can't we just be mates?"

I sighed. "I can't say I've ever had a mate I wanted to shag as much as you, but uh–I suppose we could give it a go."

"Well, in that case, would you like to come in for a cup o' tea?"

"Let's not push our luck, shall we?" I stepped back. "I'm very drunk, and I am only human, after all."

"Now that's the spirit!" She handed me a slip of paper with her number on it. "Ring me up some time and we'll tip a few more." She slipped inside her apartment and began to shut the door before adding, "Mate!"

I leaned back against the wall and took a deep breath. This was going to be interesting.

2

Regan stayed true to her word. For the next couple of years, we really did become mates, and she never did let me shag her, although it took some time before I no longer wanted to. She wasn't like any girl I'd ever met. She was smart and beautiful to be sure, but she had this way of seeing right through me and calling me out on all my messy parts. It's not like she got in the habit of apologizing for it either.

We told each other things no one else knew. Things I couldn't tell another man. She became more like an older sister (once I stopped wanting to shag her) and I started to feel protective of her beauty and her heart in a way I'd never felt about a woman before. Ways I didn't even feel about Eiran.

Had to use that protection a few times too. I've always had a funny way of knowing things about a person, and some of the lads that would come on to her gave me a bad sort of feeling. On those nights I'd slide in next to her at the bar and wrap my arms around her shoulders. If he didn't get the hint right away, I'd kiss her neck, call her by some cutesy term of endearment then introduce myself to whichever bloke was the problem.

Often times she would get mad after he stalked off, but I never apologized. I would merely tell her the truth, just like she always told me. "That one was no good. I've just saved you from a heartache, now shut up and drink."

I was protective of Eiran, to be sure, but more because she was my baby sister and I was her older brother. This was different. The more I got to know Regan as a person, the more I respected her choices and understood her motivations. She didn't require me to share her values, but she absolutely demanded that I respect them.

Many a night she sat at the pub and shook her head, smiling indulgently as I paraded by her with beautiful women. She had a good sense about her as well though. She could see when a girl was getting too clingy and starting to latch on. She'd follow them to the bathroom and warn them off about me–tell them about how I'd done her wrong and never bothered to call, that sort of thing.

We became each other's mutual excuses. It certainly was convenient, not to mention a fair bit of fun. You might say we saved each other. She never would tell me if she was a virgin or not. She always changed the subject, or started talking about my sex life instead, and it was just as well. That kind of a challenge was hard for a bloke like me to pass up, and I'd just as soon not have that extra knowledge pounding down on an admittedly weak door. Like I said, it took a long time before I could put my fraternal feelings before my instincts.

I did ask her once if she was a female eunuch. We were sitting in the flat she shared with some other law students at Oxford, but none of them were home at the time. We were enjoying a bottle of cheap wine and she laughed out loud, nearly spilling her glass. "Be serious, Finn. Don't you know me at all?"

"A lesbian perhaps?"

She found this idea similarly hilarious, then got a very serious look on her face. "I kissed you back once. You tell me."

She had me there. "Good point. That was definitely not the kiss of a woman who isn't fond of men."

"Well, don't flatter yourself too much. I was also very drunk that night. Besides, you kissed me first, remember? You caught me off guard. Anyway, I was curious. You had quite the reputation, you know."

"Were you worried I might disappoint? As I recall, you said I was a *surprisingly good kisser.*"

"Well, you know how reputations go. Sometimes it's all beauty and no brains, and you've got to have good brains to be decent in the sack."

"And you know this how?"

She swallowed. "Or so I've heard."

Sufficiently vague. She really wasn't going to give me the satisfaction of knowing one way or another. She had the makings of a top-notch lawyer already.

"So, because I'm a good kisser, that means I'm also good in the sack, does it?"

"Usually, yes, but even good has its limits."

"Now this I've got to hear."

"You laugh, but when you really ask your heart the question, would you rather have good or great?"

"Explain, please."

She tucked her legs up under her, and I found myself trailing them with my eyes, trying to keep my focus on what she was saying, but only catching about half of it.

Again, merely human.

"Good is like the *now* kind of satisfaction. Microwave sex. Instant gratification. But nothing you ever heat up in a microwave will ever taste as good as home made."

She winked and I found myself pushing back against the craving for a quick slice of cold pizza.

"Great is the *not yet* kind. The slow cooked stew, the sauces that simmer all day long."

"Am I supposed to be feeling hungry right now?" I winked back and she shook her head, smiling.

"All I'm saying is, care more about the future than you do about the now and you've got it licked." She took a sip of her wine. "No pun intended."

I chuckled at the image that popped up in my head unannounced. I certainly didn't need any help in that department.

"The anticipation can be every bit as exciting as the actual act. Why do you think men are so overly fond of lingerie?" She reached into her shirt pulled out her bra strap, which was black and lacy and completely unfair.

I shook my head. "I'm sorry, counselor, but I've got to disagree there. Foreplay may have its place, but anticipation, by very nature of the word, merely brings the *promise* of satisfaction, not the satisfaction itself."

Her eyes narrowed a bit. "And what would the likes of you know about foreplay?"

"Why don't you try me?"

"And–that's the difference between boys and men." She laughed, mocking me.

"Come again?"

"A boy wants what he wants, and he wants it right now. He'll say or do just about anything to get to that point of release, because that's all he can see. He can't broaden his scope enough to take in the entirety of the game."

"It's a game now, is it? I thought we were talking about food."

"Just stay with me here. A boy," she gestured my direction, "masters a few key moves, plays only the part of the field he knows well, and drives straight for the goal every time he gets the ball." She poured herself another glass and held the bottle suspended in midair for a moment. "But as soon as that ball is in the goal, he's setting up for the next ball. More wine?"

I held out my glass for a refill. This was a fascinating new perspective. "All right then, what would a *man* do differently?" I asked, genuinely curious.

"Oh, I don't know–dribble a little, pass the ball once in a while." She smiled knowingly. "Show some finesse."

I decided right then and there that if we were going to be *just friends,* I was going to take full advantage and ask her the kinds of things I could never ask another woman.

"Tell me then, is it so very different for a woman? The desire part, I mean. And I'm being serious now."

"How do you expect me to answer that with any confidence? I don't know how a man feels. I'm not a man."

"No, but you are going to make an excellent barrister." I fought to keep my eyes on hers. "All right then, tell me what it's like for you, and I'll compare it to my own experience."

"You really want me to discuss my sexual feelings with you?"

"Come on now, according to you we're *mates,* and you've already vowed never to sleep with me. How often do you get the opportunity to be so honest? A non-sexual conversation about sex. What could be more academic?"

I watched her consider the idea. After a while she leaned back against the couch. "We might need more wine."

I crossed one leg over the other, trying to look as if I were ready to take notes. I was, after all, a hot-blooded young man. This was valuable research!

"It's simple really, and if we're going to continue with the sports analogy, men are all about putting points on the board. The thrill of the goal and the roar of the crowd. Women, on the other hand, love the drive down the field. A bit of footwork, the back and forth. The... changing of possession."

She blushed a little trying to find those last few words and I blinked a few times. "This is quickly becoming the most arousing non-sexual conversation I've ever had."

She laughed out loud. I always could make her laugh. "I'm being serious now; do you want to learn your man lessons or not?"

I put my hand up to my temple and held it stiffly in salute. "Not another word, madam."

"I personally think men could learn to enjoy themselves immensely more if they would just slow bloody down."

Slow was not a word previously associated with my vocabulary when it came to women. I enjoyed the thrill of the chase, sure. But a fast chase it was, and the quicker the better by my terms. If there was one thing I was completely unfamiliar with, it was the concept of slow.

"You blokes think it's all about the destination, when really it's all about the ride. Every step, every touch, every..." she licked her lips absently, "kiss, is an opportunity for building a great tidal wave. Go too fast and you'll miss all that goodness, and your end result will only ever feel like every other end result."

"Well, now hold on. It's not like we blokes don't enjoy the getting there."

"Yes, but what I'm talking about is a different *kind* of enjoyment. Oh bollocks, I keep forgetting that you haven't found anyone you want to get lost in yet. You will. Trust me. You'll come back to this conversation in your mind and you'll thank me. And so will she." Regan winked at me and stood. "I have to use the toilet. Be back shortly."

She was a puzzle, this girl. She never talked about her previous relationships, and since I'd known her, she'd never done anything but date casually. Based on her obvious firsthand knowledge, I had to concede that there was a possibility of more. I just couldn't imagine anything *less* appealing than getting lost in just one person, when there was so much beauty out there to be explored. I might never get the chance to understand what the devil she was even talking about.

I thought about what she said, but it was hard to imagine anything better than the end result. When Regan came back from the bathroom, I'd poured the rest of the wine.

"Any chance you're willing to show me what you mean on a practical note? I mean, I've never personally met anyone who fits that description before."

"What description?"

"Someone I'd want to get *lost* in. Come on, you know me better than anyone. Why not teach me? I'm a fast learner, I promise you that."

I put up a very silly grin and she laughed at me. I loved the sound of her laugh, but she just shook her head, smiling.

"Any chance you're ever going to stop coming on to me?"

I tried to look offended. "I'm just trying to embrace a new concept, is all, and sometimes a little *hands-on* experience is the best way to learn."

"Sure, and I'm the Pope sitting here talking to you."

"So, no then?"

"No, Finn."

"All right." I put a hand up in the air. "In that case I'm just going to have to take your word for it. I mean, I respect your opinions and all–I just don't share them."

I can still see her sitting there. She was wearing a light green sweater and a delicate silver necklace that dropped nicely down the front of her cleavage. I watched her slender arms cross against her chest and again found myself wondering if I'd ever be able to look at her without wanting her.

If she noticed my desire, she ignored it completely. She was too busy feeling sorry for my inexperience. "Well, I've never held it against you before, and I don't mean to start now. But I'll still be there to hold your hand the first time your heart gets broken."

I raised my glass, and she did the same. "Deal."

It was just a silly toast. A formality, really. I had no intention of having my heart broken, then or ever.

AND SO IT WENT. She never agreed to show me personally, and I ignored the fact that anything other than meaningless shagging existed. Oh, I did a little experimenting here or there – dribbling a bit, passing the ball, that sort of thing. It was definitely a far more interesting experience, if in fact there was time to be killed, but these attempts at 'changing possession' became little more than a study in personal methodology.

The application may have seemed similar, but the motivation was completely different. I wasn't experimenting for the sake of establishing a commitment, I was merely perfecting my technique.

Regan's method made relationships a lot more complicated, and complications were something I had little use for. Taking your time implied something more, so I reserved my 'expertise' for the hard-to-get types and left it at that.

A perfected technique was a useful tool, though. By the time I graduated Oxford I had a full complement of instruments at my disposal, and I could use them on almost anything that walked on two legs. They used to call me the Escort of Exeter. Playing football didn't hurt my chances either. Showing up to the pub banged, bruised, and bandaged elicited a kind of gentleness and nurturing I made sure to appreciate fully at every opportunity.

Regan finished her law degree the year before I left Oxford. She took a flat in London and a job with a firm there. We never really lost touch, but she had her life and I had mine. She was still waiting for Mister Right, and I was too busy being Mister Wrong. We may have been at cross-purposes, but we made time to have a little fun together, now and then.

In fact, on my twenty-first birthday, Regan came and picked me up. She said I was getting too old and too heavy to do the birthday bumps, so we were going to pretend I was an American and this was my first night of being allowed to drink legally.

She took me to a trendy place in London that catered to American tourists and sat me down at the bar. We lined up every American shot or drink we could convince the bartender to attempt–based on a pocket guide to bartending she brought with her and then gave to me as a gift. It even had colored pictures of what each one was supposed to look like when it was finished.

Because I had examinations next morning, we decided to split up the shots and take turns trying them. In honor of it being *my* birthday and not hers, we were only doing shots whose names referred to either women, sex, or the destruction of morals and good character in general.

Since we were obviously on a suicide mission, we started with a Kamikaze, then moved on to a Dirty Girl Scout, a Slippery Nipple, a Red-Headed Slut, and ended with Sex On The Beach. At least, those are the ones I can remember. I was langered but Regan was worse than I'd ever seen her. She got a bit friendly when she'd been drinking so I kept having to stop her from taking chaps home with her. We pulled each other back to her apartment, and she fell up the stairs going in. We laughed so hard I nearly had to carry her the rest of the way up.

"Why is it you always have to have your apartment on the upper floors?" I stopped halfway up with her under my arm, trying to catch my breath. "It makes it much more difficult to get you home this way."

"It makes me feel safer" she whispered into my jacket.

It was a rare admission for her, and it caught me off guard. Growing up with seven brothers probably felt extremely safe, but living on one's own after that must have been something of a shock. As a man, I rarely considered such a thing, but perhaps a woman never got used to that part.

When we got to the top, she handed me a single key and asked me to unlock the door. I did as she asked, then led her through the door and tried to hand her back the key.

She shook her head. "That's yours."

"No, darlin'. It's not. You just handed it to me to unlock the door. Now put it back in your pocket."

She looked up at me and smiled. "No, I mean it. It's yours. You're twenty-one now. I'm giving you the key to your freedom. You can live your own life and come and go as you please."

"Are you asking me to move in with you, love?" I winked.

She tried to hit me but missed, which was sad seeing as I was standing right next to her. "No, you wanker! It's symbolic of our friendship. If I was your mum, this would be the day I'd give you your own key to the house."

"You don't look *anything* like me mum" I slurred, pointing my finger at her face and then up toward the ceiling. "But that's not a *bad* thing."

"I'm just saying, if you ever need a place to stay, a listening ear, that kind of thing. You're welcome here, is all."

It stopped me cold. It was a tradition I'd bypassed a long time ago, since Da had seen fit to give me a key at fourteen and at Grand mum's, I just used the servant's entrance when I came in after hours. It was a heartfelt gesture, and it speared me. She and I had truly become best mates over the years, and I loved her like a sister, although at the moment I was considering a bit more than that. I looked around the apartment. It was neat, sweetly decorated, and very 'Regan'. She had such a good heart.

"You know," I brushed a stray piece of hair from her forehead, "it's too bad you're so very beautiful. It must be hard."

She tried to hit me again, but I stopped her hand. "I'm being serious."

She swallowed and looked up at me.

"All your life people must have seen that first." I smiled, tipping her chin up. "Okay, maybe not before puberty, but definitely since."

She looked down, although I wasn't trying to wound her.

"They must have trouble taking you seriously, even as a barrister. And now you're just waiting for someone–anyone–to see past the curtain and want you for the beauty that's inside you."

When she looked up again her eyes had started to tear. "You stop that right now, Finn McCarthy! I'm not one of your easy marks."

I held her hands gently but said firmly. "I know, all right? I know that. I'm just...genuinely trying to pay you a compliment. I see who you are on the inside, and I'm...so amazed that no bloke worth his salt has ever even tried to push past the obvious. You deserve so much better than that."

A TEAR FELL from one of her eyes. I wiped it away and leaned in to kiss her cheek, but she grabbed onto my face and kissed my mouth instead. I pulled away, shocked.

"Now wait just a minute, I've never seen you this drunk."

"The drink's got nothin' to do with this." She kissed me again, this time like she meant it. I picked her up and set her against the wall.

Her kisses were like nothin' I'd had with other women. Maybe it's because we knew each other so well, but the connection was astounding–overpowering. I was suddenly on fire with no rain in sight.

I pulled back, out of breath. "What do you think you're doin', love?"

"You're a grown man now, Finn." She looked up at me from under those beautiful lashes. "I think it's time I showed you what I meant."

She pushed my jacket down off my shoulders and let it drop to the floor, then caressed my rough and stubbled face with her hands, tracing a finger down the front of my shirt and sliding it easily out of my pants. When her hands slipped up underneath, my skin electrified and everything slowed down, like I'd been caught in some kind of a trance.

She kissed me again and again, slowly unbuttoning my shirt until her hands had free reign. I watched with amazement as she drew her sweater up over her head, completely unashamed, and pressed herself up against my bare chest.

She was wearing a pink and grey bra that was somehow innocent and incredibly sexy all at the same time. One of the straps slipped down her shoulder and I couldn't breathe. All the times I'd fantasized about kissing her. Touching her.

There for the taking.

Her head tilted back and over to one side, revealing the porcelain skin of her neck, inviting me to partake. I traced it with my fingers before following with my mouth. She tasted like honey and I wanted to devour every inch of her.

I slid my hands around her waist and pulled her in. She was soft and insistent, fragile but strong. A perfect storm of sensuality, and I lost myself in her depths.

Regan was more beautiful than I'd ever seen her. Passionate and vulnerable and completely open to me. I'd been dreaming about this moment for years, but moments stretched into hours as we made the most incredible love I'd ever had. I'd never let myself go like that, but with her it was easy. She knew all my faults. She'd seen me at my worst.

She allowed me time to make a few plays, but then she taught me things I'd never learnt before. Slow things. Changing possession things. We hit the goal a few times, but my God, the drive down field...

I couldn't get enough of the feel of her. The feel of us. I'd never been so consumed, so...lost in another person. And in that moment, nothing else existed. No personal history, no examinations, no jobs or keys or birthday celebrations.

I knew for the first time that I was completely wrong. There really was something more. Something that made every other woman I'd ever been with fall completely out of my mind.

I may have blacked out hundreds of similar drunken experiences, but even if this *was* a product of Kamikazes and Sex On The Beach, it was a night I would never forget.

3

Unfortunately, Regan did.

She had absolutely no memory of that night. I tried to take care of her at her flat, but she threw up for three days straight and ended up in hospital for rehydration therapy. It was the sickest I'd ever seen anyone from alcohol. After that, she wasn't quite the same. We didn't go drinking nearly as much, and she settled into her job and became an adult, of sorts.

It all seemed so pointless to me. By the time I finished my degrees, I felt utterly useless. I still loved women and whiskey, but I had to start thinking of what I was going to do with all my smarts and unfortunately, I hadn't a clue. So much was going on in the world and I did nothing but play around on someone else's dime. I was basically a super-educated freeloader with no desire to run on the wheel of a crippled capitalist society.

I decided to join the army. It seemed logical at the time.

Regan was the first person I told, and her face went completely white. "You've what?"

"I've joined the army."

She studied me for a moment. "You're serious, aren't you?"

"Quite."

She flagged down the bartender and ordered two glasses of

Jameson's and told him to leave the bottle. "Please, please tell me you're joking. Is this payback for the night your friends had me turn you down?"

It was endearing, her level of agitation at the thought, but it was already done. There was no going back. I shook my head gently and put my hand over hers. "Surely you're not upset, darlin'? We rarely see each other anymore. I just didn't want you to find out on the street."

She handed me my glass, which had more than two fingers worth of brown liquid in it. "Don't make me drink alone."

"All right. Suit yourself." I downed my glass all in one shot. "There'll be none of that in basic training. I might as well live it up now!"

Regan turned an icy stare on me. "It's not a game, Finn! How can you make light of it?"

"I know it's not a game. But this" I looked around the bar. "This is the game!" I let my voice rise to match her intensity. "And I'm tired of it."

"So tired that you're willing to risk dying? *That* tired? Our boys are playing at actual war right now, or haven't you heard?" She swallowed the last of her whiskey and poured herself some more, leaving me to fend for myself.

I looked up at her, incredulous. "You're angry! Why?"

She turned her gray-green eyes toward me, and they were filled with unshed tears. "Because I've been telling you for years now not to play *this* game." She swept her arm in a semi-circle. "But you wouldn't listen to me. Now that you've finally come to it, it's by way of a suicide mission! If you're so fond of Kamikazes, why don't you just drink a few more!" She threw her whiskey right in my face and stormed out of the bar, but before I could pay for the bottle and run after her, she was gone.

I walked a few blocks in the direction of her flat and found her weeping on a bench. I took her in my arms and just let her cry. When she seemed to have the worst of it out, I brushed back her hair and kissed her forehead. "There now. Are you better?"

"No." She looked up at me, pouting. "I still want to throttle you."

"I don't understand."

"One of the secretaries at our office lost her son just last month. He joined the army a year ago and they sent him to Afghanistan. He was driving in a supply truck. Just delivering supplies. His truck hit one of those mines that are buried in the road and it blew up. He wasn't even fighting, Finn. He wasn't supposed to be in danger."

I searched her face then looked into her eyes. "You're not going to lose me."

"How do you know?"

"I don't know, I just...know."

"See that's the thing. You don't."

"I'm going to be right here for a few more weeks before I start my training. You can draw up my will, and we'll get everything settled, just in case." I smiled halfway, and she slapped me in the chest.

"Stop that! You're making it worse."

"See that's the plan" I smiled down over her head and kissed her hair. "I'm making it worse so it can only get better."

"That's an awfully big gamble."

"I'm an all or nothin' bloke."

"Aye." She shook her head, smiling for the first time since I'd given her the news. "That y'are." She sat up and wiggled out of my arms, drying the tears from her face. She looked almost embarrassed. "Sorry about that."

"I'm not." I shook my head and winked.

"Still trying to get in my knickers, are you?" She put on her best British accent.

"Always." I smiled. *Or rather, back in...*

I still remembered our time together as if it were right there between us. One breath of her scent and I was right back there in her flat, stretched out against her skin, trapped in her atmosphere, a willing prisoner just waiting to be flogged again and again by the exquisite pleasure of a love I'd never known. Every other kiss had turned sour in my mouth, and I was ruined. My heart knew it, but my stubborn head hadn't quite gotten the message.

She didn't remember a thing, and now wasn't the time to bring it up. I wasn't sure it ever would be. Telling her would only make things incredibly awkward between us, and that was the last thing I wanted–especially since I'd be leaving soon.

Truth be told, this entire transformation in me had really started that night, but I couldn't tell her that either, so I just sat there with an arm around her shoulders, thinking about it all.

"Well, you'll be at Sandhurst for nearly a year, and by then maybe all this silly business in Afghanistan will be over."

"I'm not going to Sandhurst."

She sat up abruptly. "What did you say?"

"I'm not going to be an officer."

"Why the bloody hell not? You've got two master's degrees, for pity's sake!"

I pulled the bottle of Jameson's out of the deep side pocket in my pea coat. "Fancy another drink?"

She just sat there blinking. "Not until you explain just what the hell you're talking about. What do you mean you're not going to Sandhurst? Have you joined for Ireland then?"

"No, you were right the first time. I've joined the Brits; I'm just not putting in to be an officer."

"You've joined the regulars then? Enlisted? You're not joking, are you?"

I shook my head, confirming what she already knew.

"I mean, how *could* you? You've been through Eton and Oxford. You've been to school with royals and ambassadors' children and heirs to Fortune 500 companies."

"Yes, but you know who I really am!" I switched over to a thick Irish accent to match hers. "We come from the same home town. Don't tell me you look at me now and don't see that feller at all?"

"Stop it, Finn! You're both men. You'll always be both men, but when it comes right to it, you fit better here in England, and you know it. You've done the English bit longer, and more sober too I suspect. I'm surprised you can still speak with the Irish at all."

"Now that hurts." I took a swig right out of the bottle. I could switch between the two accents at will, and she knew it.

"You're a card-carrying member of the blue blazer club!" She grabbed the bottle out of my hands and tipped it back then sat hard against the bench. "You can't just...pretend all this isn't a part of you."

"I'm not pretending. I'm just saying it doesn't matter."

"Well, if you don't want it to matter then why don't you just move back to Ireland? Join the army there if you're so bent on proving your roots!"

She had a point, but I wasn't ready to concede it. I could have joined in Ireland, or I could have claimed my Irish heritage and joined the British Army as a part of The Royal Irish Regiment. Instead, I chose to claim my British citizenship and be counted amongst the regulars.

When I didn't respond she crossed her arms over her chest. "That's what I thought."

I unfolded her arms and turned her toward me. "You of all people have to understand this."

She refused to acknowledge it. "You weren't supposed to come to it this way. You were supposed to figure it out and become a normal sort of human someday."

Her words fell hard against the wall I'd built around my feelings for her. I felt the rumble of it down to my toes.

"What would you have me do? Work in an office by day and live the life of a drunken gigolo by night? It gets old, you know?"

"At least it suits you." She pouted.

"Now you're just being spiteful." I took another drink. "I think I'd rather get shot at by the enemy."

"Don't. Say that."

"How can you expect me to lead a group of soldiers when I'm not even ready to lead my own life?"

She looked down at her shoes.

"Why do you think I've spent so much time in the pubs, bedding every female from here to Dublin?"

"I happen to know why. It's you who hasn't a feckin' clue." She sighed loudly. "But tell me Finn, do you really have to put yourself in harm's way to figure it out?"

I wasn't going to dignify her petulant jabs with a serious answer. "Apparently so."

We were both silent for a long time, her long blonde hair blowing between us. Regan slapped her hands on her knees and then stood. "What do you say we get out of here?"

"Desert? As in AWOL? I've already signed on the dotted line. They'd send me to the Glasshouse for sure."

She shook her head. "I was thinking more along the lines of dessert. As in chocolate? I think I need a pick me up. Besides, I'm bloody freezing."

"Whatever you say, love." I slipped my arm around her shoulders in a decidedly brotherly fashion and we walked on.

I hadn't expected such a vehement reaction, but it warmed my heart to know she cared enough to run me down about it.

The hard part was going to be telling my parents.

DA HAD BEEN HOPING I'd join him in the family business. While the pub life was definitely in my blood, my heart just wasn't in it. He didn't hide his disappointment, but I can't say he was surprised either.

He knew me better than most, and when I told him about joining the army, he took my hand and just looked at me for a long time. He called it *reading me*. It was similar to having your luggage searched. You felt a little violated after it was over, but everything mostly gets put back the way it was. When he was done staring me down, he let go of my hand and nodded once.

"Aye." Was all he said at first. "For the Brits?"

I nodded.

"The Royal Irish?"

"No."

Da grabbed his chest as if I'd stabbed him proper. "What are you doin' to me, lad? Are you forsakin' your country completely now?"

I tried to explain, but he just kept talking.

"I understand you want to go fight. I understand you want to be where the action is, but why not stand together with your Irish brothers and fight for the same cause?"

I'd been thinking about this question since my conversation with Regan, so I was ready with an answer, although it came across with a little more gusto than I intended.

"I'm tired of being defined one way or another. Irish. British. Eton. Oxford. Pieces of paper that tell other people who y'are before they even get to know you! I just want a chance to be in the regulars."

"Well, with all that schooling there's little chance they'll take you in the regulars. You're to be an officer I'm sure."

"Don't be."

"What's that?"

"I...respectfully declined the commission."

Da narrowed his eyes at me. "Are you daft, boy? Don't you know the difference? They're gonna put you in the worst of the bombing over there."

"Then I'll fight alongside men who don't care where I went to college or that my grandmother paid for me to attend Eton."

He conceded my point. He'd never agreed with that part of our arrangement, but Mum was the one who insisted on boarding school, and by the time that was done I was so entrenched in the culture that Oxford became the obvious next choice. He wasn't opposed to the quality of an English education– he just wasn't a fan of the influence it took to get it.

I elbowed him in the ribs. "Come on, you know what it's like to fight for the other side. Back in the day you played against a lot of your own mates in football."

"Aye, back in the day. That was a lot of days back."

"Yet you also chose to play for the Brits."

That stopped him in his tracks. "Aye." He nodded thoughtfully. "That I did."

"And why was that, exactly?"

"That's a very long story."

"Well then, it's a good thing basic training doesn't start for two more weeks."

I WENT to see Mum to tell her in person. To say she was shocked would fall a bit short, I think, especially once I told her I was joining the regulars. That I would refuse the opportunity to go to Sandhurst was, to her mind, unthinkable. They all thought I was crazy, and maybe I was. She didn't talk to me for two days straight. Grams was another story.

Grams was a tough old broad with a soft spot for the needy. A true noble who had never taken wealth and privilege for granted. In the war she volunteered to nurse wounded soldiers even though her father strictly forbade it. He was worried she might get hurt or contract some sort of disease, but she went anyway. She'd seen things I could only imagine–things that changed a person. Her life had made a difference.

Truth be told, I chose the British Army for a number of reasons, but mostly because I knew it would make Grams proud. She was fiercely patriotic and genuinely grateful to Britain's soldiers. My grandfather had been one of them, and she had an entire shrine of ancestral military portraits hanging along one of her hallways. She'd been telling me for years that I needed to grow up, to learn a sense of honor and duty to king and country, so of all the people in my life, I felt sure she would understand.

Grams sat me down in the library. She talked, and I listened. Even at four-foot eleven she commanded quite a presence, but I had to keep myself from smiling at how adorable she was. I loved her deeply and held a tremendous amount of respect for her, but we just weren't going to see eye-to-eye on this one.

Especially with me standing just over six feet.

She talked about respect for humanity and the crown, and my

responsibility toward future generations. I was informed that she'd already commissioned a painter to make my portrait for the hall-way–all we needed was the proper uniform. Apparently, she thought this was a small adjustment and one that could be easily made.

All of our ancestors had commanded regiments and been decorated leaders. This departure from tradition was, as I said, unacceptable to all of them, so I tried to explain my side, but she wouldn't budge.

"You cannot run from who you are, Finnegan."

"I'm not trying to run from anyone."

"Then why would you not take your rightful place as a leader amongst your fellow soldiers?"

"If they're to respect me, then shouldn't it be because of the kind of man I am? Not purely out of rank and title?"

"They'll respect your title first, that's true, but titles are earned by more than chance or money. It is an expected distinction. Part of your duty to this family!"

"I'm not disrespecting my heritage."

"Let me finish, young man. The respect of a title only gets you lip service. You still have to earn their hearts, and you do that because of who you are as a man. The only difference between the two is where you start and how long it takes to work your way into a position of influence."

She was talking about more than just the military, and I knew that, but I wasn't going down without a fight. If she wanted to slip in double meanings, so be it. "I can serve my country just as well being a good follower as I can a good leader."

She sat there with her back straight and those steel gray eyes staring me down. "That may be true, but you will never have the God-given influence you were meant to have unless you take your rightful place and accept it." She balled her tiny hand into a fist and pounded it into the arm of her chair.

"Being born into this family wasn't my choice. It was happenstance."

"Happenstance, you say. You believe your birth was happenstance?"

"If I'd been kept in Ireland and never met you and never known these portraits existed, we wouldn't even be having this conversation!"

She nodded thoughtfully, smoothing the folds of her skirt. "And what a privilege it is to know your family—to know who you are and where-you-come-from." She drew these last words out one at a time for emphasis.

"I just want to earn my place in this world, same as every other bloke."

Her head shook in defeat. "Earn it you will, Finnegan. Make no mistake about that. One way or another it all comes around, you know."

"I'm sorry Grams, I respect your opinions, but I need to do this on my terms."

"And I respect yours." She nodded firmly. "And I'm still proud of you." She took one of my hands in both of hers. "So proud."

"So, you're not angry?"

She sat quietly, studying me. "You know I'm not a big fan of the French." Her hands trembled as she tried to finish her thoughts. "But they were right about a few things."

"Wine, women..." I winked at her, trying to ease myself out of the conversation, but she just sat there, stoic and determined. Somewhere in my gene pool was a deep well of perseverance, and I found myself hoping I'd inherited at least a few drops.

"A very old French poet once said that a man often meets his destiny on the road he takes to avoid it."

I smiled my charming smile. "What makes you think I'm trying to avoid it?"

Like a good aristocrat, she ignored my bait. "Duty. Honor. Integrity. Those values were placed inside you, even if you don't want to acknowledge them. You were meant to make a difference."

"Well, at least we can agree on one thing, because that's exactly what I'm trying to do."

She smiled sadly. "When you come home from your time of service, we'll do your portrait." She looked out at the hallway with its wall of paintings. "In whatever uniform you end up in."

I lowered my voice, hoping Mum wasn't listening in on our conversation, and took one of Grams hands. "There's a good chance I'll be going to Afghanistan. I might not come home all in one piece."

This didn't faze her. "Then we'll paint the parts of you that are left." She stated with all the confidence she could muster. "Our men always come home."

All the officers, she meant. The ones on the walls had surely been kept from the battle, far from the front lines, but I wasn't going to argue with her any longer.

"All right then. We'll do the portrait when I come home."

4

U p until the day I joined, I didn't have any specific desire to fulfill the values she described, but something about serving your country changes all that. Military service teaches you three things mainly: gratefulness, discipline, and honor, but not necessarily in that order.

The first several weeks of training were brutal. I found I had a great tolerance for whiskey and almost none for exercise. I was lax and flabby and the only push-ups I was used to...were hardly ever done in multiples of twenty.

My muscles screamed in pain on a daily basis, every nerve ending awake and standing at full attention, but I felt more alive than I had in years. What I hadn't counted on was the mind-numbing headaches, nausea and night sweats that accompanied the subsequent detoxification. There were no drinks for the recruits. No women either–at least, not in my particular regiment. Nothing but pain and deprivation, and a lot of schooling on guns and first aid and strategic warfare.

Not since my first kiss had my body shook and my palms sweated like that. For some reason the withdrawal symptoms surprised me. Then again, maybe that should have been my first clue. My body could do without women, but it began to cry out for the whiskey.

Forcing it to shut up was just another form of discipline I would have to master.

A guy named James was in the bunk next to mine. We became good friends, he and I. The first night I began with the shakes and the vomiting, he asked if I was sick. The second night he asked how long I'd been drinking.

After a trip to the infirmary for IV fluids and a bit of medicine for the nausea and stomach pain, I felt a good deal better, but it was a hairy first few weeks, to be sure. The staff in the infirmary never said as much, but I'm certain it wasn't the first time they'd come across it, and seeing as I was determined to keep going, I guess they saw fit to help me along.

James never told the officers what was really happening, or I could have been kicked out before I even got started. The army didn't always attract the most reasonable sorts of fellows.

It also had a way of purging a man of all his sins.

The soldiers in my unit got to know each other pretty quickly over the weeks we were together. I kept quiet for the most part. Plenty of men seemed eager to talk and that was fine by me. If someone asked where I was from, I told them a thin version of the truth. That my da was Irish and my mum was a Brit and I'd basically grown up half the time in each country. If they asked what I studied in school I simply told them I was good with computers. It was true, after all.

The men I served with were top notch. Although I missed many of the luxuries of Grams' place and even the house I'd shared with Da in Ireland, I learned a different kind of comfort. Physical convenience was stripped away during basic training. Systematically. Intentionally. What was left bound us together as a single group that lived and breathed and moved and fought as one. Theoretically, of course.

We were the scraped-clean leftovers of a fat generation. We were different, at the end—purified, and I guess that was the point. What was revealed in each man told a lot more about us than any degree-granting institution could put on a single piece of parchment. Our lives couldn't be summed up and framed. They were now. In the moment.

Shortly after graduation, our moments became even more important. James and I, at least, were headed to Afghanistan. We were deployed to the same battalion, along with three other guys from our same group at basic training.

By that time, I could run five miles without getting out of breath, do fifty pushups without blinking an eyelash, clean, take apart and reassemble most combat weapons, and sleep standing up. Hell, I could even create clean drinking water out of a puddle of piss if I had to. I learned all my lessons, even some I hadn't meant to.

I learned I had a bit of a temper, a serious aversion to foot odor, and a soft spot for underdogs. This last bit came to light our first week in Helmand Province, and it started with one of our own–a young kid named Jasper. I'd gotten to know Jasper on the way over to Afghanistan and liked him immediately. Barely eighteen, he was a bit on the smaller side for a soldier, but what he lacked in stature he made up for in side-splitting hilarity. He kept us laughing the whole ride over.

Being around him reminded me of carefree days and nights spent pub-side back home. The uncertainty of our futures felt anything but carefree, and Jasper was a much-needed relief. When we got to base camp, however, there wasn't much laughter.

IN HINDSIGHT, I suppose we should have come in with a bit more respect. This was the most dangerous province in Afghanistan, and some of these men were on their third or fourth tours. Some looked sick, or maybe they were just tired. Or both. One bloke named Cooper had a particularly nasty attitude, and he started in on Jasper before we even got unpacked. Jasper was obviously used to it, but that didn't make it any easier to witness.

"Well, look what we have here...Surprised they found a uniform that fit you. Or maybe Mum was able to hem your pants before your first day of school?"

Some of the other men laughed. I didn't.

I was never overly fond of bullies, so I stepped right into the middle of something that really wasn't my business. "How 'bout we all get settled before we start talking about each other's mums, eh? 'Cause if that's what we're to be about, I've got a real interesting story about yours."

Cooper looked over. "Who the hell are you?"

I stuck out my hand and gripped his arm with all of my newfound strength. Cooper did the same. We were fairly evenly matched.

"I'm Finn, and I'm happy to know you. Unless of course, you mean my friend Jasper here any harm, that is. Last I checked, mate, we're all on the same team."

Something close to an acknowledgement flickered in Cooper's eyes as he growled back his response. A few of the others looked up. Ten minutes in, and I was already in a pissing match with the alpha.

"I don't need you to fight my battles, Finn." Jasper straightened. "I'm perfectly capable of defending myself against any enemy, foreign *or* domestic."

I had to give it to the kid. He had some chops.

Cooper stood over poor Jasper and made a point of bending his head down to get face to face. "Round here every man proves himself. Carries his own weight. Just seems like Jasper here will be carrying a little less than the rest of us, is all."

Jasper stood as tall as he could manage. He was probably five foot seven or so, but he could have been Cooper's shadow. "I can carry my own and then some. Just try me."

Cooper took a look down his nose at Jasper. "Yeah? Well, see that you do. I don't fancy dying out there."

"Neither do I."

Cooper backed down after that, but I realized I'd been standing at the ready to beat the tar out of him. Self-discipline had never been my strong suit, but I needed to hold my anger in check for use against the real enemy. While bullying was frowned upon, getting court-marshaled was just plain stupidity.

Out there I had plenty of opportunity to witness the brutalities of bullying and oppression against innocent people, many of whom were women and children. It twisted something deep within me that came up black as coal. I tried to justify it, but I wanted them dead, and not just to keep the peace. I wanted them to pay for what they'd done to their own people.

Daily contact became a welcome release for the mixture of anger and hatred that boiled beneath the surface. It was a piece of my heart I'd never known, and one I had hoped never to encounter. I began to wonder if every man met himself on the battlefield, and how many of them won their own personal wars.

For me it was a mix. Some days I won, and some days the enemy within me won. I imagine that's how it went for most of us, and I suppose that's how it was for Cooper too. He wasn't a bad guy, once you got to know him. I guess we just met him on the wrong day.

I carried around a small video camera and told the fellas I'd be making a movie someday so the world could see what being a soldier was really like. I told them they could leave messages on the film, and if anything ever happened to us it'd be saved for our families and the like. Even the officers joined in. I figured if they were going to call it theatre, we might as well have a few movies to show for it.

Most of them had left girls behind. Some, I imagine, had left boys behind. Some came out with it, and some kept quiet. Some left messages for their mum or even their dog, but everyone had a message for someone.

I thought about it, but never filmed a message myself, mostly because I didn't have a clue who I'd send it to. I'd left things as right as I could with Mum, Da, and even Grams, but Eiran was a little more difficult–even worse than Regan.

She cried real tears for hours as I rocked her in my arms liked I'd done when we were kids and she used to climb into my bed on stormy nights. I would sing to her, and my terrible voice always made her laugh. Soon the storm would be over, and she would fall asleep curled up next to me.

She was so small and frail. Even as an adult she remained petite, as if she stopped participating in the growing-up process and chose instead to remain childlike. She was still so loving and trusting. I don't know how she grew up untouched by the world's hatred, but she did.

Thankfully, Regan agreed to draw up that will for me before I left. Even though we joked about it, the army regularly encouraged everyone to make sure their affairs were in order, to make it easier on the families back home. I left anything I had to Eiran. It was simple, really, and simplicity does have its advantages.

The sergeant found me a computer so I could offload the videos. It was contraband, of course, purchased by a friend of his after dark at the edge of a nearby camp that housed American soldiers and brought to us buried in the supply truck. It all felt very MASH-like and Sarge was like our very own Radar.

He was a genius at acquisition and acquired several flash drives that I mailed home to Da every time they got filled up. Da would transfer the information onto an external hard drive for safekeeping and mail the empty drives back to us again.

These were the backups, of course, just in case anything happened to the computer during contact. I know how that sounds, but it's reality. The first month we were in Helmand, we lost two men, one to a roadside bomb and the other to a sniper. The first man was Jasper. The second was Cooper. I sent their messages home to their families, just like I promised.

I HAD a special affinity for intelligence work, so they put me in charge of communications. Our battalion ran reconnaissance missions, and I ran radio communications with the Intelligence Corps as frontline eyes and ears to what was going on.

There was one officer I seemed to communicate with frequently.

Her call sign was Eagle, for radio purposes, and mine was Groundhog. It made sense, I guess, as she was somewhere off in Intelligence Land with a bird's eye view of the war, and I was just a rat on the ground, running through the maze of gunfire trying to feed her information.

I can't say it didn't burn my ass that I was more than capable of doing her job, even if I had *chosen* not to. She was professional, if not a tad sarcastic, but I had to respect her focus. She was there to win a war, and we seemed to make a decent team.

All the details matter when it comes to intelligence. If there was dissension in the camp of our enemies, we could exploit their weaknesses. If there was dissension in ours, it could make us vulnerable to an attack. All of it was relevant to winning a war. Sometimes she asked about morale, or the state of our supplies.

She asked me once about my accent. "Irish or British, soldier?"

"Both, ma'am."

"I see. Well, it's a bit confusing. You meld them together sometimes. Makes me think I'm talking to two different men."

If she only knew...

"Well, which would you like me to do more? Sure and I kin do the Irish bit" I lilted. "But if you prefer, I'm quite fluent in your language as well" I finished in my best Oxford English.

Her laugh came over the radio. It had been a long time since I'd made a woman laugh. I thought of Regan and decided I should probably return her latest letter, announcing her engagement. I just didn't know what to say.

"I'll take both please. One or the other just doesn't suit you as well."

"I'll take that as a compliment...ma'am."

"And I'll use you for target practice if you think you're going to start flirting with me, soldier."

"Understood, ma'am. My apologies." I tried to make the words come out like a soldier would speak them to a commanding officer, but I'm not sure I accomplished it. There was a brief silence before she came back on the line.

Our daily communications played with my head. I hadn't been with a woman in months, and for all I knew this one could be fat and hairy, but I began to fantasize about her all the same. In my dreams she had long blond hair like Regan, and she kissed like Regan, and she...well, you get the picture.

The days and weeks and months started to run together. James and I managed to keep our heads on, but we were involved in a near miss that should never have happened. We were on night patrol when our installment was bombed as they slept. Nine dead and fourteen wounded. If we hadn't been on patrol, it would have been us. The computer was destroyed in the blast. Good thing we had those backups.

The attack shook me. I'd been tracking the enemy's position and had a hunch something was amiss. It had been too quiet. I should have known. After that I had trouble focusing and started stumbling through my communications. The army sent reinforcements, and my commanding officer gave me a four-day pass to Qatar.

I stepped off the plane and was greeted by a soldier who gave me my papers and a change of clothes, then put me on a bus full of other soldiers. We were dropped at a hotel near the center of town to check into our rooms.

I took two showers. Turns out I had dust in every imaginable crevice and some even I hadn't thought of. I waited until the noise cleared out of the hallways, then donned my borrowed outfit and ducked out of the hotel to find a barber. After a good haircut and a clean shave, I was finally feeling human again. I was also bloody exhausted, so rather than go out exploring, I planted myself in the hotel bar and ordered a bottle of whiskey.

The initial whiff brought back the memory of the heaving shakes, but after that first sip it was like liquid gold, sliding down my throat, and after the first glass, I couldn't remember any of the reasons I'd wanted to join the military.

Lucky for me, I didn't want to remember. That's not why a man drinks whiskey.

5

I'd polished off about a quarter of the bottle on an empty stomach when I heard the clacking of heels on tile behind me. My senses perked. I hadn't heard that sound in what seemed like forever, not that a man forgets. It sparked a small flame that had been dormant for months. Still, I was afraid to turn around. Could have been my grandmother walking around in heels, for all I knew—or some commanding officer's wife. I just kept quiet and let myself imagine it was Regan.

It wasn't.

"Nice hula shirt, soldier. Wasn't aware they did many luaus in England. Or is it Ireland?"

I knew that voice, but I kept my back turned. After all, I wasn't a soldier at the moment. I was a civilian. At least, that's what I kept telling myself.

She came up next to me and leaned on the bar. Out of the corner of my eye I could make out auburn hair and a well-fitted blue dress. I swirled my glass and turned toward her in my best James Bond. "The Eagle has landed, I presume."

She was a knockout. If there was a God, he liked me very much.

"We could use a man with your deductive reasoning skills in the Intelligence Corps...Finn McCarthy."

"I'm sorry, but I seem to be at a loss. Had I known you were coming, I'd have ordered *your* background check."

"It's Kathleen."

She stuck out her hand, and I gripped it gently. "Can I buy you a drink?"

"I'm sorry, but I can't do that."

"Oh. Right!" I held up my glass. "Too many birds on your sleeve. I get it." I couldn't for the life of me figure out what the hell she was doing there.

"But, seeing as we are, coincidentally, at the same bar, there's no law against having a conversation. Especially out of uniform. I'll just order my own drink." Her hand signaled the bartender but her hazel eyes never left me.

I tried hard not to show just how much I noticed her lack of uniform. One long leg crossed over the other as I swallowed down another sip of whiskey. Coincidence my ass.

She ordered a glass of vodka, on the rocks, with a twist.

"So, how did you find me?"

Her smile was more of an indulgence. "I'm a senior-ranking officer in the Intelligence Corps. It wasn't that difficult."

"Well, bully for you." I held up my glass in mock salute. "In that case, I guess the real question is why?"

"Indeed. That is, in fact, the question of the day."

"Excuse me?"

"Well, don't all the best questions begin with why? For instance," she leaned a bit closer as she looked me up and down "why would a chap with two masters' degrees from Oxford be fighting on the front lines in Helmand Province with the regulars? And better yet, why would he be so bent on keeping it a secret?"

"It's not a secret. Obviously."

She had me at a disadvantage, seeing as I'd never laid eyes on her, but evidently she'd seen all my pictures dating back to diapers.

She stared at me for so long I started to feel self-conscious. "What, do you think I'm a spy or something?"

"No. I'm just trying to figure you out."

"How 'bout you start by answering my question? Why are you really here?" I leaned in close enough to smell her perfume, which caught me off guard, but I recovered easily. I got close enough to her face to make her nervous, then pulled slowly back, drawing her with me until she shook her head. She may have read my files, but she'd never seen me in action.

"I know what happened in your unit, and I know you've had a hard time with it."

I turned back toward the bar. "Yeah? And you know that how?"

"It was obvious from your communications, but even if it wasn't, there was a request from your CO."

"A request for what?"

"The leave. And that someone would make contact with you. See if you needed anyone to talk to. See if you were...still fit for duty."

I scoffed. "So they sent me a beautiful woman?"

She blinked back her surprise at my candor. I stood and came close to her. The dress, the perfume. It made a lot more sense that way.

"I can assure you," I whispered, close enough to her ear that I could feel the heat pouring off her skin "that I am always, and at any time" I pulled my head back slowly and looked her in the eye. "Fit. For duty."

She slapped me right across the face. I suppose I deserved it, but hey, she started it.

"I'm not here to bed you, you pompous arse! I'm here as a professional!"

"A professional *what?*" I started to walk away from that bottle of liquid gold, then thought better of it and turned back to grab it. She caught my arm as I did.

"I happen to have a degree in clinical psychology."

"A shrink? You're here to shrink me?" That deserved at least another shot, so I poured one in my glass and downed it. "I'm afraid you've worn the wrong dress for that."

She snatched the bottle away. "And I think you're over your three-drink limit, soldier."

I wanted to get up, but she put her hand on mine and the heat was undeniable. I was making her very nervous, though I wasn't sure which side of her brain it was coming from.

"Sit down, or we'll continue this session in my office with a guard at the door!"

"Session? It's a session now, is it? Last I looked I was on leave from the military. I was supposed to relax and unwind–not think about it anymore. If that's how you're going to play it, why don't you just cuff me and get it over with?"

My chest was heaving, and it felt like being in a firefight. The room went fuzzy and I started to sweat, trying furiously to blink the images away.

Her demeanor changed almost immediately. She slid her fingers gently around my hand and brought out this soothing voice I hadn't heard in any of our previous communications. "I'd rather we just talk. Can't we just talk? Two people, having a drink, sharing time together. Would that be all right?"

My focus came back to her hand still touching mine. I brought my pulse down and slowed my breathing. It was over, for the moment, so I sat back down.

"Can I have my bottle back?" I was trying to be polite, but it came out through closed teeth.

"Well that depends."

"On what?"

"On if you're going to play nice."

She was probably nervous I might lose my temper, but I wondered if it wasn't all wrapped up together. Suddenly I wanted the warmth of a woman like I hadn't wanted it in a long time. "I *always* play nice."

She seemed to sense the shift but turned away and took a long sip off her vodka. "How about we get some food into you?"

"Suit yourself" I replied. "I'd just like to ask one thing."

"What's that?"

"We're just normal people. Not commanding officer to subordi-nate or shrink to patient."

"Sure. No problem."

"And one more thing."

"Yes?"

"Forgive the delivery, but I don't like being blindsided, and the fact that you seem to already know my life story is something you could have kept to yourself rather than mashing it in my face."

Her eyes hit the floor. "You're right. I'm sorry about that."

"I already know you out rank me so there's no need to prove it, and I don't want to be treated like a test subject. I just want to be treated like a human being."

Her eyebrows went up. "Fine."

I asked the bartender to cap my bottle and have it sent to my room, which he did. We moved from the bar to the restaurant, and I pulled out her chair, like any gentleman would. She thanked me and put her napkin across her lap.

"See how nice this can be? We're supposed to be on a break from the military, so we should act like it, don't you think?" I ordered a bottle of red wine and looked at her for approval.

"Definitely."

Her head never moved, but her gaze flitted back and forth nervously between the menu and me. It made me chuckle.

"What? What's so funny?"

"Nothing." I picked up my menu. "Have you eaten here? What's good?"

"Okay...small talk."

"What, you're incapable of being on a date?"

"This is *not* a date."

"At ease, Captain. I'm just making light of an obviously awkward situation."

She shook her head. "How did you know I was a captain?"

"Well I've addressed you enough times over the radio. I think I should know your rank by now. Besides, clinical psychologist? I did the math."

"Something you're very good at, I hear."

I folded my hands in my lap. "And what else have you heard?"

She closed her eyes for a moment, then opened them and looked straight at me.

"I know that your father was a footballer, your mother prefers Britain to Ireland, your grandmother paid for both Eton and Oxford, you refused a commission, for reasons which I hope will be forthcoming, and..." She looked down at her napkin. "You've been in love with a girl named Regan since you were about eighteen."

I swallowed down some wine. "But *why* do you know those things?"

"Because we want to move you into the Intelligence Corps, but we had to do a thorough background check before we asked."

"I enlisted."

"And yet you could be my peer." She was genuinely baffled. "Why aren't you?"

"Why don't we talk about you instead?"

"We're not here to talk about me."

"You said we were going to talk like normal people. You obviously know all there is to know about me. It's your turn."

"All right. What do you want to know?"

I put my elbows up on the table. "Well, as a soldier, I'd like to know why you want me in the Intelligence Corps, but as a man, I'd like to know why you chose that dress."

"Pardon?"

I maintained absolute eye contact as I spoke. "You could have come here in uniform, or jeans, or even a hula shirt, but you came here in a fitted blue dress with a drop pendant hanging to just the right height in your cleavage, matching earrings, expensive perfume, and no stockings under those high heels. That tells me you're a woman who just might be looking for more than answers." I leaned back. "Not that I'm against the idea. Quite the contrary. I'd just like to know what angle we're supposed to be going at this from."

Her face turned bright red. She picked up her napkin and pretended to dab her mouth as she covered her face. "And that, Mr. McCarthy, is why you're an excellent fit for the Intelligence Corps."

"No, the reason I'm a good fit is that I've already assumed you know the rest of my history, otherwise you wouldn't have tried to appeal to the player in me with such an utter...lack..of mercy" I said, conceding her beauty.

Her face got even more red.

"If you'll excuse me." She stood, so I did too. "I have to..."

I inclined my hand away from the table. "Be my guest."

It wasn't easy, being dapper in a hula shirt, but I had to give it a go. When the waiter came around, I ordered us salads, steak with baked potato and vegetables, and a plate of shrimp as an appetizer.

It took quite a while before she returned, but when she finally did, the shrimp was waiting, and the salads had already made their appearance.

"What's this?"

"Dinner, of course." I stood and proceeded to seat her. "I took the liberty of ordering."

"You did, did you? And what, may I ask, are we having?"

I shrugged. "A simple steak dinner. I'm sure it'll be delicious after eating dust and ration packs for the last several months."

"I see."

"Is that all right?"

She smiled with her lips closed. "It's fine. I'm not very hungry, though. I ate before I came."

"Well, I hope you won't mind if I eat mine and yours then, because I haven't had a steak since I left Ireland."

She picked at her salad and sipped on her wine. "Tell me, Finn, about growing up. Was it mostly in Ireland?"

"I feel I'm at a disadvantage, seeing as I don't really know when you're asking me a question to which you already know the answer."

She sighed. "Let's make a deal, shall we? No more games, and if I ask you a question, it's because I really don't know the answer."

"Good. At least we're done talking about my childhood."

"Excuse me?"

I gave her a tight-lipped smile as they took our salads and put down our dinner plates. She hadn't eaten one shrimp and barely touched her salad.

"I think I'd feel better if you just asked me what you really want to know, and what you really want to know is if the bomb that killed most of my platoon tipped me off balance. The answer you're looking for is yes. It did. How could it not? I'm having anger I've never felt before. Guilt, like I shoulda known it was coming. I see and feel things in my dreams that sometimes come true the very next day, and it's never happened that fast before. I can't–"

"Wait a minute." She held up her hand to stop me from talking. "What do you mean it's never happened that fast before? What are you talking about–your dreams coming true? Are you having nightmares?"

"Something like that."

"Well, I'd like to–"

"Look, I'm not unstable, if that's what you're thinking. Every man out there in Helmand Province will tell you the same thing. You can't...go through what we go through and not have it affect you, and the ones who tell you it doesn't are lying through their teeth. But that doesn't make me unfit. I just needed a break is all. I needed to unwind and have a drink and have a nice steak dinner with a beautiful woman and remind myself I'm still human. It's what we all need, once in a while."

She nodded and it got very quiet for a few moments. "In that case, when you're done with your four days of leave, we'd like to move you out of your present post and bring you over for some specialized training. If what I know about Oxford's math and science departments are true, you could probably *give* these classes, but since you insist on remaining enlisted..." She stopped and made a point of looking straight at me "...you'll begin training to operate with our team directly."

"And *you* want me on your team?"

"I do."

I snickered. "As a direct report? Don't you think that could get a little complicated?"

"You flatter yourself, Mr. McCarthy."

"Do I now?" I'd seen that look on so many women's faces, it was unmistakable. She just needed a little persuasion. This was where Regan's lessons came in handy.

"I think you'd better take some time to consider your options." She stood, making it clear that the date was over. "I've rented a beach house about an hour from here for the next three days. I need to get out of the city, feel the sun, touch the water, that kind of thing. You can reach me at this number when you've made your decision."

"What makes you think I need more time?"

"Because this won't be the easiest assignment you've ever had, that's why, and because you still have a lot to learn. Especially about women."

I laughed out loud and rolled out the brogue. "Really now! Do tell…"

She slid the card my direction and leaned down, putting both hands on the table in front of me and giving me a good look down her dress. "Because I'm allergic to shellfish, I can't stand Italian dressing, I'm a card-carrying vegetarian, and because Finn, as a woman I have to tell you that assuming you know what I like is a gross overestimation of your ability to please me."

With that she stood and walked away from the table, leaving me to eat two steak dinners and finish an entire bottle of wine by myself.

6

The next morning, I woke with a food hangover and a half-drunk bottle of whiskey staring at me from the dresser. I got dressed, pocketed her card, checked out of the hotel, and took a cab to the seaside. It wasn't hard to find the rental house she'd indicated, but she wasn't there, so I walked the beach barefoot, then planted myself in the sand to wait and watch the waves for a while.

As it happened, the waves were worth watching because she came up out of them sporting a string bikini and a couple of tattoos her dress had hidden nicely. She smiled as she stood in front of me, wringing out her hair.

"Hello, Finn. Back so soon?"

"You're the intelligence expert. You tell me. Or wait." I got up and brushed the sand off my shorts. "Is it the psychologist I'm talking to today? You know, sometimes I feel like I'm talking to two different women." I grinned.

"All right, you've had your fun. Would you like to come in for lunch?"

"That all depends."

"On what?"

"On what vegetarians eat for lunch, of course."

"I'm sure we'll find something you like."

"Well, if you don't mind, I think I'd like to go for a swim first."

I began to strip off my shirt, and when I grabbed for the button on my shorts Kathleen held up one hand.

"What do you think you're doing?" Her head turned quickly to the side.

I popped the button and dropped my drawers, revealing of course the bathing suit I'd bought in the city, hidden safely under my shorts, for just this effect.

She laughed as I started to run away in my swim trunks, tossing a handful of sand after me. "You *are* unstable! Just remember that!"

Swimming in the warm salt waters of the gulf was soothing in a deeply satisfying way. I wanted to float there until all the desert grime was cleaned away, along with all the images that dirtied my mind. I hadn't been swimming since childhood, which seemed more than a lifetime ago. I got out and laid on the sand, letting the sun bake my skin until I knew I'd had enough.

Just off the back porch was an outside shower. Kathleen was sitting in a hanging chair in the shade watching me as I came up the beach, with a glass of white wine in one hand and a book in the other. She was still wearing the bikini, although she'd wrapped a see-through sort of sarong around her waist and tied it at the hip.

"What a gorgeous day!" I called out. "I'm just going to wash the sand off." I pointed to the barely enclosed space with a spigot hanging over it.

She nodded, without looking up from her book.

I stripped off my swim trunks and jumped tentatively into the stream, assuming it would be cold. It wasn't. It was just as warm as the ocean–maybe warmer. Still, it felt good to stand there. It seems I couldn't get enough of the feeling of being washed clean.

Purely out of curiosity, I snuck a peek at Kathleen and was surprised to find her watching me with little shame, despite her show of embarrassment at my drawer-dropping session earlier.

"Are you enjoying the show?" I quipped.

"Immensely, yes. Thank you. Much more interesting than my book."

I wasn't sure I liked the turnabout. It made me feel abnormally awkward, although why it should have didn't make any sense at all. Women were what I did best. If she wanted to stare, let her. I had nothing to be ashamed of. Still, it was slightly unsettling. Something didn't feel right.

I could handle the man and woman bit. The hard part was this blurred line between commander and subordinate, doctor and patient.

I found a towel and wrapped it around my middle, emerging from the small space to find Kathleen gone. I hung up my swim trunks and pulled a clean pair of underwear out of my pack, along with another pair of shorts and a t-shirt I'd bought along with the trunks. While I appreciated the army's effort on my behalf, I wasn't really a hula shirt kind of guy.

I found Kathleen in the kitchen of the little house, pouring some more wine into her glass and offering one to me. "It's warm. Seems ice is against the law here."

"It's fine, thank you."

Kathleen sat on a stool at the counter. "So, have you considered my offer?"

"Which one?"

She wasn't amused by this. "The only one I've made you."

"Yes, I am interested in transferring out of my unit, and yes I would like to join the Intelligence Corps, although I'm not a fan of leaving my mates out there high and dry."

"You have the potential to help them more overall as a part of our team than you do boots on ground. Not that where we go or what we do isn't dangerous. In some ways it's more so. They know we're running intel and when they find out where we're at they try to bomb us, just like we do them. We don't stay in one place very long, though. It's much harder to hit a moving target."

I nodded. Military Strategy 101 said that wars were won and lost because of Intel. The ability to wipe out entire armories, weapons factories and command centers would do more to cripple our enemy than anything. If the enemy was confused and scrambling, they wouldn't be shooting at my friends. The sooner we won, the sooner I could save what was left of my original battalion.

Grams was right. My talents were being wasted on the ground. As an eagle I could track my prey, see the whole picture, and affect change. As a groundhog, I'd eventually become dinner.

Suddenly I regretted refusing that commission, but those were thoughts for another day. I was standing in front of a beautiful woman in a string bikini who might just be willing to provide me with the ultimate distraction from the war and all its pain. "Can I ask you a question?"

"Of course."

I swished some wine through my mouth. "Now that we've got that settled, the bit about the transfer, do you want me to leave?"

"You are absolutely free to go, soldier. My role as a commanding officer in requesting your transfer is finished."

"Yes ma'am." I saluted her and took a step closer. "And your role as a clinical psychologist, is that finished as well? Have you determined that I am, in fact, fit for duty?"

"I believe you are indeed fit for duty." She smiled. "A bit off balance in general, perhaps, but I doubt it's the army that's done it to you. And some time I'd love to talk to you about your dreams, but I'm willing to save that for another time if you are."

Another step closer. "So, I guess it's settled then."

"Yes, it is." She looked away, sipping her wine. "You could've just called, actually."

"So now that all that military stuff is out the way." One more step. "As a woman." I tipped her chin up "Do you still want me to leave?"

She took a deep breath and it stuttered into her chest. "No. I don't."

I leaned in close to her face, speaking softly. "And why is that?"

She smiled up at me. "Because I was hoping to shag you, of course."

As I started to kiss her, I remembered her comments about over-estimating my ability to please her, so I let her lead.

"You're the ranking officer here. Why don't you just tell me what you want?" I smiled, ever so willing to oblige her.

She had no problem satisfying that request. I was a good little soldier, and did exactly as I was told and then some. After all, every soldier is encouraged to improvise when necessary to achieve the overall goal of the mission.

She was an interesting sort. Seemed to love the chase and the sport of lovemaking and that suited me just fine, but she wasn't attached in an emotional way to any of it. I could have walked away and seen her on the street two days later and it wouldn't even be awkward.

As afternoon wore into evening, we were laying on the bed letting the breeze from the ceiling fan cool our overheated bodies. I looked over at the closet and saw the blue dress on its hanger.

I pointed at it, as understanding dawned. "That dress."

She looked over at it and smiled. "Yes?"

"It had nothing to do with the army's desire to get me to join the IC, did it?"

"No. Not a thing. But I am good at my job." She traced a finger up and down my chest. "I'd seen your pictures. Did a little digging into your history." She rolled back onto the pillows. "Good help is hard to find out in the desert. There's a war on, you know."

So, she was using me? That felt strangely backward. I blinked a few times.

"Oh, don't look so shocked! It's not like you haven't done the exact same thing probably hundreds of times."

"Well, I don't know about hundreds. That would be excessive, don't you think?"

She pushed up onto one elbow. "Tell me about Regan."

She could have knifed me in the back and it would've felt better than that particular question at that particular moment. "Excuse me?"

"What's she like?"

"And how exactly is it that you know anything at all about her? Do I even want to know?"

"If you're going to be part of the IC, you're going to learn a lot of things that will probably shock you. You'd best get over it now."

"Well it has no bearing on my work with the IC, and besides that it's none of your business."

"Look, we can be friends, can't we? It's all right. You can tell me about her."

"I'm sorry, but now that I know you're a psychologist, talking about anything personal seems very...I don't know, clinical. And that subject in particular is very much off limits."

"Suit yourself." She rolled on top of me. "Perhaps we should change the subject."

"I do like the way you think though."

THE TWO OF us had a lot of fun together. Three days' worth of eating, drinking, swimming, sleeping and shagging, in repeating cycles. I almost forgot where we were, and why we were there. Almost.

The return to reality was not going to be easy. It seems the whole captain/corporal thing was going to be a bigger deal than I realized. When we went back to our posts we couldn't act as if we had anything but professional communications. Coming out of theatre and into her unit was not as easy as I thought it would be on either account.

She was there constantly, in the training sessions and drill sessions and on missions and debriefs. It was interesting to watch her in her role as captain. She obviously loved her job and it wasn't as if she treated her subordinates badly, she was just too busy trying to win the war to care about anything else. It seems she had an enormously handy work/play switch she could turn on and off as the need arose.

The beach house hadn't been the end of it, either. The escape was just too tempting, for both of us. If there were a couple hours of downtime available, we'd find a way to sneak off separately and meet up for a little R & R of our own. Somehow, we were good enough at our respective jobs to keep it a secret. They were like mini missions hidden within the greater scope of my education.

We started doing real missions back in Helmand Province, but in a different area than I'd been in before. I fell easily back into soldiering mode, and our small group of operatives worked well together as a team. For the first time since my enlistment, I felt like I was making a real difference.

After about two months in the field with little time to rendezvous, Kathleen asked me to meet her off-compound near the supply depot. It was dangerous. Night patrols were numerous, and they tended to shoot first and ask questions later.

I waited in the back of a supply truck until I heard her whistle. I started to climb down but she signaled me to stay where I was. I did as I was told. When she appeared again, she stepped quickly into the truck and pulled me back into the darkness.

I began to pull her shirt up out of her cargo pants, kissing her neck. "God, I've missed the taste of you."

"Finn, wait." She pulled out of my arms. "I need to talk to you."

I tried to focus on her, letting my eyes adjust to the darkness. "What is it, love?"

She was completely silent, so I grabbed onto her hands. "Well, don't keep me waiting. What's the trouble? Have we been found out?"

"No. It's worse than that."

"Bloody hell, what could be worse than that? I'll be thrown in The Glasshouse for shagging an officer."

She held my hands firmly and pulled me into a part of the truck that was a little brighter so we could see one another's faces. "I'm pregnant."

My heart stopped momentarily. I kept waiting for it to restart, but the blood wouldn't flow to my head so I could think about what she said. "You're–" I stammered. "You're...what?"

"You heard me. Don't make me say it again."

I sat on a box of some sort, hoping it was booby trapped and would just blow me to smithereens. A baby? I looked up and said it out loud. "A baby?"

"Usually, yes. That's how these things tend to end up." She was nodding in her captain sort of way.

"And you're certain? I mean, we are out here in the desert under stress and all that."

"It's not just a missed period, Finn. I've had a blood test."

"By whom?" I stood up. "Do they know–about us?"

She shook her head. "No, I've a friend who's a nurse. She kept it confidential and I didn't tell her who the father was. We can't tell *anyone*, Finn."

"But we have to fix it."

"Fix it how, exactly? We're in the middle of the war, in the middle of the desert, and I'm the highest-ranking officer out here at the moment. If I announce this to anyone there'll be an investigation."

"Can't you just say it happened in Qatar, and you don't know who the father is?"

"Qatar was four months ago. The story won't play out. Besides...I don't want an abortion."

In all my years of playing the field I'd never once been faced with an unwanted pregnancy. I was raised Irish Catholic, for God's sake, and of course I valued human life but...

"How did this happen, love? We've always been careful. I've used protection like it was a religion."

"You mean to say you've never had anyone come to you like this before? Ever?"

"Not once."

She raised her eyebrows and crossed her arms over her chest. "Well, statistically speaking with a two percent failure rate, given your lifestyle, it was bound to bite you in the arse one of these days."

"Oh, that's rich, comin' from you, Miss *Good Help is Hard to Find*." I started pacing in the back of the truck.

She tugged at my arm. "Sit down and lower your voice! We start shaking this truck and there'll be a patrol on us in no time."

I took a deep breath in and out and tried to clear my head. "How long have you known about this?"

"Couple weeks."

My eyes went wide. "Couple *weeks*? And you're just now gettin' round to telling me?"

She bent down. "You know you default back to the Irish when you're angry? It's cute." She kissed me and our foreheads leaned together.

I pulled away and put my head in my hands. "Don't you see? You've got to go home. You can't be out here and be pregnant. It's not safe. I can't protect—"

"You know, you're not obligated to do anything about this Finn. It's not your problem, it's mine."

"Not my problem! Not my problem? Are ye *mad*? Of course it's my problem!" I looked at her. "It is...my problem, right?"

She stood abruptly. "Of course it is, you daft prick, what do you think? Just because you've bedded every female from London to Dublin doesn't mean... I mean, yes, I've had my share of... It's yours, all right? There's been no one else. Not since we've been together."

I put both palms in the air. "That's absolutely what I thought. I was just...checking."

When I looked up at her again, there were tears in her eyes. The captain was gone. Standing before me was a woman whose vulnerability I'd rarely witnessed, and it broke me. I tried to go to her, to comfort her, but she shrugged me off.

Who could blame her? I'd been selfish, rude, and now insulting. Instead I put my hands on her shoulders. "Look at me. Please." She did as I asked. "I've done this all wrong."

"What's that?"

"I've lost me marbles." I sighed, the Irish coming straight out of my heart. "There's a wee babe comin' into this world with my name on it, and I've done nothing but think of myself. I'm an arse and I'm sorry for it."

I slipped my arms around her neck and swallowed hard. We were great in the sack and not much else, but that didn't matter at the moment. Right was still right.

"Marry me."

She wiggled out of my arms. "No."

"I won't have a babe in this world and leave it without a name."

"No." She went and sat back down. "It's not you, I just...I don't want to be married."

"Why not?"

"I don't know - my parents are divorced, my brother's divorced, even my grandmother is divorced. Hasn't worked out all that well for anyone I know, how about you?"

I thought about my parents. They weren't divorced, but maybe they should have been. "Just because others have tried and failed, does that mean it's not worth trying? That's a whole other *life* in there!" I pointed at her stomach for emphasis.

Her hands covered it protectively. "I know that! Don't you think I know that?"

"Do you want to raise a baby alone?"

"No."

"And you don't want an abortion."

"No."

"Then say you'll marry me. It's not like we're not...compatible."

She smiled over at me. "Well, that's true."

"I know how you like your toast and that you prefer coffee with cream over tea with milk." I thought some more. "And that you're allergic to shellfish, you hate Italian dressing, and you're a card-carrying vegetarian to boot! We'll learn the rest as we go." I threaded my fingers through hers. "Come on. What do you say? We don't have to tell anyone, but we'll know. I'll know. And then when all this is dover, we'll make a life, the three of us."

"I don't know. I don't know what I want."

"Say you'll think about it."

"We're not in love with each other, Finn. I know it. You know it."

She was right, but there were consequences to our actions and a tiny babe wasn't going to pay the price for my arrogance. "Just promise me you'll think about it."

"I'll think about it."

We sat together on one of the boxes and I held her for a long time. Neither of us said anything else.

7

A fter we parted that night, all hell broke loose in Helmand. We had a week or more of aggressive firefights. We lost three men. Every time I even looked at Kathleen an intense fear rose up in me for her and the innocent life inside her. A baby. My baby. And already we were raising it in the middle of a war zone.

It wreaked havoc on my mind as I thought about all the children caught in a fight that wasn't theirs. I wanted to kill everything in sight and end the war immediately. I nearly lost my mind with worry.

I wanted her out of there.

Then they gave us orders to break camp and regroup at a command post away from the fighting. After two days of discussions and strategy meetings, it was announced that our group would go on another mission into Helmand. Another dangerous mission, and they gave every man (and woman) a forty-eight-hour furlough before we left. That should have been my first clue.

WE GOT on a transport and went back to Qatar. After everyone split up to go to their hotels, I doubled back and met Kathleen at a church complex on the outskirts of the city. It wasn't much, but it was anonymous. It also wasn't my idea.

She looked at me. "Now what?"

I took her hand. "Now we wait."

A half-hour later an army chaplain showed up in a cab. "Hello Finn."

"Hello Bryce."

Kathleen looked at me. "Friend of yours?"

"Oxford."

"Ah."

I shook Bryce's hand and then pulled him into an embrace. "I know we talked about it, but this stays very much on the down low, eh?"

"I am, as it were, sworn to secrecy." He gripped his collar for effect.

"Brilliant. Bryce? This is Kathleen Collins."

He took her hand. "Happy to meet you. Now, I realize you're in a bit of a hurry. Where would you like to go?"

I looked around and found the Anglican Church. Kathleen wasn't Catholic so it would have to do. "How about on the steps over there?"

"Fine with me." Bryce smiled at Kathleen, who looked petrified. "Are you all right?"

She nodded. "Perfect."

Bryce looked skeptical, but we kept moving. It was hot and we'd already been waiting for a while. Thankfully, the sun was in just the right position to shade the steps, so we climbed them and stood at the top.

Truth be told, I wasn't feeling all that well myself. It's one thing when you make a decision like this and you're thrilled about it. It's a whole other story when you're gettin' it legal for legal's sake. I'd thought it through a thousand times. Mum would've demanded that I do the right thing. Even Da would've insisted that I lie down in the bed I made.

I wasn't questioning the morals of it, merely grieving the

stupidity of my choices. It was absurd to think I could carry on like I had indefinitely and without consequence. The odds had been against me for years, I'd just chosen to conveniently ignore them. Kathleen was right.

So was Regan.

I never did return her letter. She was likely married by now, and for all I knew, had a baby of her own on the way. I started to wonder– if I'd listened to her earlier, would things have been different between us?

Then again, I was a firm believer that everything happened for a reason. A pregnancy like this would've crushed Regan, and I was so very thankful that it hadn't happened accidentally on a night she never even had the good sense to be thankful for.

That part of my life seemed so very far away now.

The desert came back into focus right around the time Bryce started with the "do you, Finn McCarthy" part. I said I did, and I meant it. Kathleen didn't back down either, but she looked like a hooked trout, and when I kissed her it was like kissing Eiran. We were in for a heap o' trouble and we both knew it, but it was done and that was that.

There were no rings. No reminders. No remembrances. No real promises of any kind. What could we possibly promise, except the till death do us part...part? We were down to thirty-six hours. It felt like a life sentence with nothing but capital punishment to look forward to. Perhaps it was a mistake, but there was no turning back.

BRYCE'S CAB had been waiting the whole time, and it took the three of us back into Doha, where it dropped me and Bryce off at a bar on the far side of town, then continued on with Kathleen, so as not to raise any suspicions.

I paid the driver and gave him specific directions to her hotel, then stood there with my hands in my pockets as it drove her away. I didn't know what else to do. We couldn't risk spending our "honey-moon night" together. She had to meet up with some of the other officers later that night and continue to make things look as normal as possible. She tried to smile at me as the cab pulled away from the curb, but I could tell she was in a bad way.

"You all right, mate?" I felt Bryce's hand on my shoulder.

"Not really. I feel awful. I'd rather go drown myself in The Gulf."

His face was gentle and understanding as he hooked me with his arm solidly around my neck. "How 'bout let's drown in the water of life instead, eh?" Bryce was a good mate.

While we were at Oxford, he studied theology, obviously, which made for some interesting conversations on the nights we both happened to be studying whiskey. We joined the army right around the same time, although I'm sure his reasons were better than mine. He got his commission through an abbreviated officer's training designed for doctors and clergy and the like. I never dreamed we'd end up in the same part of Helmand Province, but then again, Da always said that God has a way of bringing people 'round at just the right time.

Bryce knew the kind of man I'd been. Still, he didn't judge when I'd come to him asking for help and discretion. Like I said, he was a good mate.

We stepped into the Sheraton, and he directed us toward the lift. We rode down one floor, and the doors opened into what looked and felt exactly like an Irish pub. Bryce sat me down at the bar and ordered two pints of Guinness and a couple glasses of Jameson's, neat.

I looked around, astonished at how much I missed Ireland. I would've given just about anything to be back there, before any of this happened. "How ever did you find this place?"

He grinned. "We are allowed to talk to Catholics, you know."

I raised one eyebrow. "Pardon?"

He shook his head, laughing. "I have a friend who's a chaplain for The Royal Irish. He tipped me off."

I turned on the accent. "Well, are you certain an Englishman won't be killed on sight in an Irish pub?"

"No more so than an Irish traitor, I imagine."

I grinned at Bryce, placing my hand over my heart. "I'll have you know that my mother's family has served the British Army for centuries. I was bound by duty to do my bit for king and country."

"Well then, perhaps we're both foreigners here after all." He held up the Guinness and took a sip.

I felt that. Like a foreigner. I'd never had a good sense of where I belonged, and though I'd probably always call Ireland home, I felt an equally strong kinship to the UK, which is largely why I found myself in these circumstances in the first place.

I looked at the Guinness and Jameson's sitting side-by-side and chuckled. "You remembered?"

"Finn, my boy, you aren't an easy man to forget."

"What's that supposed to mean?"

He slapped one hand down on the bar. "If I hadn't been set on serving the church, you were my idol."

"I haven't a clue what you're talking about." I couldn't imagine being anyone's idol but held up the glass anyway "To the water of life."

"The water of life."

I took a sip. "What are you talking about–your idol?"

"You're joking, right? You were the shining example to which all Exeter men aspired. Every man there wanted to be you." He just looked at me.

"Oh! You mean the women."

"Of course I mean the women! Isn't that what you were there for?" He snickered.

Unfortunately, I was in no mood for kidding, even if he wasn't. Kidding, that is. "What I was *there for* was an education." I drank the entire glass of whiskey and set it down on the bar. It was promptly refilled.

"All right, mate" He set his drink down. "My apologies."

I rested my elbows up on the bar. "I've just married a girl I knocked up but I don't love, and my Irish Catholic roots are bumping up against my love of the Anglican Church's convenient liberality. I'm having a bit of a crisis at the moment, so forgive me for cutting short the banter."

Bryce nodded to the bartender, and he left us the bottle. We sat in silence for a while, the sights and sounds of the pub bringing me back to younger days–carefree days–when all I had to worry about was which girl I might go home with that night.

"You know what I still don't get?" I asked him in all seriousness.

"What's that?" Bryce burped as he poured himself another drink. "Sorry. I'm a bit of a lightweight these days."

"Why now? I mean, why, in the middle of a war, on the cusp of a mission that may cost me my life, is this happening? And what kind of a God puts a pregnant woman in the middle of a war-torn country?"

Bryce just swirled the brown liquid in his glass. He didn't try to answer, which was fine, because I didn't expect he knew.

"And why did I go all those years in school shagging everything in sight with never an incident and now...Now!"

"Finn. Mate. *Why* is the one question everyone asks, and it's one of the only ones we can't answer. Why is one of the most dangerous questions in the English language, and it's best not to ask it, believe me. It'll drive a man mad."

"I guess."

"Besides, I don't have the answer."

"I know."

He hesitated. "But you do."

I finished another shot. "Believe me, mate, if I had the answer I'd have changed something by now."

"Maybe it wasn't time for it to be answered until now."

I shook my head, defeated. "Let's drink." I grabbed hold of the Guinness and took a long draft. "And eat. Do you think they have any food here? I'm bloody-well starving, and if I don't eat soon I'll be talking to you from the flat of my back."

Bryce laughed and put a hand on my shoulder again. He signaled the bartender who brought us out some bread and hummus, then hot bowls of what passed for a pretty decent Irish stew.

It was as close as I was going to get to home for a while, and I was thankful for it. Of course, in the army you're thankful for just about everything. To be sitting out of the dust and the blazing hot sun, sharing a pint and some stew with a mate from home was pretty close to heaven.

I was weary to the bone, with no idea how I would ever gather the energy to balance the intensity of this upcoming mission with my new responsibilities as husband and father.

I finished my stew and looked over at Bryce. "Thank you. I meant to say it earlier, but..."

"No worries, mate." He smiled as he finished his pint. "So whatever happened to that girl from Oxford?"

"We just established there were more than either of us could count so–." Suddenly it dawned on me. "You mean Regan." My voice dropped, and I instinctively reached for the whiskey.

He watched my hand with interest. "Sore subject?"

"Not by any fault of yours." I took a long drink. "I don't know whose fault it was. Probably mine."

"Did she break it off, or you?"

"We were never together."

His face registered shock and awe. "That simply cannot be true. You were together all the time, and I don't know of any woman capable of resisting you past the first date" he chuckled.

"She's not just any woman. We were mates." I sipped my whiskey and let the obvious hang out there for him to grab onto. "Nothing more."

"Not even once? That doesn't seem quite like you."

"There was once." I sat there staring at the top of the bar. Memories swirled and landed at the bottom of my glass. "But we were both very drunk, and only one of us remembers it even happened."

Bryce slowly nodded his understanding. "And I'm guessing he likes to drink whiskey as he reminisces."

"He does indeed."

"Where is she now?"

"London. Finished her law degree and works as a barrister for a firm there. Marrying one of the partners, last I heard."

"What, you're not to be the 'Mate of Honor'?"

He had a goofy smile on his face and I had to laugh. "It's probably done by now. Just as well."

"You don't sound very convinced."

"No, really!" I answered. "While that night remains, to date, the best night I have *ever* spent in the sack, we weren't meant to be together any more than Kathleen and I. She's kind and virtuous and absolutely brilliant, and yet we laugh all the time and she's great fun to drink with. I just–wish I were more like her, I guess."

"Best night in the sack...*ever*? Really?"

I looked at him, incredulous. "I'm pouring my heart out here, and that's the point you choose to stick on?"

"Coming from someone who has admittedly bedded more women than I can even fantasize about, that's pretty high praise. I mean, I may be a vicar, but I'm not exactly a saint, and I'm certainly not dead." He grinned.

"Yeah, well." I looked into the bottom of my glass. "She taught me things I'd never learnt before."

He snickered loudly. "Now this I've gotta hear!"

"How *old* are you?"

"Sorry." He laughed. "It's the whiskey, I swear!"

"Listen, I don't know how to explain it, but she wasn't the kind of woman who was easily satisfied. And I don't mean sexually."

"Obviously."

"Come again?"

"Well, just look at you!"

Frustrated, I rolled my hand in circles, trying to pull the right words up to the surface. "She wanted more than sex. More than I knew how to give, anyway. She challenged me to see it as some sort of transcendental, spiritual experience. For her it was all about knowing someone so well that you got...*lost* in one another."

Bryce tipped his head in agreement. "She's right about that."

"Oh bollocks, not you too?"

"That's how it is with me and Anna."

"Anna? Sod it! I'd forgotten you took a wife! I'm so sorry I haven't asked about her till now. How is she?"

"She's good. Hates the war, but keeps the fire burning for me."

"And it's...like that for the two of you?"

He nodded. "When you find the person you're supposed to be with, it takes it to a whole other level. It's supposed to be based on a relationship that exists before all the shagging comes into play."

"So all these years, I've been doing it backwards, is that what you're saying?"

"No, I'm just saying that up until now you've gotten a good taste of how the other half lives and...if I may be so bold, found it lacking? By comparison?"

"You could say that."

He swirled his glass again. "I think she proved what you didn't want to admit."

"And what's that?"

His voice gentled. "That there's more to women than sex."

"Don't be silly. I've always known that."

"In your head yes, but until the night that only *you* remember, that knowledge hadn't made it to your heart yet." He poked his finger into my chest, and I turned away.

"And now, here I am, married to a woman I barely know, about to be a father, and any chance of learning that for myself has been blown away with the desert sand." I wasn't usually one for pity parties, but I felt strangely justified, even if it was my own damn fault.

He slapped me on the back. "Don't be so hard on yourself. You're doing the right thing. Give love a chance, mate. After the war, when things settle down, you might find love suits you. Half the battle is letting it inside."

"What's the other half?"

Bryce shrugged. "Keeping it there."

8

Later that night, full of whiskey and Guinness, I snuck up to Kathleen's hotel room and knocked gently on the door. It took her quite some time to open it, and when she saw me, I was pulled quickly inside.

"What the hell are you doing here? Don't you know we could be found out?"

"It's two in the morning. Anyone who's still awake will be convinced they dreamed me." I pulled her into my arms. "How are you?"

She shook her head into my chest, trembling. It broke my heart to think she was miserable on her wedding night. I was her husband. I needed to do something about that.

"Come and sit. Let me get you something to drink."

She let me lead her over to the bed, where I set her down carefully and went to fetch some water. Ever since I'd heard about the baby, it was like she was made of glass. The hard-nosed captain I'd met over the intercom I had no problem sending into theatre. This person sitting on the bed was frail and unsure, and she was carrying my child.

I was terrified.

She needed protection. Provision. Rest. I could give her none of those things. I couldn't even tell anyone what she was going through–what *we* were going through.

She was holding some papers in her hands, but I moved them to the bed so she could hold the water.

"I've been gathering information for you."

"Information?" I didn't understand.

"In case anything happens to me."

I gripped her shoulders. "Stop it."

She shrugged out of my grasp. "No, Finn. We've got to be realistic! I know where we're going–what we're risking!"

"Well, I'm risking it too."

"I know that. I know. But I'm leaving these things here–in a safe deposit box. Just in case. It's a list. See?" She picked up the papers, trying to appear encouraging. "These are all my family members, and where they live, and their addresses and phone numbers. These are my bank accounts. Since we're married now, everything will be shared. I have a good deal of money saved from being single for so long. If either now, or sometime in the future I don't survive but the baby does, I want you to put it in trust for him...or her."

"Please, stop talking like this." I rubbed a hand over my face. I was much too drunk for this conversation. I'd been hoping we might consummate the union, but apparently not.

"I've sent an email to my best friend in England with the location and number for the safety deposit box. I'll mail her my extra key tomorrow, and here's one for you." She closed it into my palm, along with a card that contained the number and location of the box. "If you want to put your information in there too it might be...well, it might be good."

I took the papers out of her hands and set them on the bed again. "My parents don't even know I've been married. No one does. This is ludicrous!"

"I know it sounds irrational, but there are so many things I never thought of before. I've never had to worry about anyone but myself. Now there's this–baby. And I don't know, I–"

I pulled her into my chest again. She cried, and so did I. It felt like I was coming unglued. I stroked the top of her head and kissed her hair. "We'll make it right, don't worry. We'll get it all sorted."

I don't think she was convinced. I know I wasn't. I didn't want to add my information to hers. I didn't want any part of this. I just wanted to go back to England, or Ireland or both.

Anywhere but the Middle East. Anywhere but Helmand Province.

There was only one way I knew to truly comfort a woman, and that was distraction, so I took her mouth and kissed her until she melted into my arms. She was vulnerable in a way she'd never been with me before. She didn't try to take charge, she just let me make simple, gentle, unprotected, beautiful love to her.

Knowing I was making love to her with my child already growing inside her was startling, and the lack of a barrier changed the experience entirely. It was vulnerable and–strangely sacred, and afterward I went in the bathroom and wept in the shower.

In the morning I left her a note and slipped out to buy some breakfast. I ordered a tray for her from the hotel dining room, to be delivered with a flower. It was the best I could do without raising suspicion. She could do what she wanted with that safety deposit box, but I wasn't going to add to it. That was like admitting we were already dead, and it wasn't in me to give up that easily. I wasn't going anywhere without a fight.

Instead I went to my hotel and slept most of that day away, fitful as it was. I dreamt about Kathleen. There was an explosion and she was lying on the ground, bleeding to death and I held her head in my hands as the life drained away from her. I watched the blood seep into the dust and saw the face of a child appear and disappear within the blood. I woke up drenched in sweat and sat on the edge of the bed, chest heaving. I felt like I was losing my mind.

Regan had drawn up a will for me, but if things were reversed and Kathleen lived on without me, I would want to provide for the child if I could. I wrote a letter to Da, with instructions on the outside of the envelope:

Da,

Only open this letter if for some reason I don't come home from the war. Otherwise I'll explain it all to you in person one day.

Finn

Da would understand. He'd keep it confidential and would contact Regan and Eiran and make it all right, if need be. I put the card and the key inside the envelope and mailed it off.

That night Kathleen met me for dinner in a restaurant on the other side of the city, away from where military personnel usually stayed. I took a room there so we could spend our last night together before we went back to theatre. She fell asleep almost immediately. I held her the entire evening and through the night as silent tears slipped down my face. I tried to sleep but it just wouldn't come. This was no way to begin a marriage, and a war was no place for a pregnant woman–especially one who was secretly pregnant.

We had breakfast together at the hotel the next morning, but my nerves were raw from lack of sleep and worry. I sat there, frazzled and unshaven, with my head in my hands.

"You have to tell them. You have to go home."

"I can't do that Finn."

"Why not?" I leaned across the table.

She sat shaking her head, staring into space. "I keep hoping the war will be over soon and none of it will matter."

"But what if it's not?"

"We're going in with plenty of ground support and air support if we need it. It's going to be fine." She said the words, but her heart wasn't in them.

"Is that what you were thinking yesterday when you were making out your will?"

"It wasn't a will, it was a precaution. And if you're smart, you'll do the same." She dabbed her face with the corner of her napkin.

"What will you eat while we're out there on this mission – ration packs? How can you be sure you're getting the right foods for the two of you? And what if you get hurt and no one's there to tell the medics you're with child? It could be disastrous!"

She glared at me and pushed her plate away. "I'm not hungry

anymore."

"Can't you see what this means? How can you be so stubborn?"

She put on her captain voice. "I don't want to talk about it anymore. We're going back to base today. Let's just take things one day at a time."

"One day at a time. Great. That's just great."

I was furious and my emotions were barely in check as I put her in a cab. I gave the driver directions to her hotel so she could gather her things. The next time we saw each other would be at the airstrip. Once again, I stood with my hands in my pockets and watched her pull away from the curb.

I DIDN'T SEE her for the rest of that day. Back at base, our unit was hurrying to gather supplies and head out into the desert. It was hot. Hot enough that we had to take electrolyte drinks and salt tablets or risk dehydration and shock. I had no idea if electrolyte drinks were safe for pregnant women, and had I been home, I would have looked up a whole list of do's and don'ts, but when we did have access to computers and global networking, it was strictly monitored. I didn't know any of the medical personnel enough to trust them with our secret, so I kept my mouth shut, but it was eating me alive. I couldn't think straight.

A few short months ago I was ready to die. Now I wanted out, but for what seemed like all the wrong reasons. Jasper and Connor had already made the ultimate sacrifice. James and my other mates were still out in the desert, continuing to put themselves in harm's way.

I wasn't the only husband and father out there. My unit had been full of them, and this group was no different. Some of these women were mothers with multiple children waiting for them back home. I watched them all with renewed interest, understanding perhaps for the first time, that every one of us had a story, a family. Maybe she was right. We were all in the same boat, all putting life and family on the line. We had a job to do out there. I just hoped I could do mine without losing my mind.

Soon we had a full complement of personnel at the ready. It was the middle of the night and we were just about to head out into the desert. Kathleen pulled me aside.

"I'm not going."

"You're not?" I was thrilled, but I tried to maintain professional decorum.

"Command–" She stopped and looked straight at me. "Isn't willing to risk my going out on the mission. I'll be communicating with you from here as needed. Simpkins will be running things out there and a few of us will stay back and relay information. In fact, they may be reassigning me. I'm to wait for more specific orders."

She didn't look happy about it, so I tried not to smile.

"In the event that I'm called elsewhere before your return, good luck out there, and stay safe."

"Yes, ma'am." I saluted her with a wink and she blushed, then looked away. The relief was palpable. Like someone came along and decided to carry my pack. I turned to leave then looked back at her. "You stay safe too."

"Will do."

Even at base camp we were closer to the action than we had been in some time, and we were heading right into the thick of it. By the looks on the faces of this group, what was normal for my former battalion was a little too close for comfort for these folks. Pushing myself into survival mode, I tried to focus, to shut out the hushed conversations and questions floating between bunkers and makeshift barracks. As far as we knew, the enemy wasn't aware of our presence. We were on strict radio silence.

The next night, our patrols saw suspicious movement in a nearby village. We gathered what we knew from satellite images, radio intercepts and talking with the locals, and decided to move in a little closer. Turns out we'd done our job well because a pre-dawn raid on the house in question revealed a bomb-making operation. Our troops were able to go in and shut it down, with no casualties on either side. That raid gave us crucial information to plot their next steps, but we never got to use it.

The next morning as we were returning to the base camp, they retaliated with a pre-dawn ambush. Bombs were going off all over the place as we called for backup. I didn't know where Kathleen was or if she was still safe, but adrenaline wouldn't allow me the luxury of worry. I had a job to do, and the war depended on it.

I tried furiously to send as much information as I could back to base and to headquarters, in case our security was breached, then grabbed as much as I could carry and headed for one of the foxholes. Our troops were fighting back, but it was no use. As the firefight got closer, I heard someone yelling for everyone to fall back, so I ran, dropping a grenade into the hole behind me to destroy anything that might cripple us, and as a distraction to help me gain some distance.

If there was a time for me to pray, this would have been it, but all I could do was run. They had us pinned down and were still coming. We launched what we could to hold them, but they were firing right back.

A guy named Phillips hung up the radio and announced that air support was on its way, we just had to hold tight for a few more minutes. I took up my weapon and prepared to return fire, my chest still heaving from my quarter-mile sprint. I spotted Kathleen about twenty-five feet behind me and I motioned furiously for her to get out of there, to take cover. She was crouched behind a jeep with her helmet covering her head. She didn't even see me waving at her.

Suddenly a bomb exploded right in the middle of all of us. A direct hit, and I went flying.

I CAME to with the sound of airplanes and cannons overhead, realizing our help had arrived just seconds too late. My helmet had been blown off and there was still debris raining down around me. I looked to the left and my buddy was dead, so I pulled his helmet off and covered my head, crawling through the debris on elbows and knees. I had to find her.

Right away I noticed a searing pain in my right shoulder, and I couldn't bend my right knee. I may have had injuries that needed attention, but I was alive and the guy next to me was dead. If I could move, I had to try. Crawling was excruciating. I basically had to pull myself along on my left side. There were bodies lying in the dirt, some of them still alive and screaming for help. I tapped the helmet I was wearing and got static, but it was still a signal, so I began to try calling for medics–as many as we could get. Injured men were grabbing at my legs as I inched by them. I promised I'd be back.

Finally, I spotted a shock of auburn hair flapping through the dusty air. When I came up on her I could see a huge hole in her middle. I tried to stuff it with a bandage from inside my coat but when I reached down into her gut, I knew.

She blinked when I touched her, but she wasn't really coherent. "Kathleen!" I called into her ear. I propped her head up out of the dust. "Kathleen! It's me, it's Finn!"

She attempted to swallow, and her eyes tried to follow my voice. "Finn?"

"I'm here."

"I'm sorry..." she whispered. "You were right. I shouldn't have stayed. Now it's too late."

I stroked her hair back, crying. "Shh! Shh...Just be still. We're gettin' you some help." The sun broke through the horizon, illuminating all the dust in the air and surrounding us in a strange glow. Suddenly my dream came back to my mind. I looked down at her stomach and watched the blood soak into the dust around us. I waited, but no image of a child appeared in front of my eyes. Maybe it would have, had they not been blurred by tears.

The sounds of war dulled in my ears until all I could hear was my own heart throbbing against my temples. I kept stroking her hair and screaming "Medic! I need a medic!"

I hit the side of my head, trying to get the radio in the helmet to crackle to life, but in the end it didn't matter. She closed her eyes and went to sleep and took my dream with her.

The light faded unexpectedly, and I remember thinking how odd it was, seeing as the sun had just come up.

9

The next thing I remember, I was in a mobile hospital somewhere away from the front lines. I could still hear the gunfire in the distance, unless I was hallucinating. Maybe they'd given me morphine or some other drug that was keeping it all in the background.

"You're all right, soldier. I'm Doctor Stuart and you're at Bastion."

Camp Bastion. Field Hospital. Okay, so that was a good sign.

The noise was muffled until I turned my head. Then everything got louder. I blinked a few times to see if I was actually awake. It was like someone was turning the volume dial as I moved my head from side to side.

"I can't seem to hear out of my right ear."

"That's not too surprising seeing as your right side took the worst of the blast. It may come back. We'll just have to wait and see."

"What's wrong with me?"

"Well, for one thing your shoulder is shattered. We had to fish a lot of shrapnel out of it. The knee too. We've done what we could out here in the field, but you're going to need some more extensive repairs."

"Repairs?"

"You'll need some reconstructive surgery. They may need to replace your shoulder completely. The knee is also a mess. There's shrapnel embedded in the bone. When the medics picked you up, you'd lost a fair amount of blood. We weren't sure we were going to be able to save you, but you were one of the lucky ones."

"Lucky, sir?"

He put his hand on my arm. "In a manner of speaking, yes. You're alive. You survived. You have to be thankful for that. We're soldiers and this is war. Wars have casualties. We keep going."

I didn't respond. What did he know about keeping going? Had he lost a child in this war?

"Infection is the big risk now, and the sooner you get everything all straightened around on the inside the better. You're being put on a transport to the hospital in Birmingham."

"England?"

"Yes. You're going home, son."

Home. Was England home? Was Ireland? Was anywhere? If they were sending me to England, they didn't expect me to return to the fighting any time soon–if ever.

"When?"

"Tomorrow morning."

Dr. Stuart started to walk away. "Sir?"

"Yes?"

"The others in my unit. How many...casualties?"

"The chaplains keep those lists. Would you like me to send someone by to see you?"

I looked up at the ceiling and nodded. He made a notation on my chart and walked away.

I was in an open ward with several other patients, all on stretchers like mine, with varying degrees of injury. We had all given of ourselves for our country, because our country asked us to participate in an effort to free the oppressed. Collectively, we had done a good thing–a noble thing. We'd done what was asked of us. We'd served. Sacrificed. Some gave their sight, their hearing, or their limbs. Some...gave all.

I looked at the defeat in their eyes. The fear. The shame. The anger. Nothing in our training had prepared us for this feeling of helplessness, and I wished to God there was a clinical psychologist around to talk to.

Sleep came easily. I'd never been so tired. I'm not sure how long I slept but when I opened my eyes Bryce was sitting next to my stretcher.

"Hey there, mate. How's it going?"

I turned my good ear toward him. "What are you doing here?"

"I'm an army chaplain. For another six months, anyway. What better place for me than an army hospital in the midst of a war?"

"Right. Sorry."

"The doctor said you were asking about the casualties from your unit."

I nodded my head.

He hesitated just long enough for me to know the truth. "Unfortunately, mate, it would be faster to tell you who lived."

My stomach dropped. I knew what was coming but I tried to put it off. I started naming some of my better friends. "Phillips? Jamison?"

He shook his head.

"Connelly?"

Negative.

I swallowed, trying to get closer to the officers' list. "Grayson."

Silence.

"Crummer."

Still nothing. "Let me get right to the point Finn, because I know what you're asking."

I already knew it inside my head. Of course, I knew. But I had to hear it from someone else's mouth to make it come true. "She's dead, isn't she?"

Bryce looked around. "Yes."

I could feel the firestorm of emotions rising up within me, threatening to overwhelm every nerve ending. I wanted to scream, cry, and kill people all at once, and yet I knew in my heart none of it would do any good. None of those things would bring her back. None of those things would help me to see the face of a child I would never know.

I stared up at the ceiling, tears running down both sides of my face. Bryce grabbed my hand and held on.

"I was with her at the end, you know. She said she was sorry. That she should have listened to me. She told someone about the baby, and they were supposed to be reassigning her."

Bryce nodded.

"But no one knows we were married, and what does it even matter now?"

"It matters that you did the right thing. It matters to God."

"I don't want to talk about God."

He looked down at his shoes.

"Was it even legal? I mean, you have the certificate we scribbled on, did you do anything with it? Did you file it away somewhere? Does the Church of England even know we've done this?"

"It's been less than a week, and we're at war. No, I haven't done anything with it yet. What are you saying?"

"I'm saying annul it. Make it like it never happened."

"Finn..."

I turned my head toward him. "Look, it was a bad situation from the start. What do you want me to do? I can't tell command now, and I can't mourn her publicly."

"That doesn't change the facts."

"What if I told you the marriage was never consummated?"

"Wasn't it?"

"Answer the question."

"Look, it's not that I don't want to help you, it's just..."

The indignation was rising up faster than I could put a lid on it. I whispered, trying to be cautious, but it was difficult. "I can't go to her family, a complete stranger and tell them about some grand affair in a dust-ridden country that got their daughter pregnant. What do I have to comfort them with? That I married her out of guilt and obligation, and now she's dead and so is their unborn grandchild?"

Bryce knew I was right, but he was conflicted.

"Better for them to think she died a hero than a trollop."

"I don't know, mate. I don't know that I can do it, ethically speaking. You married in good faith, under the eyes of God."

"What we were *under* was duress. A desperate measure in a desperate situation. Look, I'm a miserable Catholic and a horrible Protestant. I don't even know if I believe in marriage as an institution."

"And yet, you said *I do*. So did Kathleen."

"I can't believe you're giving me a hard time about this! You were more than willing to be discreet about it when we stood on the steps of that church in Doha. The three of us are the only ones who knew about it. It was never filed, never made official. *Please*, Bryce."

I tried to turn more fully toward him and felt the flesh of my shoulder scrape against bone. I gritted my teeth against the pain and let out a growl that sounded more like a wounded animal than a man.

A nurse came over and asked about my pain.

"Suddenly quite unbearable" I said between short sips of air.

She took a look at my shoulder dressing. "It's seeping through. You may have torn the stitches. I'll have the doctor come take a look, but in the meantime, I'm going to give you something for the pain."

She took a syringe out of her pocket and put something in my IV. Within seconds I felt a rush of peace and calm.

"Why don't you rest?" Bryce said. "I'll check back with you later."

I couldn't talk to him. I couldn't think of anything. I made my mind go blank and closed my eyes. I just wanted to float away.

AFTER THEY CLEANED, re-stitched, and dressed my shoulder wound, I slept most of the day and night. Bryce never came back. It was just as well. There was nothing left to say. I was going back to England.

If there was a God–and at that point in my life I didn't know what I thought–surely he understood my situation. To me the more unforgivable sin had to have been the act that landed me in that spot in the first place. The fact that I tried to make it right had to count for something.

The next morning as I was getting loaded for transport, I was given a letter-sized manila envelope along with my personal effects. It was sealed and addressed as confidential for my eyes only. I thanked the medic who delivered it and held it under my blankets until we took off.

The aircraft was the most massive plane I'd ever been on. There must have been fifty of us packed in side-by-side on stretchers with nurses and doctors and myriad staff all on this enormous military transport. I swear they could have performed surgery mid-flight if they had to. There wasn't much privacy, and there wasn't a lot of light, but I pulled out the envelope and tore it open best I could with one shoulder completely immobilized. Inside was a note from Bryce. It said:

Best of luck to you, mate. Look me up when the war is over for you.

-B

It was an awfully large envelope for such a small note. I looked inside again, and there, at the bottom, torn in half, was our marriage certificate. Her name was signed on one side and mine on the other. Torn in half. I sighed, putting the pieces back into the envelope and resealing it.

It was done. Finished. Like it never happened.

THE FIRST SEVERAL weeks at Queen Elizabeth went by in a blur. It didn't feel anything like the facilities at Camp Bastion. This was a brand new, state of the art hospital that served the general public as well as military personnel injured in conflict zones. I was thankful to be out of hostile territory, where the only things waking me up in the middle of the night were IV pumps and blood draws, rather than patrols and gunfire, but that doesn't mean I stopped hearing them in my head.

I would dream about the war and wake up in a cold sweat or come out of a drug-induced haze thinking we were under attack, writhing in the bed and swinging at the air with my good arm. I kept ripping my stitches open, so they gave me medication to keep me still. In fact, they put me down so many times that I started to think it might be better if they just drugged me altogether until it was over.

I had my shoulder replaced, then my knee. Eventually they put new pieces of bone in my right ear and implanted an amplifier in the ear canal. It worked, for the most part. Slowly my hearing improved, until it was only slightly worse than the other ear.

I felt less and less myself as more and more of me got taken out and replaced with other peoples' parts. It was a peculiar feeling, knowing I had other people's joints and bone grafts melding with my own. It was also strange to think that I could never go backwards, to a time when all this wasn't a part of me yet. I would carry it forever.

Somehow.

When I wasn't having flashbacks, I was tormented by dreams about Kathleen and a sweet baby girl, with strawberry blond hair and deep green eyes. Why I was so convinced it had been a girl, I have no idea, but that was how it played out in my mind. I thought about how I'd feel if a daughter of mine had been made pregnant out of wedlock by the likes of me.

I hadn't wanted to be a father, so the grief didn't make any sense to me. They tried to counsel me, but I couldn't be honest about everything I'd gone through. It was a secret, and it needed to stay that way. I didn't want to soil Kathleen's memory, nor cause any trouble for Bryce.

Six weeks after I got to Birmingham, the pain started to increase substantially, and I couldn't figure out what was wrong, because they'd already replaced enough parts to make me bionic. As it turns out, I had a significant fever and when the nurse took the dressing down, the whole shoulder was swollen and red and felt like it was being ripped apart from the inside. They gave me something strong to knock out the pain, and when I woke up again, I was in the ICU with a morphine pump and a button I could push every ten minutes for pain relief.

The hallucinations got worse after that. I couldn't tell what was dream and what was real. Pain, faces, sights, sounds, smells. I had entire conversations with Kathleen and Grams, and I have no idea if I was speaking audibly or not. The infection was overwhelming my system and I was fighting for my life, and the only reason I know this is because I lived to tell the story.

Also, because Da was sitting next to me when I finally came back around.

I'd put him as my emergency contact for the army's sake, and evidently they thought it was enough of an emergency to call him. I would have told him eventually, but the last thing I'd written was an "only open if I don't come home" letter, so I wanted to make sure I was coming home before I contacted him again. The army didn't see it that way.

Neither did he, apparently, because he was sitting with my letter open in his lap, holding onto the key. I looked over and let my breath out in a huff. He looked older somehow, and more worry-worn than I'd seen him in some time.

"That bad, eh?"

He nodded once. "Aye."

"I can explain."

"No need."

I took a mental inventory of my systems. The pain was still significant in my shoulder, and my knee felt like the new joint was glued in place and wouldn't even bend with a crow bar.

"When did you open the letter?"

"Last night, when I thought I'd lost ye."

"Have you shown it to anyone? Talked to anyone?"

"No, why?"

"Don't."

I watched him fold the letter and put it all away in the pocket of his overcoat. He was nothing if not discreet, a quality I had always admired. Da was never in a hurry to have serious conversations. He knew they'd come around when the time was right, so we were quiet for a long while.

I was so tired, and all my muscles felt sore and stretched, as if my skin was pulled too tight. When I tried to look out over myself, I could see my cheeks rising up into my field of vision, and my hands looked puffy and strange. I tried to swallow and even that took effort.

"Why am I so swollen?"

"Infection. Your body's trying to take care of it."

"She's dead, you know. They both are."

Da looked down at his lap. "I'm sorry."

He waited to see if I wanted to tell him more, but there was nothing else to say.

"I'm going to sleep for a bit."

"Aye. You rest."

"Does Mum know?"

"That you're in hospital?"

I nodded.

"I came alone. Didn't want to worry her until it was time to do so. Would you like me to call her?"

"Wait till we see if I live. I don't want her seeing me like this for the last time."

"That's no way to talk."

"It's how it feels—like all the life's draining out of me and it's not finished yet."

He stood and grabbed onto my puffy hand, leaning over the bed and looking me straight in the eyes. "Well then, you keep fightin' Finnegan Colin McCarthy. You're your father's son and sure I never gave up on anything in my life. Don't you give up, you hear me?"

I stared at him. He was serious, in that way he gets sometimes. His eyes bore into me like he was driving his will directly into mine. I felt a cold tingle travel up my left arm, sending tiny electric shocks all the way through me.

"Now's the time for survival. The grievin' will come later. McCarthys don't quit. We fight."

With that last word I felt the change. It was like the air shifted somehow. Things felt the same, but somehow, I knew they weren't. He waited for me to acknowledge him, then dropped my hand back onto the bed. The electric shocks ceased, and a peace washed over me that put me right to sleep.

10

All in all, I spent four months at Birmingham, and then they let me go. By that I mean that I was medically discharged from the British Army. My knee was good enough to walk on and after months of physical therapy for the shoulder, I'd still never have the strength or ability to hoist a weapon and fire it properly.

On top of that, my hearing only returned partially in my right ear. They could have given me a desk job, I suppose, but my heart was no longer in it. Besides, I was battling depression and nightmares, not to mention a decent addiction to painkillers.

Mum came up and visited a couple of times. Da was kind enough to wait until I was out of the ICU and no longer looked like a puffer fish before he told her where I was. I could tell she wanted to say *I told you so*, but she didn't. She just let me heal and said she was glad I was alive, which I'm sure was true enough for her, I just didn't share the sentiment most days. She said Grams was anxious for me to come home, and I promised to come and visit as soon as I felt stronger.

When I finally got out, Da picked me up and took me back to Ireland with him. I spent most of my time wandering down to the local pub, drowning my sorrows in whiskey and then taking the painkillers on top of it all until I ended up in a stupor.

I even went to London once, but I didn't visit Grams. Instead I looked up Regan and her new husband Michael.

Turns out he was a fairly likable chap. We shook hands at the door, but he was in the middle of a legal case at the time and ducked out with apologies and a promise to return for dinner, leaving Regan and I plenty of time to catch up.

They had a lovely flat in a popular part of London, and as soon as Michael walked out the door, she sat down across from me. "You look like shite, you know."

"Feeling every one of these twenty-six years, thank you very much." I stretched. "Sorry I uh...missed the wedding."

"Don't be. You were serving our country, and that's plenty excuse for me."

"Oh, so it's *our* country now, is it?" I winked.

"I wasn't sure you even knew, since you didn't respond to my letter."

"About that..." I sat there stupidly. I couldn't even form the words. "I have no excuse, really, other than the fact that I am the world's most deplorable human being."

"Deplorable isn't a word I'd choose for a wounded warrior. And probably a decorated one at that."

I had in fact been given several medals in honor of my service, but none of them meant anything to me. Decorations were just shiny things that sat in boxes and reminded us of our pain.

The silence hung between us. I didn't know what else to say. I wasn't trying to be melancholy; I just didn't feel much like a hero. "And look at you! Married, a distinguished barrister. Why, you've lost nearly all your Irish. Become an honorary Brit, have you?"

"You should talk, Mr. Chameleon." She gave me a sly smile and relaxed back against the couch. "I always figured that must have been what made you such a good lover."

I knew full well she'd been pleased by me that night, and still found it funny that she had absolutely no recollection of it. I toyed with the idea of sharing it with her just to see how she'd respond, but she might not even believe me.

"And what would you know about that?" I asked.

"Nothing, of course, but I figure all those women talking behind your back at the bars couldn't have been wrong."

"You interviewed them all, did you? That must've taken *years.*"

She ignored the sarcasm. Never was one to take my bait.

"You've always been able to make yourself into whatever you needed to be at the time. When you're with an English girl you sound like a Brit but if you're with the Irish you roll out the brogue like it's no big thing. You just...become what they want you to become and voila! You're in bed!" She snapped her fingers for emphasis.

"So, it's the accent, is that it?" She wasn't completely wrong; I just didn't like it when she referred to me as a gigolo. Especially now.

Her smirk reminded me of how well she knew me. "I'm sure you have a few useful talents as well, but getting there is half the battle." She held up one finger. "Except when you're drunk of course, because then you mix the two accents and it gets very confusing. Still, that's my personal favorite. I like it when you're both men at the same time. Feels more like the real you."

It was hard, being reminded of the depth of our history together. Frankly it was easier to forget she was in my life than to remember with regret.

She smiled as I looked up. "Speaking of which, are you feeling your Irish enough to want a spot o' whiskey?"

She didn't have to switch accents on my account, but it was kind of adorable. "I thought you'd never ask." I smiled my charming smile and she turned on one heel, ignoring me completely. When she came back, it was with a bottle and two glasses.

"Aye and that Michael's a good lad if he lets you keep the Jameson's right out in th'open." I winked.

"Aye, he is at that." She poured us each a glass and we toasted. "To Irish whiskey in English glasses."

"To Irish whiskey" I said, drinking mine down all in one gulp.

"Easy there, soldier." She looked me over once again, concern written across her beautiful features. "What seems to be the trouble?"

"How long will your husband be out?"

"A good bit I should think. Why? Are you still trying to shag me then?" She winked again, trying to keep things light.

She was all fun and games, but I had to hold back my reply. Instead, I poured another shot. "Because if I start the telling, I don't want to have to stop halfway."

She took the bottle from me. "This is all I've got. Will it be enough?"

I looked at the bottle in all seriousness. "I don't know. I guess we'll find out."

"Tell you what" she announced. "I've some Guinness in the icebox as well. Let me get us each one of those and it'll be just like old times." She disappeared again and called from the kitchen. "Can I make you a sandwich?"

"Please. And thank you."

She came out carrying two bottles and handed one to me. "You don't have to be so damned polite, you know. We're old friends, you and I. Be right back with your sandwich."

I stood in her living room looking at her wedding pictures. They'd married out of doors, in Ireland by the looks of it. Her family and some of the people from our town were standing by with smiles as wide as the sea. *These people went on with their lives. They haven't seen, touched, smelled or tasted war. They've gone to their jobs and cooked their meals and looked after their wee ones and nothing much has changed for them.*

Regan and Michael looked happy–and very much in love. I hoped for her sake he was a good match. Someone she loved enough to get lost in. I swirled my bottle and brought it to my lips. Likely the only thing I was destined to get lost in was the drink.

"Here we are. I'll have you know being married has been good for me. I've actually learnt how to cook."

"Cooked me up a sandwich, have you?" I sniffed it cautiously and she knocked me in the arm.

"Very funny. Now sit down. Seems we've got a lot to catch up on."

"What we have to catch up on isn't very funny, I'm afraid."

She sat down on the sofa, crossing one leg under herself. After all this time, she still took my breath away. I didn't dare sit next to her, so I kept my distance and stood by the fireplace. "You look happy. Are you?"

She smiled. "Very. Michael's a wonderful man. I hope you'll get to know him while you're here."

I tried to return the smile, but it wouldn't come.

"How about you? Any women in your life? Or should I say, how many women are in your life?" She laughed at her intimate knowledge of me, but her laughter fell silent when she saw my face. "Finn, what's happened?"

I poured another glass of Jameson's and felt the burn soothe my frazzled nerves. I just wanted to forget, but there was a story to tell, and if anyone deserved my confession it was Regan.

I pulled the manila envelope out of my coat pocket and handed it to her.

"What's this?"

I couldn't say the words, even after all that time. I just let her look inside. She pulled out the note from Bryce and gave me a quizzical look. "Is this a friend of yours? Was he killed in action?"

I shook my head and took another drink. Regan reached her hand back inside the envelope and fished out the two halves of a marriage certificate, then read the names.

"You got married? Why didn't you tell me?"

I sat down hard on her sofa and the dam broke. I put my head in my hands and began to weep–huge, wracking sobs that had been buried these last months under layers of dust and grief and secrecy. I had no secrets with Regan, but I don't think she'd ever seen me cry. Hell, I don't think I'd ever cried that hard myself, but it all came pouring through in enormous, overwhelming waves that threatened to take all my breath and leave me trapped under the water.

She came immediately to my side and pulled me into her chest like a mother would. She held my head and spoke soothingly into my hair. "Hush...hush...It's all right now. Shh...I'm right here, love...shh..."

As suddenly as the emotion had hit me it was gone. There, in the safety of her arms, I stopped weeping, as if my emotions had been turned off at the switch. I rolled out of her embrace and we both leaned back against the couch. I couldn't face her, so I looked straight ahead, telling her my story in a monotone, disconnected voice that was, in fact, somewhere between a Brit and an Irishman.

"I met Kathleen at a hotel bar in Qatar. She'd been assigned to recruit me for the Intelligence Corps, only she wore," I chuckled out loud at the memory, "the tightest fitting blue dress I'd ever seen." I shook my head.

Regan looked at the two halves of paper again and verified that Kathleen was the other name next to mine. "Knowing you, I imagine she's quite beautiful. Am I right?"

"She was" I said simply. Emotionless. Immediately I was back in the dust, holding her head in my hands and watching the lifeblood of our child slip into the cracks in the thirsty ground.

Regan's hand went to her mouth. "Oh my God. No! Finn—no! I'm so sorry. Is she dead?"

My head moved with just the tiniest affirmation.

She opened her arms and drew me in again. "Oh, my Lord, how long has it been?"

"Four months, twelve days and—" I looked at my watch "—several hours. You can't feel too sorry for me, though. You haven't heard the worst of it yet."

"If there's worse than this, I'm not sure I want to know it. Why wouldn't I feel sorrow for your loss?"

"Because I didn't love her."

She pushed me away so she could look into my face. "You what?"

"I only married her because of the baby."

Her hand went to her mouth again, and this time her own tears stained her fingertips. "Oh my God."

"Please stop saying that. I'm not sure God has anything to do with it."

She took my hands. "Of course He does and you know it as well as I do. You were married by a vicar–his seal is right here. If you didn't care about what God thought you would've asked just any old barrister to do this for you."

She had me there, but still...

"There were...extenuating circumstances."

"Such as?"

"Such as, she was an officer and I was not."

"I see."

"We needed discretion."

"So you went to the church?" She laughed out loud. It *was* a bit comical, saying it that way.

"I had an old friend from Oxford who is now, conveniently, an army chaplain."

She held up the paper. "Not the same Bryce you used to pal around with? We've been to the pubs together, haven't we?"

"The very same."

"Okay, so that's making a little more sense I guess, but... Are you telling me you kept it a secret?"

I nodded.

"All of it. Even the baby?"

"I tried to get her to tell them, but at first she didn't want to get in trouble or get me in trouble. A lot of good that's done her."

"But...a pregnant woman in a combat zone? What was she thinking?"

I stared at the coffee table again, as if the answers were carved into the grain of the wood. "In short, I think she was overwhelmed and didn't want to really acknowledge it to herself, much less anyone else. She never wanted a child, and didn't want to get married either. In the end she did tell them the part about being pregnant. That's the irony of it all. The day before she died, she told me they were making plans to transfer her away from the fighting."

Regan's head dropped to her chest. "Then it's guilt you're feeling?"

Good old Regan, a fantastic marksman, she was. "Yes, guilt, but it's more than that. Before all this happened, I never wanted a child either, but now all I can think about is how I should have become a father, and it doesn't make one lick of sense." I drained my glass.

"Sure it does. It's what I've been telling you for years now. Your heart wants what's right, and everything else has been emptiness. Your love was meant for one woman, and hers for you. That's the way it's meant to be. You'll find her Finn. I promise."

I looked down at her hand and picked up her ring finger. "You can't promise me anything anymore."

She pulled my face up to meet hers. "I never could, Finn. It's not like that, and you know it. You're grieving is all. It's normal."

"Well then, I guess grief leaves permanent scars." I held up my arm and pulled back my sleeve to reveal a tattoo I'd gotten on my right arm, next to my mangled shoulder. It was a picture of a heart with an arrow through it and the name Annabelle inscribed across the arrow.

"Who's Annabelle?"

"That's what I named her."

"It was a girl?"

"In my mind, it was."

"I see."

"Do you?"

She stopped. "No, I guess I don't, really." Regan put her hand on my arm, rubbing her fingers tenderly over the surface of the tattoo. "I may not be able to feel what you feel, but I've always loved you, Finn. You're closer to me than my own brothers, and it hurts me to see you hurting."

I loved her too. I always had, even if she was the one female that had never responded to me as a man. Or maybe because of that.

I took hold of her face and kissed her. It was stupid. It was impulse, but I needed a woman. I needed warm arms and a release from this torment. I needed someone who knew my heart, and she was the only person that had ever truly satisfied my soul.

She kissed me back momentarily, then pushed me away, wiping her mouth afterward. "What do you think you're doing?"

"I'm sorry, I just…"

"Get out."

"What?"

She stiffened and pointed toward the door. "Please leave."

"Look I said I was sorry–it won't happen again, I just–"

She took a deep breath and her eyes were like steel. "I'm sorry for your loss Finn, I truly am. But I don't think you're stable right now. Go home. Go back to Ireland and figure yourself out. You need to get this sorted."

I stared at her for a long time and she didn't say another word. Didn't she know? Of all the people in the entire world, for her I would've given my own life. But she didn't want my life. She wanted her own life, with her own husband, in a modern little flat in London. And I wasn't a part of that. Not anymore.

I got up and walked silently to the door, hurt and anger mixing in dangerous proportions in my heart. Then I stopped and turned back. "I've been in love with you since I was a boy of eighteen, and not because I wanted to bed you, but because you're the only person on the planet who knows the real me. So, forgive me for not being able to shut that down."

Her eyes welled up, and I wanted to go to her. To hold her, to kiss her tears away and drink from the sweetness of her mouth. The taste of her had brought me right back, and I wanted to carry her up the stairs and make beautiful, uncomplicated love to her. It pulsed through me and I fought it back and still it rose up.

Michael had seen past the curtain, conquered what I hadn't be able to manage. I would have to buy that man a drink someday, but today was not that day.

I thought I was done, and I should have just walked away, but I said it anyway. Out loud. Like a jackass.

"You know what? Even after everything, I have to thank you for that one incredible night you did give me. You were right all along, and I'll be eternally grateful, because it changed me, and I needed to know the truth."

"What?" The question came whispering out and I watched her

face turn from wonder to shock and then to fear. The part of me that wanted her to suffer for that knowledge was strangely, sadistically satisfied watching her brilliant brain trying to deduce the obvious.

"I may not be perfect, but I'm nothing like I would have been without you. Goodbye Regan, and thank you."

I walked out and she called after me. "Wait! Finn, what are you talking about! What night?"

I turned around and walked backwards with my hands stuffed in my pockets, but I didn't answer her. I just stared and kept moving.

"Finn!"

I walked away from her that night. I left her standing there in the cold, wondering. She should have to remember, like me, and if she couldn't, let the question haunt her instead.

11

I probably shouldn't have done that. I shouldn't have given her cause to doubt herself–to doubt me. But if that was the last time I was going to see her, I wanted her to know why.

I walked into the first pub I saw and picked up a glass of whiskey and a woman, just about as quickly. Or maybe she picked me up. It was hard to separate sometimes. I was obviously upset and ordering my whiskey straight...these were telltale markers. I knew her game, because I'd played it too many times myself. She was trolling, and I was an easy mark. It made me sick to think about how many times I'd done the exact same thing.

A part of me wanted to have sex with her, just to quell the need Regan had stirred, but I couldn't bring myself to go home with her. It was just too nauseating. Images of the night Regan and I spent together looped through my mind. I could still smell her, taste her, feel her underneath me. Hell, her perfume was still on my shirt.

I apologized and paid my tab, then left the bar and caught the tube out to Oxford, where I walked the campus in the fading daylight, trying to remember where it had all gone wrong. I'm not sure how long I walked but I was sitting on a bench when one of my old mathematics professors strolled by.

"Finn? Is that you?"

"Professor Smythe, sir!" I stood. "I'm surprised you remember me. Especially in the dark."

"There are some students you don't forget, my boy. You're one of them!"

"Should I take that as a compliment, sir?"

"If you like..." He winked at me. "How've you been? What are you doing these days?"

"I've just been medically discharged from the army sir. I was... wounded in Afghanistan."

"Oh my! I'm so sorry." He shook my hand. "Thank you, for your service."

I nodded. I never knew what to say when people said things like that. I suppose a simple "you're welcome" would have sufficed, but the words always got stuck in my throat.

"I was just heading home, but my wife's out of town visiting her mother and I've nothing but a frozen dinner waiting for me. Care to go for a bite? Catch up a bit?"

I had nothing better to do. Literally. I had no place to stay and no plans whatsoever. "Why not? Thank you."

We were walking across campus, just enjoying the evening, when Professor Smythe said "How about the Bird and Baby?"

I wasn't really paying attention. I was just trying to remember how it felt to be a college student again. "Wherever you like, sir."

Had I even been thinking straight I would have suggested something else entirely, because in just a few minutes we were standing at the entrance to The Eagle and Child. Nicknamed *The Bird and Baby* by the likes of C.S. Lewis and J.R.R. Tolkien, this pub had been an Oxford haunt since the sixteen hundreds. It wasn't the professor's fault; it was just that my eagle hadn't landed. She'd flown away and taken my child with her.

I swallowed hard as I went inside. I'd been there plenty of times over the years, so it felt familiar enough, and once I stopped thinking about the name of the place, I settled in to the warm atmosphere and likable staff. We ordered some dinner and a couple of pints.

"Tell me, Finn, how are you holding up?"

"Sir?"

"Don't *sir* me. I was in Afghanistan too, you know."

"You were? But you don't..."

"Look young enough to fight?"

"That's not what I was thinking."

"It's all right. I am a bit of an old goat. I'm forty-five you know—came to Oxford right after I got out."

"How many years did you serve, sir?"

"Twenty. Exactly. The last two in Afghanistan."

"And why did you get out, if I may ask? Were you wounded?"

"No. I had just seen too much. I wanted to have a bit of a life left. I wanted to be 'normal'. What a joke that is, eh?"

"Sir?"

He looked across the table at me. "You and I both know the word normal is completely redefined once you've been where we've been and seen what we've seen."

I thought about some of the things we probably had in common. My losses, nightmares, and altered perceptions were probably not much different than any other soldier. But they were still mine. And they still tortured me.

I swallowed hard. "Does it ever get better, sir?"

"Better? Yes. Gone? No."

I nodded. I could see that being true.

"Once you've been a soldier, you're a soldier for life. It's in you. The honor, the integrity." He looked at me pointedly. "The nightmares."

"You have them too?"

He tipped his head. "Not as often, anymore. Where were you deployed?"

"Helmand Province."

He dropped his head. "I'm sorry, son."

"What did you do in the military, sir? With a background in mathematics?"

"Intelligence, risk assessments, strategy."

"We have that in common as well then."

He raised his glass to me. "I figured as much. The IC tends to recruit smart, clear thinkers and you're perfect for them."

I looked down at his hands and noticed his wedding ring, trying not to think about the married woman I'd just left wounded and wondering. "You're married then?"

"Yes."

"Even while you were in?"

He nodded gratefully. "Only thing that kept me sane, I'm afraid."

I looked down at my plate and pushed the food around on it, still nauseated from the day's activities.

"How about you Finn? Have you married?"

He looked at my ring finger, probably guessing the answer, but he asked it all the same. It was tricky to answer, but I wasn't about to tell my whole life story to this poor man who just wanted a bite and a pint and then home to bed.

"I'm not married. Not sure I ever will be."

"If memory serves, you had quite the reputation with the ladies."

I blushed a little. "Yes, well...I was a bit...*overzealous*, for a while."

"You're young. It happens." He smiled indulgently.

"I don't feel young. Not anymore. I feel like an old man who's past his prime. No offense, sir."

"None taken and quit calling me sir!" He clapped a hand on my good shoulder. "The first six months or so are the hardest. You have to stay busy and be around people who are normal. You need to have a purpose, my boy. Have you decided what you'll do with your degrees yet?"

"No, I haven't."

"Would you like to come and teach? I could probably pull you in for some lectures. Or possibly there's a position they'd consider you for?"

"Thank you, but I don't feel I'd be a very good teacher."

"How about a research assistantship while continuing on for your PhD?"

"I'll have to think about that. Thank you, though." We were almost finished with our dinner and a very cute waitress was eyeing me. It was tempting, but I was exhausted and just wanted to sleep.

"Actually, I'd like to start a company that will combine mathematics with computers for the film industry."

"Really?" The professor put his fork down and looked at me in earnest. "Now that sounds interesting. I'd love to hear more about it."

I pushed my plate away. "Well, I'm sure you'd love to get home to bed as well. I won't bore you with it. Besides, I've got to procure a room for tonight before it gets too late."

"Nonsense! You'll stay at my place! Like I said, my wife's out of town and we've a spare room for just these occasions. Please. Say you'll come. We can talk on the way."

"Thank you, sir." I didn't know else to say. It was certainly more kindness than I'd experienced back at Regan's. He wouldn't let me pay for my portion of the meal either, and soon we were on our way to his flat, which, as it turns out, was only a few blocks away.

It was a cozy place that was tucked in between a dozen or so other cozy places on his street. "We've lived here for the last five years and have loved every minute of being so close to everything."

"Do you have children, Professor?"

"No, and how about you call me by my given name, which is Roger? I'm not your professor anymore, am I?"

"No, sir. I mean, Roger." I laughed. "*Sir* is a holdover from the military."

"I understand. Just trying to put a lighter note to it." He smiled and gestured for me to enter.

"It's a lovely flat."

"That's all the wife's doing, I'm afraid. I'm not much for textiles and colors."

He showed me where to put my things and where the facilities were, then we sat across from one another in the living room. He slapped his hands onto his knees with a bit of excitement. "Now tell me about your ideas. I love to see students combine their talents and knowledge into something unique and useful."

I had to chuckle at his enthusiasm and wished for a moment that I shared it. "Do you know what CGI is?"

"Computer Generated Imagery–used in science fiction films and video games."

"Exactly. Well, when I was in the Intelligence Corps, we were always analyzing films and night vision feeds. We needed to recreate a visual of the landscape using satellite generated images to plan and create strategic advantage."

"Go on."

"I've always been fascinated by movement on film. I've got an idea of how to possibly create a new technology for doing CGI in films that uses the same principles of satellite feeds to obtain fairly immediate relayed images and combine those with the real time filming. The idea is to insert computer generated images into the shot real time that can appear to move and interact intuitively with the landscape, rather than using multiple static images and running them all together to create the feel of movement."

"So where does the mathematics come in?"

"Creating algorithms that take the constantly changing coordinates as an image moves along the landscape and inputting calculations that will allow the other images to adjust their position in space based on those calculations."

"Fascinating. And you want to create this technology. Patent it?"

"Yes sir."

"Incredible. How far along are you?"

"Not very. It's all just ideas rumbling around in my brain right now."

"Well count me in! I'd be happy to consult on the project–perhaps even invest in it if you end up bringing it to terms."

"Really?" I shook my head, astonished.

"Absolutely! It sounds fantastic!"

That was twice I'd found myself out of words. "Brilliant. Could I have an email address for you? I'm likely headed back to Ireland tomorrow."

He slid a business card across the table. "I look forward to hearing from you!"

We talked for a bit longer before turning in, and in the morning I left a note thanking him again for his hospitality. I made my way to the train station, planning on heading west toward Ireland. I wanted to head toward home and away from everything I'd known for so many years prior, but I just couldn't.

There was one more thing I had to do, so I headed back toward London instead, and caught the first flight to Qatar.

12

When the plane landed, I almost couldn't disembark. Like a zombie I made my way through the airport, then caught a taxi to the bank that held Kathleen's safety deposit box. I didn't stay long inside the velvet-curtained room, but rather dumped the contents into a bag which was much too big for what was left. I'd brought it all the same, not knowing what I might find there in the sterile black box with the key.

The fact that she was dead didn't seem to matter to anyone but me. The people at the bank were going about their business as any other, normal day would have dictated. They came, they went, I came, I took, and no one really noticed the passing. I didn't read through any of the letters, though there were several. How long she'd spent writing them up until that day I'd probably never know.

I went to the hotel where we first met, with the bag slung over one shoulder, and sat at the bar with a bottle of whiskey, but the woman in the blue dress never came. I toasted her anyway.

After putting a decent dent in the bottle, I headed to the restaurant and ordered two steak dinners and almost finished both of them. I wasn't quite as ravenous as I'd been the first time, after months in the desert eating nothing but ration packs. I went ahead and ordered a bottle of wine but preferred the whiskey instead. In my ritual there was some room for variation.

The next day I checked out of the hotel, bought some swim trunks, and took a cab out to a little rented house by the sea where I swam, sat on the beach, and watched for the woman in the bikini to walk up out of the ocean, but she never did. I washed off the sand in the outdoor shower, made some food and drank some more, and instead of lovemaking, spent the next three days reading through her letters and instructions. They went something like this:

 Finn,

If you're reading this instead of Penelope then the unthinkable has happened, and I'm so very sorry. I guess this is the place where I should tell you all the things I loved about you, but neither of us are really capable of that kind of love—at least not yet. I hope someday you will be, because Finn, you're a good man. I can feel it in my soul, and if you're reading this, it means the child we have somehow fashioned out of our collective brokenness is no longer in your life either.

I think you would have made a fantastic father, regardless of the circumstances. I know not all families are perfect. Ours wouldn't have been either, but I'm so very proud of you for being the kind of man who was willing to give it a go rather than give up.

You're not a quitter Finn, so don't quit now. Don't give up. Promise me you won't give up. Please. If you're all that carries on of the three of us, then there's a reason. Don't let all of this be for nothing. You're strong, and you must let that strength carry you. Take your time, but don't stop living. Not forever.

With Love,
Kathleen

THERE WERE letters to her parents, her brother, and one to Penelope, who I assumed was the best friend she talked about giving the other key to. At first, I wasn't going to give them to anyone. No one but Penelope even knew they existed. I read the other letters. They didn't talk about me or the baby. They were just personal letters that said goodbye. I supposed a family who lost a soldier to the war would be comforted by that last goodbye, so I sent them, in plain envelopes with no return address, to each of the people on the list.

I didn't learn much about Kathleen from the letters, just like I hadn't learned much about her while we were together. I wondered what our sham of a marriage would have looked like–two people who barely knew each other trying to raise a child together. Anyhow, it didn't matter. None of it mattered anymore.

I would have liked to take the information about her bank accounts and put all that money into the Army Benevolent Fund, but I couldn't. I wasn't her husband. Instead I just enclosed the sheet of paper with the bank information into the letter to her father. He could take her death certificate, which they would surely send to him, and do with it what he wished.

I didn't want it. I didn't want any of it. Not the knowledge, the money, the memories. If I could have made it all disappear from my heart I would have. When I left Qatar, I took the key to the safety deposit box and threw it into the ocean. The only thing I saved was the letter she'd written to me. I folded it into my wallet and flew back to Dublin.

When I showed up at her door, Eiran threw her arms around me and wouldn't let go. She was just out of nursing school and hadn't been able to visit when I was in hospital, due to her exam schedule.

She pulled me into her flat and pushed me down on the couch. "Let me have a look at you." She stared up one side of me and down the other.

It was good to see her, even though I couldn't tell her all the things that had happened to me. Aside from Regan, Da was the only one who knew about Kathleen, and it was going to stay that way. I just wanted to see Eiran's face. I wanted to remember what it was like when we were kids, in a cottage near the sea, before Mum moved in with Grams and we were still a family.

"Are you satisfied? Do I look whole to you?" I chuckled.

"I suppose so." She put her hands on her hips. "Now where the hell have you been, and why haven't you called me?"

"I've been busy."

"Yes, well I've heard that all before."

"I don't want to talk about the war."

Her face fell in disappointment, then softened. "At least tell me about your injuries. I am a nurse now, you know. I'm interested in these types of things."

I told her about my knee and my shoulder, and she made me take my shirt off to have a look at the scars. When she saw my tattoo she said, "Who's Annabelle? Some girl you were shagging, no doubt. Are you still seeing her?" When I didn't say anything, she assumed the worst and I let her.

She pushed and pulled around the skin and bones on my shoulder. "Right then. What's next? The knee? Did you go through all your rehabilitation?"

"Yes, would you like to see those scars too?"

She seemed to take the question seriously, then shook her head. "No, I suppose that's fine."

"They replaced some of the bones in my right ear as well. Have you got one of those funny little scopes with the light on it? Perhaps you could see in." I teased, tilting my ear in her direction.

She put her hands on her tiny hips again. "Is it a crime for me to want to make sure my brother's got all his parts? After all, you did go off to war and almost got yourself killed."

I put my head down. "I'm sorry. You're absolutely right. Now, have you got anything to drink?"

"It's ten in the morning!"

"Right. Sorry. I've been traveling. Must be my body's a little off. Jet lag and all."

"Traveling? Where to?"

"I had to go back to one of the areas near Qatar to get some paperwork squared away, is all. I just flew in this morning. It's a few hours later there."

"Let me make you something to eat instead. I've got work at three, but here–I'll give you a key. You're welcome to stay for a few days if you like. The sofa pulls out."

I took the key gratefully and felt around in my pocket for the other single key I still carried–one that went to another apartment in another life, or so it seemed.

"So, tell me about your schooling and your new job."

Eiran could talk a blue streak if you let her, and I did. The endless noise of her voice drowned out all the other voices vying for my attention. I found myself laughing as she animated her stories using great, billowing gestures that made them seem bigger than life, and certainly bigger than her five-foot frame.

The entire morning and into the afternoon, we cooked together and talked, and I got lost in her hilarious tales. Oh, how I'd missed her. We talked about the days when we would travel to all of Da's pubs, tricking drunken old men out of coin that we used to buy sweets and games in the many museums and shops we visited.

When I was a child, I didn't care a lick about history, but my mother instilled something in us that even Da in all his Irish glory hadn't been able to accomplish: the importance of knowing what's come before.

All those museums we ran circles around and monuments we climbed on, bringing Mum to tears for our lack of decorum–all of it left something in me. I hadn't realized until that moment, but there, in Eiran's kitchen, I suddenly had an insatiable thirst, and it wasn't for alcohol. I wanted to know who I was. Where I'd come from.

"Do you know Nana still asks about you?" she said, as if on cue.

I smiled at the memory of Da's mum, her long hair flowing wild and free, tied back with a blue ribbon. "How is she?"

"Her body's not so good, but her mind's still sharp as anything."

"Is she still living up north?"

"Aye. And she's still crazy as ever. I used to go and visit more, but with school I haven't had the time." She cleared our dishes and put them in the sink. "If you go, be forewarned. She makes strange piles of stones in her yard and will talk your ear off about the history of our people. How's your Irish?"

"Not much better than it's always been, I'm afraid."

"Well then, you can always just smile and nod." She grinned at me. "I have to go shower and get ready. You'll be all right then?"

"Absolutely. Go!"

That night after Eiran went to work, I went up to Dublin to the pub Da had named after me. Finn's Place had a great location in historic Temple Bar, but over the last several years it had become nothing more than a worn-out version of itself. Somehow Finn's Place had gotten lost in the shuffle of progress. Life went on around it, but it stayed stuck in its own kind of comfortable rut.

It was, I realized to my own amusement, aptly named.

I sat down at the bar and a new face with a tight sweater came over to me. She didn't know who I was, so I thought I'd keep it that way for as long as possible.

"Something I can do for you?" She smiled that *I'd like to take you home later* smile. I knew it well.

"Shot of Jameson's and leave the bottle."

She looked me up and down. "Sure thing."

The deal could have been sealed right there, if I wanted it to be. Problem was, I didn't. Even the thought of casual sex was absolutely repulsive, which was ironic, given my history. I chuckled out loud as I drank, shaking my head. If only I could get myself to react to whiskey the same way, I'd be just about ready for the monastery. Maybe that was what I really needed–some type of deep, spiritual, self-actualization.

Or maybe I just needed that whiskey.

"So, what brings you to this *fine* establishment?" She leaned across the bar, giving me a good look straight down her sweater.

My body responded but my mind shut it down.

"What do you mean?"

"Well, a young, good-looking man like yourself ought to be in one of the other pubs 'round Dublin that has some life to it. There are plenty to choose from. Just not sure why the likes of you would come to a place like this." She swept her arm in a circle and I followed it, noticing perhaps for the first time how lifeless it felt. "Unless of course, today is my lucky day."

She winked at me and stepped down the bar a bit. "Hello Paddy. The usual?"

The old man nodded, and she poured him some whiskey.

She was right. There were a few old-timers there. Colonel McKenna and his wife still sat a table near the window, Gil Reedy and his brother-in-law, Kenny, were at the end of the bar, and Father Flanagan was over in the corner. The place seemed almost frozen in time.

A stained, outdated menu sat wedged between salt and pepper shakers every few feet along the bar, and although there were ten or fifteen tables in the place, most of them stood empty. The lighting was terrible, even though the street front was completely made of glass. There was room out on the sidewalk for an awning and some tables, but nothing had been done.

The place was as unknown and as boring as the old man sitting next to me. Perhaps it was the whiskey, but I began to see the place with new eyes. So much potential. Such a waste.

Like looking in a mirror, it was.

I thought about telling Da—maybe I could give him some ideas to boost the place, but at the moment all I wanted was another shot of whiskey and maybe a–

"Finn! Is that you?!" The door to the bathroom swung back and hit the man in the arm, but he just stood there looking at me.

It took me a minute before his face registered in my memory. "Shane?"

He came over and clapped a hand on my shoulder. It was still a little damp from his visit to the john, thank God, seeing as last time I was there, Shane was the cook, and I was rather comforted by the fact that he washed his hands after using the loo.

Tight sweater came over and leaned on the bar. "You know this bloke?"

Shane laughed heartily then, so hard he nearly doubled over. "You can't be serious, Brandy. Don't you know who this is?"

I was laughing because Shane was laughing, but then I said "Wait! Your name is Brandy?"

She stuck out her chin a little. "Aye."

"And you work in a bar..." For some reason this made me laugh all the harder. Soon Shane and I were holding onto each other to keep from falling down. I don't even know why it was so funny. It had been so long since I'd laughed. Really laughed. Brandy just kept looking at us.

Shane put a hand over his chest trying to catch his breath. "Brandy? Allow me to introduce you to Finn. This is his place." He couldn't get through that last part without snickering and snorting while he talked, which made it kind of hard to understand him.

"Poor Brandy doesn't get the joke." I dispensed two more shots and we raised our glasses to one another before tossing them back and then slamming them down on the bar.

"Here's to the world's best bartender!" Shane yelled. "*Pour* Brandy!"

I thought I might wet myself, but it had just been so long since I'd found anything silly enough to laugh at.

"Okay you two. I don't know what's going on here, but you'd best settle down, and Shane you'd best get back to work. I've put an order or two up in your absence."

He held up a finger to stop her from turning away from us, trying to catch his breath. "Let me try this a different way. Brandy? May I introduce to you *Mister* Finn McCarthy."

She flushed pink. "You mean...Mr. McCarthy's–"

"Son, yes." Shane's head was bobbing up and down and the snorting started again.

I stuck out my hand. "Pleased to meet you Brandy. Now don't mind me–I'm not about any kind of official business. I'm just havin' a drink here."

She took my hand and shook it weakly. She looked me up and down again, as if she still wanted to shag me and maybe this new revelation had merely sweetened the pot.

By this time her face was bright red, although it wasn't really fair–there was no way for her to have known. She looked at me and stammered. "Well then, why don't *you* tell him to get back to work!" She dismissed us and went down to the far end of the bar to talk to the customers down there.

"Did you know who he was?" she called to Father Flanagan. He looked over at me and nodded. "How about you?" she said to Colonel McKenna, who just grinned at her. "Does everyone here know Finn McCarthy but me?" she called out. A round of "aye's" with raised glasses followed. Only Paddy stayed quiet and sipped his whiskey.

She brought me a second bottle of Jameson's and set it down next to us. "I guess this one's on the house."

I grabbed her hand before she could walk away. "Now don't be cross. I'm not a bad guy."

"Is that an English accent?" She grabbed onto the neck of the bottle. "Are you pulling one off on me?"

I don't know why the English accent came up. Must have been created as a default when trying to charm women. "I'm a half-breed. Or didn't you know that about my family? How long have you worked here?"

"Six months. But your Da doesn't come in here that often and he certainly doesn't tell me stories about his wife and kids." She pulled her hand away. "Now, if you'll excuse me."

She was just the fiery sort I'd have considered a challenge a year or two before. But I let her go with little more than a thought. *I really am a sick bastard.*

Shane leaned in. "So what brings you to our neck o' the woods?"

"Just visiting."

"I've got to get the grub on, but you'll be here for a bit, no?"

"As long as there's whiskey flowing and I'm still able to sit straight on the stool."

"Right then! I'll see you in a bit."

Shane's *bit* turned into more than an hour, and in that time, I'd started wandering around, looking at the walls and floor and table arrangements, sketching ideas on napkins, and making notes on my phone.

Brandy watched me with interest. "Not on official business, eh? Looks fairly official to me."

"Just thinking, is all."

"Well are you thinking about some food? Because you've had enough whiskey to put a horse down."

"Aye." I turned too fast and stumbled a bit. "Have Shane put something together for me."

I ate a basket of fish and chips and took a few pictures. I couldn't stop thinking about the potential this place had with the right renovations. The ceilings were quite high, making more modern, hanging lights an interesting option. If we managed to resurface the bar and polish the floors it could have a totally different vibe. New stools wouldn't hurt either, and maybe a chalkboard menu and a couple of large mirrors to expand the feel of the place.

Who was I kidding? I wasn't Da, and while my name may have been out front, it wasn't my money in the till.

I took a rain check on the rest of that bottle and left some money on the bar. I wasn't about to pull privilege, no matter what Brandy or the others thought of me.

I took the bus back to Eiran's and slept fitfully. I dreamt of sailing voyages on open seas and figured it was my heart telling me to just sail away from there. Would have been nice at that point. Instead I got up early and went down to walk on the beach. I'd always loved watching the sea with its soothing, perpetual motion.

I wondered if the sea had a memory, or if it all washed away and sank into the depths once the tides carried it out. All my memories were blurred together. I tried to remember different pieces of my life. Trips to the west side of the island with Nana, and her belief in everything mysterious and supernatural. The constant excursions with Mum and her incessant ramblings about the differences between the Celtic cultures. Da's focus on business trips and little else.

My childhood had been spent everywhere but a home base, my adolescent years rocked back and forth between both countries, boarding school, and two very different homes. Then came university, followed by the nomadic life of a soldier. I didn't even have my own apartment. Everywhere I went I was just visiting. It made me sad to realize I had no real sense of place.

13

When I called Da to tell him I was going on a tour of his pubs around Ireland, the other end of the phone got quiet for a while.

"Do you want me to come with you?"

"No need. I'm my father's son, after all, and it's not just computers–I've a degree in business as well, don't forget. Do you trust me to check on things for you? Make some changes if I see fit?"

"Changes?"

"It's a whole new world out there. Take your place here in Dublin, for instance. I was there just last night, and it's too old-fashioned. The international crowd won't come near it–it's all old men and drunkards at that. But your location is cherry. With a few structural changes, some decent advertising, and an expanded wine list, you just might start making a name for yourself."

"That what you think?"

"That's what I think."

Another bout of silence on his end. "Well, let's talk about it when you get back, then. And check in once in a while, will you?"

I don't know why he bothered saying that last bit. All the managers of those pubs had known me since I was a wee lad, and no doubt they'd be reporting back to him just as soon as I left their establishments.

And so it went. I spent a few days at each place, depending on the circumstances. Starting with Dublin I made my way south, down the coast. Initially everyone was glad to see me. Colin's boy made good. Fun-loving. Oxford grad. Army hero.

Admittedly, my methods were a bit different from Da's. Turns out I was a very good bartender–for the first part of the night, anyway. Once people started buying me drinks, I think I lost more money than I made. I slept it off in the storerooms, in cots pulled out for just such occasions. Until it started to get out of hand.

The army had no problem continuing to fill my prescriptions for pain pills. They said I'd likely always have issues in the shoulder, and although the knee was better, there were no guarantees. Being awarded a medal for bravery that sat in a box did nothing to ease that pain, but the pills did.

They dulled everything nicely, and when I added in a little whiskey, I usually didn't remember a thing. Got in three fights the first two weeks. Woke up with cuts and bruises and no recollection whatsoever of what I'd said or what I'd done.

The only thing I couldn't stomach was the women. Every one of them, no matter what she looked like, reminded me somehow of Kathleen. I thought about my unborn child–my Annabelle–and realized what I would do to a bloke that took advantage of her like I had done with so many women over the years.

They came on strong and willing, but it was my love of women that had started it all, and I wasn't going there again. I promised myself I wouldn't sleep with another woman I wasn't in love with, which at that point in my life kept me relatively safe. In fact, I came to prefer the release of a good brawl to the body of a beautiful woman. Often times I picked fights specifically with blokes just like me–good looking chaps who preyed on innocent girls.

I was my own version of Robin Hood, asking them all polite-like to step outside for a word and then sending them home bloody before they could close the deal. I tried not to fight inside the bars.

They were, after all, part of my future inheritance, and lucky for me, most of my father's mates looked the other way instead of calling the police. I even walked a few girls safely home afterwards and left them at their doors like a real gentleman, whether they wanted me to or not. If only Regan could've seen me turning them all down.

Nights don't last long when you're passed out cold, so I just made sure I was, one way or another. It was a great safety net. No woman in her right mind, no matter how desperate, wants to shag a ridiculously wasted loser who can't even sit up straight. As it turns out, drooling was *not* my most attractive feature.

Like I said, I'd known many of these men my whole life. They all saw the changes in me but gave me a wide berth because they knew I'd just been to Afghanistan. Convenient, that tortured war hero bit. I fought and drank and wandered my way through Wexford and Waterford, through Cork and Killarney.

During the day, when I wasn't sleeping it off, I would roam the hills and parks, trying to breathe with the landscape, trying to touch something untouchable. Traveling the back roads was like rediscovering a lost part of my history. For as much as I was able to feel, it felt...right somehow.

And yet, the nightmares only intensified. I would wake up more nights than not in a cold sweat, head pounding, with images from the war unrelenting in their assault on my heart and mind. I relived Kathleen's death again and again, until her face was nothing more than a blank mask. Then the blank mask became other faces—Grams, Da, Bryce, even Regan. They all died night after night, and there was nothing I could do to stop it. Their blood soaked into that insatiable dusty ground until I screamed myself awake.

The only thing that got me back to sleep was the painkillers, even though those produce their own form of bizarre dreams. Needless to say, I barely slept, and I hardly ate. Although the innkeepers' wives tried their best to feed me, I grew pale and thin. After a while I even stopped picking fights. I was getting the tar beat out of me and I just didn't have enough tar left to fill in the cracks.

. . .

AFTER ABOUT A MONTH OR SO, I landed in Limerick, at the first bar my father had ever opened. We'd lived there for a year or two and the man who ran the pub was one of Da's best mates when he played for England. A hulk of a man, he was. Played fullback, if memory serves, and got thicker from there.

I stumbled into the pub 'round three o'clock, already a bit langered from the train ride, and there was Nigel, wiping the bar, wearing a red apron over a plain white t-shirt just as he'd always done.

"Nigel! How are you mate?"

"Finnegan me boy! How ye be?" He came out from behind the bar and when I tried to shake his hand, he pulled me into an embrace instead.

He looked me up and down and sniffed decidedly. "We're celebrating, are we?"

I smiled. "I've got to use the loo, if you don't mind."

"Be my guest!" He slapped me on the back and it nearly knocked me over. "Probably still got your name scratched into the door, too!"

"Tanks."

"I'll have the missus make you a sandwich!" He called after me. "Looks like you haven't eaten in weeks!"

I think I fell asleep in the loo, because all of a sudden I heard a gigantic pounding on the door and Nigel's voice on the other side.

I came out only half-tucked, and Nigel pulled me over to a booth and sat me down with a pot of coffee. His wife, and I'm sorry to say I can't remember her name, brought out a sandwich and some crispers and set them down before she got a good look at me.

She was a large, round woman who wasn't afraid to speak her mind to anyone. She grabbed hold of my whiskered chin and yanked it over to make me look her in the eye, which I honestly tried to do, but she kept wiggling my head around, so it was hard to focus.

"Finn McCarthy, what are you on?"

I pulled my head out of her grasp and wrapped my hands around my coffee cup. "What are you talking about?"

She grabbed my chin again, so hard in fact, that I briefly took inventory of just how much tar I had to spare, but one look at Nigel's biceps and I decided to keep my mouth shut.

She pointed at my face. "Them there eyes is what I'm talking about and you know it. Is it the drugs you're on?"

I pulled the bottle out of my pack. "They've got my name on 'em. You can look for yourself."

She did. "Aye and what're these for?"

I ripped open the snaps on my shirt and showed her my shoulder. "Is this good enough for you woman?" Nigel got noticeably agitated. "I was wounded in the war! I've just come out of the army. Any other questions?"

"Well, by the look *and* the smell of you, you've been washing 'em down with something what's not supposed to be mixed with that stuff. And I'm sorry Finn, but those scars have long healed." She put the bottle down and placed both hands on her sizable hips. "You can stay out back for the night, but you won't be causing trouble 'round here. You'd best be gone by morning." Nigel started to protest but she put her hand up to stop the flow of his words. "I'll hear none 'o that. No more on the subject at all."

Chances are, word had already come through some of the other places I'd been. News traveled easily, especially amongst the women.

She walked away then, and left Nigel and I sitting there with an awkward silence looming between us.

"What's happened to you, son? Does your da know where y'are?"

"I'm twenty-six years old, Nigel."

"Aye. And you're in need of some help, too."

"I've got all the help I need, thanks." I put the pill bottle back in my pack and slammed down the rest of the coffee. I stood on shaking legs and picked up the sandwich to take it with me. "You can tell the missus I won't be troubling you for that room tonight. I'll take care o' myself."

"Finn, wait! Let me talk to her. Your Da'll never forgive me if I let you walk out that door."

I didn't even turn back around, just yelled my answer back over my shoulder. "I won't tell him if you won't."

When I opened the door and stepped back into the daylight, the sun burned my eyes. I felt like a vampire, gone out before the dark settled in. My belly ached for a bit of whiskey and I found another pub down the road that also had a room, as luck would have it. I fell headlong into the bed and passed out.

I dreamt about Nana. She was talking to me, giving me some type of instructions. I'm not sure what we were talking about, but she was speaking in Irish.

Waking up the next day, I knew I was in trouble. Without any whiskey the night before, my body shook with need. I popped a pain pill instead and laid there until it calmed things down enough to get my wits about me. As soon as I showered, I bought a loaf of bread and some coffee and caught the morning bus up to Galway.

Da didn't own anything in Galway. The Connemara region was one of those places that was still so steeped in the Irish language and culture that Mum never liked to visit. I'd only been there once or twice with Nana, when I was a child. I knew no one and no one knew me.

It was exactly the kind of place I was looking for.

At a particular spot along the way, a herd of sheep came and stood across the road, rendering it impassable–at least temporarily. The driver got out to try to move them along and I decided to take the opportunity to stretch my legs.

"No need, sir. We'll be on our way shortly."

"I'm just going up over that rise to relieve myself."

"Suit yourself, but I won't be waitin' long once the herd moves on."

"I'll be fine, thanks." I grabbed my pack, just in case, and headed for cover.

After I'd done what I came to do, I stood on top of the rise and surveyed the landscape. It was beautiful country, and as I turned toward the sea I remembered some kind of a dream where I was standing there, looking out over that same piece of coastline, and the harbor began to glow and draw me to it as the bus pulled away and left me there.

I came out of this peculiar vision and looked down to see the bus driver waving at me. The sheep were gone–and I do mean, gone. I can say this because I was standing on a hill above the road and they were literally nowhere to be seen. It was very strange, as if they'd never been there at all.

I yelled at the driver to go on without me. What on earth I was supposed to be doing there, I hadn't a clue, but I figured a glowing harbor had to mean something, and seeing as I had no real plans, I might as well find out what it was.

14

Good thing I'd packed that loaf of bread, because it took the better part of the afternoon to walk down through the hills to the harbor, and by the time I got into the village, dusk was settling in. It was just as well, because I was terrible thirsty for something to go with that bread. I procured a room and settled myself into the pub below it. Convenient, that was.

A few fishermen came in and sat down so we struck up a conversation and shared a couple of rounds. They were jolly fellows who didn't seem to mind that I was pretty well pissed, because soon enough they were right there with me. It was a Thursday and they'd just brought their fish to market, then buttoned up the boat before coming in for a pint. They introduced themselves as Peter, James and John and I laughed right in their faces.

"Are you joking with me now?"

"About what?" Peter said.

"Those are your real names?"

"Aye."

"Like in the Bible."

"Aye. Like in the Bible. This is Ireland. Every other man is named James or Peter or John."

"But you're fishermen? And your names are Peter, James, and John..." I waited for my meaning to sink in.

"Aye? You said that already," Peter answered, stone-faced.

The three of them sat there looking at me until I just shook my head and took another sip of beer. The rest of the pub got strangely quiet as I looked up at the bartender for some help and she busted out laughing. The whole place erupted, actually. The joke was on me, apparently, and so was a round for the house. They slapped me on the back, and we laughed until we cried real tears. I liked this place already.

We talked about the fishing trade and one of the men asked if I was a fisherman.

I had a good laugh at that one. I mean, I did have a bit of growth on my chin and my clothes were in need of a wash, but I certainly hadn't been there long enough to smell like the sea.

Still, I decided to play along. After all, the less I told people about who I was or where I'd come from, the easier it'd be to forget. In fact, I don't know why I hadn't thought of this sooner.

"A fisherman I'm not, but if you'd like to teach me, I'm a right fast learner."

"Looking for work, are you?" John laughed, shaking his head.

"Might be."

James grabbed onto my hands and looked at my palms. "You might be lookin' in the wrong place, mate. Those hands haven't seen an honest day's work in some time, I'd say. Nicely trimmed nails, fancy pants..." He gestured to my slacks and bowed a little to make his point.

"You're going to judge me by my pants, are you? I've seen hard times, I can assure you. Hard work too."

"That so?" James replied.

"Aye."

They looked at each other and laughed, then Peter spoke for the three of them.

"Well, how about we take you out with us on tomorrow's run, and if you don't toss your cookies, we'll consider that a good day!

But don't think your hands won't come home bleeding, fancy pants."

Again the pub fell silent while the gauntlet was thrown down. I drained my glass, slamming it down empty on the bar. "You're on!"

Amidst the applause, all three men agreed this was a fabulous idea, although whether or not any of them would remember it the next day was yet to be seen. They spent the whole rest of the evening introducing me to everyone in the pub, as if I were already part of the family.

By night's end, the whole lot of us were swaying arm in arm, singing the old songs in broken and slurred Irish until they put tar paper up on the windows to fool the police into thinking they'd closed for the night. It went on like that into the wee hours, and I laughed all the way up to my room.

A fisherman, me! Preposterous.

AND PREPOSTEROUS IT WAS, come five in the morning when I'd only been asleep two hours and yet three grown hulks of men rolled me out of bed like it was my birthday, to fetch me down to the boat. I was still drunk, so I went willingly, although I remained slightly disoriented until we were well out into the bay and the morning light broke over the hills.

They sailed on an old Galway Hooker, complete with a tar black hull and crimson sails, a high sheer and an upswept bow to handle the breaking seas. She was a sturdy boat, large enough to handle herself in the wind, but small enough to be worked by a crew of four. Three if necessary, apparently.

Luckily, I was lulled by the sea and not sick at all. Although they made for a jolly crew, on the boat they were all business. They taught me how to set the lines, measure the depths and read the wind and water. I wrapped my hands in cloth when we pulled up the nets and lines, but they still bled by day's end, just like they said. All in all, it was a good day, and it was nearly over before I started getting too thirsty.

We pulled the boat in and James and John took the catch to sell, while I stayed back with Peter, buttoning her up for the night. Peter was the head of their crew, and it was his boat. He was married with two children, but James and John were both still single. I liked Peter. He wasn't exactly a quiet man, but he seemed trustworthy, with an air of authority about him.

Bleeding hands or not, it felt good, being out on the sea all day like that. I had worked up a fierce appetite as well, which was something I hadn't known in quite a while—maybe since that original double steak dinner.

Mary, the barmaid at the pub, had hot meat pies for us when we got in. I was ravenous, and finished thirds before I even ordered my second pint. Mary stood with her arms crossed, watching me eat, smiling with satisfaction.

She was a round, warm woman, about my mother's age, yet the farthest thing from my mother's likeness there could ever be. Fiery red hair, skin leathered by the sea, and hands hardened by a life spent tending other people's problems.

Everyone's hands were hard there, because life was hard, but it was simple and beautiful too. I started to think maybe that was the problem. Maybe my life had been too complicated.

I pulled Mary aside and asked if she'd consider renting me a room by the month.

"That depends," she answered.

"On what?"

"On whether or not you can pay me, of course." She smirked, wiping the bar.

"I have money."

"Well anyone can see that, fancy pants." She looked up at me. "Question is, what are ya running from, and is it gonna come making trouble on my doorstep? We don't want no trouble here."

I looked down at my shoes, then smiled up at her. "The only thing chasing me is my own demons, but I hear they like meat pie, so I don't think they'll be any trouble a'tall."

"Well they seem fairly fond of whiskey as well, those demons." She looked down her nose at me.

It must have been the smile that won her. It was always the smile. She may have even blushed a little.

"Well, so long as they're not mean drunks I s'pose I can stomach having you about."

I laid a hand a hand to my heart and reached down to grasp hers, kissing it gently. "Much obliged, I am."

She yanked her hand away. "Oh, that's how it is, is it? It's the ladies you favor, and sure's I know why too."

I got a sour look on my face. "You won't see me married in your lifetime I'm sure."

"Who said anything about married?" Mary winked at me and went off to fetch me another pint.

Peter, James and John were sitting at the other end of the bar and after I got done making my deal with Mary on a price for meals and lodging, I stood my round and positioned myself among them.

I held up my bandaged hands and said "Well boys? What'll it be? I didn't toss my lunch, but oh what a slacker out there I was. No crew in its right mind would hire the likes of me. Still, I want to thank you for a glorious day out on the sea!"

"Making fun of us, are you?" Peter asked.

"No!" I insisted. "I'd do it again tomorrow if you'd see fit to let me."

"Well?" Peter looked at James. "Go on, give the man his wages!"

James slid several bills my way.

"What's this?"

"Today's pay, that's what." Peter took a sip of his beer. "And there's likely more tomorrow if you're interested."

"I am."

Peter nodded. "We lost a man on our crew last month. Been looking for a replacement."

"Lost?"

James leaned in to explain. "Aye. Got tangled in a net and pulled under the boat. 'Twas a terrible accident. The seas are a dangerous place."

"I'll wager I've seen worse."

He took my likeness for a few more minutes. "All right then. You'd best get a decent night's sleep. You'll be feeling it keenly tomorrow."

I raised my glass. "Couple more rounds should set me to sleeping like a wee babe in arms."

I swallowed hard after the words left my mouth. Didn't expect it to throw me for a loop, but suddenly Kathleen was there again, head in my arms, blood on my hands.

I should have kept her safe. Somehow, I should have fought harder, or known better. What kind of man allows a pregnant woman to call the shots in a time of war? Commanding officer or not, it was my fault she was dead. My fault I wouldn't be rocking my precious Annabelle to sleep.

Lost at sea sounded like a decent penance.

I ordered a double shot of whiskey with my pay and a round for the house, which included less than ten of us at the time, counting Mary. I slammed it back to the sound of cheers and applause. Then, with a full belly and a cloudy mind, I bid them all a good night.

Next morning was a storm so we didn't go out. We took to mending nets and cleaning the equipment below decks instead. In the afternoon I went to Galway and bought some clothing that was more appropriate for my new lifestyle, including some considerably less *fancy* pants, a few flannel shirts, heavy boots, and a sea slicker.

As I wandered around Galway near the docks, an old woman dressed all in black with a deep blue shawl stopped me in the street. "You there!"

I turned quickly and looked around. "Me?"

She grasped my hand and when she did, a strange look came over her face. Her eyes closed and she just held my hand in an awkward silence. I felt that same surge of electricity I had in the hospital when Da stood over my bed. I'd felt it on a smaller scale on the top of that hillside the day before. The sense of being drawn.

Her lips were moving but no sound came out at first. I waited, for perhaps she was saying a prayer. Finally, she spoke in a shaky old voice that quivered and stuttered along like her fingers as they wrapped slowly around mine. "You have the sight, but not the wisdom."

She was a crazy old woman, to be sure, but I didn't want to be rude, so I let her continue to hold my hand. I looked around, slightly embarrassed, but no one passing by seemed to think it was strange.

"You must let it guide you. The sight mustn't die with you. It must carry on."

"What are you talking about? What sight?"

"You already know what I'm talking about. You must learn to read it. Follow it. It will lead you away from the bloodshed and the tears. This is why you've come."

Her eyes opened at the end of her speech and so did mine, yet I didn't remember closing them. I blinked once or twice but found her gone. All of a sudden. Just like the sheep.

I looked around but no one was there. I was just standing in the street, by myself, looking probably quite ridiculous. There were no blue shawls, or even black dresses–nothing but an old used book-shop right in front of me. I hadn't noticed it before, but the blue paint around the outside of the storefront was the same color as the woman's shawl, so I walked in.

Immediately the shopkeeper approached me. "Oh, hello! I'm so glad you've come in! Here's the book you've been waiting for."

He tried to hand me a book, but I shook my head. "I'm sorry, but you must have me confused with someone else. I've never been here before."

"Have you been looking for this book or not?"

I looked down. It was a book about seers. "Vision and Magic? Druids? I'm sorry, but I'm not the man you're looking for."

"Are you certain?"

"Of what?"

He shrugged nonchalantly. "Anything, really."

He left me holding the book and turned, walking toward the

back of the store. He began collecting piles of books to be re-shelved, leaving me standing there in the middle of the shop waiting for God knows what else to happen. I thumbed through the copy, trying to get a sense of what I was even doing there.

It seemed to be a collection of essays about the history and traditions of seers, but instead of being all feathery and abstract, it was an academic look at the tales and legends that had been told in Ireland throughout the ages. Just the sort of book a fella like me would gravitate toward to try to explain the intersection of myth and reality. These were stories I remembered Nana telling me when I was a small child. The old woman had used the phrase "the sight", and that was in the book as well. But I didn't know anyone there, and I wasn't in Galway looking for a book.

I suppose I should have been more skeptical, but there were just too many strange and curious things piling up. Something had drawn me to that harbor. There was a reason I was in this place, at this time.

Nana wouldn't have been skeptical at all, but being a mathematics man, I headed over to the spirituality section and chose a book about quantum physics and the nature of reality. Then I selected a few other books from different balancing perspectives and added them to my stack. If I was going to figure out what the hell this woman was talking about I needed to go about the study logically. I did enjoy reading, and if I was going to get lost at sea, I might want something to do in the down times.

The shopkeeper came over to the register to ring me out. "That's good, see? Your natural curiosity will keep you moving toward the answer."

The answer? What answer?

I paid the man and walked out of the shop. Down by the water, I sat on a bench and took out the book the shopkeeper had given me. I'd been having strange dreams since I was a child. Dreams that often came true in just the way I dreamed them, but I never knew what to make of it.

For a while I thought those things happened to everyone, but it quickly became apparent that they didn't, so I shut that part down, not wanting to be viewed as a freak.

I told Da about it once and he sent me to talk to Nana, but Nana spoke only Irish and he didn't stick around to translate. I only caught about half of what she was saying, but I could tell she really wanted me to understand.

It wasn't only dreams. I had lots of strange experiences. Sometimes it was helpful, like knowing who to keep Regan away from. Sometimes I just *knew* things about a person that turned out to be true, or was able to help someone find an item they'd lost. Still, I passed these off as strange coincidences. Although the Celts are thick with it, I'd never put much stock in superstition. Probably my mother's influence.

I looked around for the old woman again. It felt like she was watching me from a dark alley or behind a curtain. Truth be told, the whole experience had me shaken, so I packed up all my purchases and headed back to that quiet little fishing village and my room above the pub. I deposited all my goods upstairs at Mary's and walked out along the docks.

James and John were sitting on the boat enjoying the last bit of sunshine coming in over the bay. James was taller and thinner than his brother, with a bushy beard that was desperately in need of a trim and only made his face look that much longer, his cheekbones pushing out over the top of the fuzz.

"Finn! What's the story?" He smiled warmly at me, as if I were the brother who fit nicely between he and John. Indeed, according to height I would've been next in line, as John was a stockier, more compact version than either of us, with considerably less facial hair.

"Just coming 'round to see if anything was needed."

"I'd say a pint was needed." John looked up at his brother, who nodded in agreement. "We were just going in!"

These were my kind of fellows. "Brilliant!"

James put on a fake British accent. "What are we, from London now?"

It occurred to me they still knew precious little about me, and I wanted to keep it that way. I put one arm around each of them and laid on an overly thick British accent of my own, just for effect. "I've passed through London once or twice, I daresay all the chaps speak like that. What say we practice a bit?"

James grinned at me and tried his own version. "I say, that sounds rather boring."

"I'd rather speak Gaelic than side with the Brits." John added.

"Well, let's go get us a pint then, shall we?" I said in as much broken Irish as I could remember.

John held onto my shoulder. "Mate? That was terrible. We're going to have to fix that."

"I told you I was a fast learner." I bowed before him. "I shall be your humble student, but I have to warn you, it gets worse the drunker I get. I've been told I start mashing all sorts of languages together."

"Well, I don't plan on being sober long enough to teach you." John said.

"Right-o." I smiled. "First one's mine then."

We headed into the pub arm in arm and I marveled at the camaraderie we'd developed in such a short time. Although I had none of my own, these felt like brothers, and Mary a mother to us all.

It went on like that for a while. The rain came down and the seas were nothin' but cold and misery, but we drank ourselves warm at the end of each day, and always had our fill of fish and stew in the evenings, bacon and boxty and Irish oats with dried berries in the morning.

Mary was always on me about why I never took the ladies up on a drink or a date, and I just told her I'd sworn off women, but I think she may have started to suspect I was gay.

One day she leaned over the bar. "Now Finn, if you don't take a lady soon, the men will be thinking you prefer their company, if you know what I mean."

"Are you insinuating that I'm gay?" I whispered back in a slur. "Because I'm not, you know."

"Is that so?"

"It is."

"Good lookin' fella like you? There's only two reasons you're not with a woman. Either you're gay or you're married, and I don't see no hint of a ring on that finger."

"I'm neither of those, trust me, and I've been with more women than there are boats in Galway Bay. Not that I'm proud of it, mind you."

"And you've had your fill, have you?"

"Something like that."

"All right." She tapped her hand on the bar. "But it might be easier to say that you are. I can't hold the women back forever. They're always in here asking about you. I tell 'em you're unavailable–you just don't wear a ring."

"Well that sounds about right. Keep that one going, will you?"

"Aye." She shook her head. "But it's a darn shame, it is. You can't hide behind that beard forever, Fancy Pants."

"I've done all right so far." I inched my empty glass toward her for a refill. "How 'bout I just marry you?"

"Don't flatter yourself young man! What makes you think I'd want the likes 'o you hanging around?"

"Ohhh...now don't talk like that Mary! What would I do without your cooking?"

"You'd be a starved little imp like you was when you first walked in my door, that's what!"

I grabbed my non-existent middle. "And look at me now! You keep cooking for me, I'll be so fat no one will ever want me!"

Mary waved her towel at me. "Ah, go on now!"

"No, I'm serious! How's about a bit of stew for old Finn?" I smiled at her and she about melted. Convincing Mary to get me what I wanted was never difficult and always fun. One of the highlights of my day, actually.

"Go sit down! You'll get your stew you little scamp!"

I blew her a kiss and she swatted it out of the air with her towel. Mary had become one of my favorite people on the entire planet.

15

Heavy lifting was one of the things the army doctors warned me about, and indeed, the pain was excruciating at times. That rebuilt shoulder wasn't made for the fishing trade, but luckily I didn't have any trouble getting the chemist in Galway to fill my prescription. I never asked for too much or to have it filled before its time, so we got along quite well.

The job increased the pain. The pain justified the meds. The meds helped me forget. It was a good system. Still, even with all of it rolled together, it was a better, fuller life than I'd ever had before. For the first time, I actually felt useful. Either way, distraction was a fantastic tool.

And that's how it went for a period of months. My beard grew thick and my hands grew rough and my heart grew dull and those books I had bought remained all but forgotten.

Until one night I had a dream. The dream was about a boat that got lost in a storm, and its crew with it. I watched the boat break apart, but I wasn't on it. In the next scene I was sitting on the shore waiting for the boat to come back in, but it never did.

I woke up heaving, with my shoulder aching so badly I thought I'd been blasted by that bomb all over again. I took a pain pill and tried to sleep. Took another and washed it down with some whiskey and finally got comfortable enough to pass back into dreamland. Not that I was in a hurry to revisit that particular scene.

James tried to roust me an hour or so later, but I was completely out of it. He pushed hard on my right shoulder to get me awake, and I came up swinging. I cried out in pain and grabbed hold of that shoulder like it was being ripped off my torso.

He looked at the open bottle of whiskey on the bedside table, then back at the shoulder and perhaps for the first time, noticed the scars and dimpled flesh from the wound. "Are you all right?"

I rolled side-to-side, grasping my shoulder. "No, I'm not all right. What the hell time is it?"

"It's four. Peter says there's a storm comin'. Wants to get out and back before the worst of it hits."

I tried to roll over and stand but something was wrong in that shoulder. I could barely move it, and the muscles were all locked up tight. I cried out again and reached for the whiskey in a stupor.

"You're not going anywhere mate. What happened to that shoulder?"

I laid back down, sweating. "Bomb blast, in the war."

"The war? Really?"

"Please just leave me alone." I groaned.

"You sure you don't want me to fetch you the doctor?"

I took a swig off the whiskey. "I've already got medicine for it."

He studied me for a moment, hesitated, then let it go. "All right, then. We'll see you on the flip side." He said in his British accent, trying to cheer me up.

I waved him on and passed back out, then woke some time later to Mary with her hand on my forehead.

"Why do people keep coming in here unannounced!" I yelled.

She ignored my anger and sat looking at the shoulder.

I opened one eye just a crack, trying to ascertain what on earth she was doing in my room. "I'm going to start sleeping with my shirt on."

She scowled at me. "Don't be smart with me, boy. Now what's

happened to this shoulder? James left me a note you were in a bad way. I've asked the doctor to come."

"I've been to the doctor. That's what got me into this mess." I tried to shield my eyes from the light where she'd drawn the curtains to get a better look.

"This here's from shrapnel, am I right?"

"James should've kept quiet."

"James didn't tell me nothin' but to check on ye. It's my own eyes telling me the rest. You're not the only one's seen a few things, Finn McCarthy."

I didn't answer for a while. "I don't want to talk about it."

"Well, you're going to have to tell the doctor 'cause he'll be here any minute now."

"Perfect," I said, sarcasm dripping.

"If you're ready for it, I've got coffee here for you." She brushed a few of the wild curls back from my face. "I'm sorry you're not feeling well, son."

I slid up on my good elbow and leaned back against the pillows, blowing out shallow, staccato breaths with each movement. She handed me the hot mug in my left hand and I tried to sip it, but even that caused considerable pain on the right.

"We're going to have to get after those curls again once you're feeling better."

"Whatever you say, mother."

She sat with me a bit while we waited for the doctor. "You don't talk much about your mother. Sure, she worries about ye?"

"She lives in England. I don't see her much."

Mary nodded. "It's been that way for a long time, has it?"

"She's lived in England most of my life."

"And you?"

"I've been here and there."

"And what of your da?

"He's here in Ireland. Lives outside Dublin now, but he travels a lot."

"And what's he do for work?"

"Same as you. Owns a few pubs."

"A few you say. Not like me then. I can barely keep the one running."

"He was fortunate–used to be a pretty decent footballer. Played in the club teams and the national team as well. Had a bit of a nest egg to start with and built from there."

"Ach! See I knew you come from royalty!"

Royalty? Not quite. Then again, if she could see the estate Grams owned, Mary would probably keel over. Best to keep that secret a while longer. Being a footballer was respectable. Being the privileged grandchild of the English ascendancy who attended school with aristocrats was a bit over the limit, I think. Even for me.

"And how 'bout you? Do you play?" Mary wondered. I assumed she was trying to help keep my mind off the pain.

"It was Gaelic Football for me. Club teams mostly. Not much more." *Nothing like, say, playing for Oxford...*

She patted my hand. "Grown up around pubs then, have you? No wonder you hold your liquor like an old man."

Did I? I'd seen those men sitting in Da's pubs all day and into the night, stumbling home to the missus. Surely I wasn't so far gone? I'd taken a few months off from life, was all. Just taking my time, like Kathleen told me to. She told me not to stop living, and I hadn't. In fact, I felt more alive now than ever.

The doctor knocked on the door just then.

"Hello Mary. Hope you don't mind I've let myself in. This here's the patient I assume?"

"This is him." She stood up and brushed out her apron. "And he'll thank me for leaving I'm sure, so I'll let you to it."

The man smiled and nodded politely at Mary, and then at me. "Finn? I'm Dr. Ryan. How are you?"

"I've had better days."

He shut the door after Mary. "Well, let's have a look, shall we? It's the shoulder, is it?"

I nodded.

He sat on the edge of the bed. "How 'bout you start by telling me how it happened and what's been done already? Anyone can see from the scarring you've had some surgery on it. Lean forward, please."

I did so, but with difficulty. "I served in Afghanistan. Was medically discharged a few months ago after a bomb blast shattered this shoulder, my knee, and some of the bones in my right ear. I've had various surgeries trying to repair it all. Spent some months in hospital at Birmingham."

"British Army then?"

"Yes, sir."

"I was in myself. That's how I got through medical school. Did my required years of service. Been in private practice since. I prefer a...quieter life now."

I looked at him and knew intuitively that he understood. "Yes, sir."

"You don't have to call me sir, son. We're not in anymore, are we?" He poked around a bit, and every touch sent me to the ceiling. "Did they replace the entire shoulder?"

"Had to. There was nothin' left of it. And too much debris embedded in the bone I'm told. Had trouble with the knee too, but the shoulder was the worst of it. Had an infection in it once before, but it didn't feel quite like this. I don't feel feverish and ache all over this time. All the pain's right in the shoulder there. Feckin' thing's all locked up. Can't seem to move it for a damn."

"Did they tell you no heavy lifting or repetitive strain?"

"Aye."

He looked at my calloused hands and arms full of rope burns and hook lashes. "And what've you been busy at since you've been staying here at Mary's?"

"I've taken work on a fishing boat."

"But certainly you don't do any heavy lifting, pushing, or pulling on that boat?" One of his eyebrows lifted.

I tried to keep the smirk from my face. "No sir. Not a bit."

He sat back, grinning. "What you've got there, son, is an inflammation issue. Overuse. Overwork. That joint is angry, and it's going to stay angry until you rest it a good long while. And I do mean rest. Completely. The life of a fisherman's not for you, Finn."

"I can barely move my arm, and it grates something fierce."

"I can give you something for that. And I'm going to bind it up for you too." He took out a large stretchy bandage and literally bound my arm and shoulder to my chest. It felt ridiculous to be a one-armed man, but I noticed a slight relief almost immediately. "This will take all your muscles out of the equation for a while. I want you to wear it like this for at least a week but take the bandage off to shower and sleep. We're looking to immobilize it until the swelling goes down. Then you can start with small movements. Do you remember your rehabilitation exercises?"

"I do."

"Good." He handed me two small slips of paper. "Here's something for the inflammation and another for the pain. I want you to take the inflammation pills three times a day, with food. The pain pills are to help you sleep." He inclined his head toward the open bottle on the nightstand. "It'll work better than the whiskey for the pain but see that you don't combine the two or it'll put you in a stupor."

"I happen to like stupors," I joked.

He ignored me, smiling. "Mary can help you with the rebinding if you've no one else. She's handy like that. Good people, Mary, and the others too. Known them all a good long time."

I took the papers from him. I really didn't have anyone else to look after me or bandage my wounds. What if I'd been truly alone? Would I have gone back to Da's? Eiran's? Regan's? Who was I kidding? Probably none of those.

"I'd like to check on you in a week or two, if you don't mind, but if you've any trouble before that, just let me know."

"Thank you."

"There'll be no working. You have to rest it. Have you another source of income? A pension from the army or anything?"

"I've got some put by. I can manage for a couple of weeks. Now what do we need to do to settle our account? Mine with you, for coming."

"I think we'll just call this one a wash. One soldier helping another. Now would you like me to have the chemist bring these over?"

"No, I can go. In Birmingham I got fairly good at eating, drinking and signing my name left-handed. I'm sure I'll manage."

"I'll see you next week."

"Brilliant. Thanks."

Trying to manage with one arm without the benefit of hospital staff was harder than I remembered. Luckily, I had the other prescription in my bag, so I took one before heading over to the chemist. It was getting on in the afternoon, and by the time I fetched the medicine, the air was icy cold, and the wind had whipped up. The rain would be right on its heels.

Winter storms were no joke on the coast.

IT WAS hard to keep a coat buttoned up with one arm, so I hurried back just before the downpour, looking forward to meeting up with the boys for a warm piece of pie and some coffee. When I finally got the door closed against the wind, there was no one there except Mary, wiping down the bar.

"What's this? Where are the three stooges?"

She looked worried, nervously glancing out the window as she rubbed the same spot on the bar with her towel. "Haven't come in yet."

"What do you mean?"

"Haven't been here. Don't know as they're back yet."

"They must be back. Have you seen the harbor?"

"Aye, and there's no boat in their slip. I've just gone out and looked again."

I tried to reach back into the depths of my early morning memory. "James said they were heading out early because there was a storm coming. They wanted to get back in before it hit."

She looked at me with fear in her eyes, and I remembered my dream. It couldn't be. Not that...

"Maybe they put in somewhere up the coast a bit. Let's not assume the worst. Peter wouldn't risk his boat. Let's just wait it out, shall we? Come on Mary, let me buy *you* a drink for once. We're not likely to get a big crowd on a night like tonight. Let's turn on the tele and watch some news."

She let out a heavy sigh that seemed to release with it some of the worry she'd bottled up inside. "Let me go make us something warm to eat first. I've got a chill in my bones what won't be chased away except by a belly full of hot stew."

"See now? Keep talking like that and I *will* have to marry you!" I winked, trying to put her mind at ease, and she waddled off into the kitchen.

I turned on the tele and sure enough there was news on every channel of storm warnings, telling people to stay in for the night. Mary came out a few minutes later and set two bowls down at our booth. She looked up at the news, then down at her bowl, making the sign of the cross on her chest and waiting for me to do the same before she'd start eating.

I tried to keep Mary talking as the news droned on in the background. I asked about her late husband, her grown children, and even her cat. Anything to keep the conversation away from the storm. When we were done eating and she'd cleared our plates, we shared a hot whiskey.

"Those boys are like my own. Been comin' in here since they were fifteen." She smiled. "Sneaking in, is more like it."

I laughed. "That sounds like James and John, but I can't see Peter sneaking anywhere. He seems pretty straight up."

"Peter is, that's true. I was at his wedding, and his wife's a real sweet one. Callie's her name. She used to work for me here, waiting tables, when my husband was still alive. That's how they met. Leastwise, that's when the flirting began." She smiled at the memory. "'Course now with the wee ones she doesn't work anymore. Seven and five they are, and cute as buttons. A boy and a girl, so rambunctious and what love my pies!" she said proudly.

"What's not to love?" I smiled and sipped on my mug.

The storytelling seemed to calm her, so I just let her talk.

"James and John, they were lost boys–always getting in trouble, needing direction. Took them boys under his wing, Peter did. Peter inherited his father's boat and taught them a trade. Been with him ever since, day and night."

"You mean they live together too?"

"Callie's father was a fisherman who knew Peter's father. You know how that goes. She inherited his house and there's an extra room in the back. They rent it out to James and John. Got her hands full feeding all them boys, Callie does, and her own wee ones as well." Mary looked out the window as lightning lit up the sky and the thunder cracked after it. "That's why I feed 'em for her every chance I get."

I always knew the Irish people to be a loving and hospitable sort, but I'd never personally known people who truly cared for one another like this. It was like a family, but no family I'd ever known.

Mum was neither affectionate nor generous beyond what propriety dictated. In her mind English children were to be proper, well-mannered, and seen but not heard. They were sent to boarding school to be instructed in culture, academics and social graces, and expected to return as well-bred, "finished" ladies and gentlemen. Mum never wanted us in the pubs, that much was true, but more than that, she wanted us to be proper, so she saw to it with Grams' money and influence. I can't fault her for it. It's just the way she was raised.

And yet, Grams was different. More balanced. Or perhaps she'd simply lived long enough to see the value in relationship over respectability. In any event, she took the time to be with me and talk to me, and I loved her for it.

Da was the sort who would give you the shirt off his back, but he was so busy with his hand in so many projects, he didn't have a lot of time to get to know people. He didn't invest in relationships like he invested in businesses. He was sharp though, with a keen intuition that served him well, at home and in business. I loved Da because he gave me the space I needed to sort myself out. I was wholly convinced that even if he did know where I was, he wouldn't come find me—not unless I asked.

Eiran was a whole other story. She loved me to pieces, but she was a mother hen. Anyone would have thought she was the older sibling and I, the baby brother. She was bossy and sometimes cross, but in the end you fell in love with her enormous heart and smothering sort of love. Still, we didn't have a lot in common.

I thought about Peter's wife, sitting home waiting for him. "Can you call her? Call Callie and find out if he's checked in? Surely he'd call her first chance he could."

Mary shook her head. "Already tried that. He hasn't called. She hasn't seen him since he kissed her and the children goodbye in the middle of the night."

"Maybe they're beached in a little cove somewhere and the phones aren't working because of the storm. They'll be fine. Peter'll see to it."

She looked straight at me. "Did I ever tell you how my husband died?"

I stayed silent. We both knew she hadn't. It was a rhetorical question.

She looked down at her mug of hot whiskey and swirled what was left of the liquid around over the lemon wedge and cloves. "He never came back in."

I swallowed down my fear. There were certain dreams I dreaded waking up from. Ones that that were so real in sleep, I knew somehow they would be true in the real world as well. Dreams like the one James had woken me from that morning.

She finished her mug and pulled down two regular glasses and the bottle of Jameson's, then waited for me to pour it. Suddenly I was the bartender and she was the patron. Lucky for me it didn't take the use of both arms to pour whiskey.

"How long ago was that?" I asked.

"Thirteen years. This week."

I swallowed down the irony. "What was his name?"

"Harry." Tears gathered in her eyes. "His name was Harry."

"Let's have a toast then. To Harry!"

She lifted her glass. "To Harry. God love him."

After she downed the brown liquid, Mary turned off the tele and collected our glasses. "I can't watch anymore, and I'm not as stout as I used to be." She swayed a bit, and I tried to steady her with my good arm. "I'm going to bed. You need anything?"

"No, I'm good. But I will need you to bind up my arm tomorrow after I shower. If you don't mind."

"I don't mind." She reached down and gently kissed me on the forehead. "Goodnight Finn. Sleep well."

"You too. I can lock up."

She smiled gratefully. "Thanks."

I took the bottle with me upstairs and added it to my collection. It was always handy to have around, of course. I pulled a chair over to watch the storm through the windows for a while, and for the first time in a long time, I said a prayer. I ask for safe passage for Peter, James and John. I asked for protection over Peter's wife and their children.

There was nothing left to do but sleep, so I took a pill from the new prescription bottle and laid down in the bed.

Peter would have called.

16

Next thing I knew it was morning, and rather than attempt a shower I pulled my coat on over my good arm and headed down to the docks. The slip was empty, but it was early yet, so I sat on a piling and waited, watching the sea. It was still terrible cold, but the sun had crept out and the waters were calm again. Surely they'd be headed home today from wherever they had pulled in.

After about an hour I went in, chilled to the bone and Mary poured me some coffee. "How's about a little hair of the dog?"

"You too, eh?" She wiped the hair out of her eyes and put a splash of whiskey in both our cups.

"I'll be taking that shower now. Can I bring the wrapping back down after?"

She nodded. "I'll make us a bit of breakfast."

So that was what it had become. Me and Mary, waiting for news of the inevitable. He would have gotten word in by now.

When I walked down after my shower in nothing but my pants, Mary was sitting with a pretty young thing in the same booth we'd occupied the night before. They both looked up and the girl turned her head away when she saw me.

"Sorry. I didn't know anyone was here."

Mary slid out of the booth. "No need. Finn, this is Callie."

Callie waved at me with her head turned, which I had to laugh at, because most women would have stared openly, not that I was much of a catch at that point. I'd gained back some of my weight, but none of my former glory. The tattoo and the scars were probably intriguing though, at the very least.

Mary's girth hid me for a moment as she wrapped my arm and bound it tightly to my chest, then helped me slip my t-shirt on over the top of it all.

"She's dropped the children at school and come to wait out the news with us." Mary whispered as she slid the shirt over my head.

I nodded and stuck out my left hand awkwardly. "How do you do?"

Callie took it just as awkwardly. "Pleased to meet you." She tried to smile. "Peter's told me a lot about you."

"All lies, I hope." I grinned at her, trying to lighten the mood. I looked between the two of them. "Any news?"

"I've called them in as missing." Callie shook her head. "The harbormaster said he received a distress call late yesterday afternoon about sunset but hasn't heard anything since. Communications broke in the storm. They're making a search this morning."

Mary simply nodded.

I looked back and forth between the two of them. They'd spent their lives in this village, this lifestyle. Callie had lost a father to it. Mary a husband. They understood this kind of waiting; this brand of torture. They were kindred spirits who needed one another, but I didn't belong.

Mary brought out some warm porridge and I ate it gratefully, but once I was done, I pulled on my coat and took a fresh cup of coffee back out to the docks. I knew what I would find, but I had to watch anyway. I had to walk the dream through to its conclusion.

And conclude it did, about two hours later, when the harbormaster and his men came calling over at Mary's.

I walked in behind them, and while no words were exchanged, I could see Callie and Mary, and I watched their faces fall.

"We found the boat," The harbormaster said quietly. "It was

dashed against some rocks about five miles up. Looks like they were trying to come in–trying to stay close to shore. Perhaps it was just too shallow, and the waves were too strong. The hull broke apart."

Mary's face went white. "All three of them? Gone?"

"We've no trace of them. Not yet. Just pieces of the boat is all, and a few personal effects that washed up on shore."

Everything happened in slow motion. First, I watched Callie fall into Mary's arms, then I watched her whole life fall apart, while her dreams floated away on the empty seas. I stumbled back into a booth across the bar and let them have some breathing space. It was a grief so large it filled the whole place and spilled out onto the street.

The men from the harbor patrol locked eyes with Mary. She'd done this routine before. Thirteen years ago. Mary, who loved those boys like they were her own. Mary, whose chest was now filled with an inconsolable widow.

"We'll keep looking."

Mary acknowledged them, and they tipped their hats and left as quietly as they came. There would still be days of searching before it would be announced. Days of waiting on tiny imagined glimmers of hope, of walking the narrow line between denial and acceptance. I liked to call that nirvana. Others called it limbo.

The ache in my shoulder intensified until I realized I was holding every muscle rigid. I tried to relax but I couldn't. I couldn't breathe. I wanted to offer them my comfort–my strength, but I had none, so I struggled up to my room, closed the drapes and wept. I couldn't bear the grief. Not again.

It wasn't long before I couldn't stand my weakness any longer. I went back downstairs to see if there was anything I could do. I was a soldier, for God's sake. I'd seen death. Lost friends.

Mary had closed the bar and locked the doors. I found her sitting in the dim light rocking Callie, brushing back her hair and wetting it with tears of her own. She knew this grief. Who better than Mary to comfort her?

I wandered into the kitchen and fetched us some coffee, which I brought out with my one good arm. Mary started to get up, but I waved her off. "I've got this. I've still got one good arm. I'm not help-less." I winked at her and she seemed relieved that I was there. The only man left in her life at the moment.

Later that afternoon Mary put Callie to work. They decided that they wouldn't give up hope until there was no more hope to be had, so they dried their eyes and put on their aprons and made some sandwiches for lunch and a pie for the kids. Callie fetched them from school and brought them to Mary's. They squealed when they saw Mary, who gave each of them a big round hug and a kiss on their cheeks.

"This here's Declan," Mary announced. "Declan? This is Finn. He works with your da on the boat sometimes."

"Is he an uncle then? Like James and John? Da says they're all like brothers on the boat, so I can call James and John my uncles. Are you my uncle too, Finn?"

When he looked up, I noticed one of his teeth was missing in the front. He looked just like his dad when he smiled and it about speared me, but I smiled back. "If you like."

I tried to shake his hand with my left and he looked at me funny. Then he noticed my other arm wasn't sticking out of my sleeve.

"What happened to your other arm?" He looked behind me to see if I was hiding something. "Is it cut off?"

I laughed. "No, no. It's in there – see?" I let him look inside my shirt and he spent a good deal of time looking for that other arm. When he finally found it wrapped in its bandage, he seemed satisfied.

"So you've hurt it?" he said.

"I did, yes."

"Is that why you're not out on the boat with Da and my other uncles?"

My eyes flinched as I looked down at Declan's face. "It is indeed."

He went back to eating his sandwich, satisfied with my answer.

Mary moved along to the tiny little girl next to him. She spun the stool around to face me and the little girl squealed with delight. "And this here, is Bree."

She leaned down and nuzzled Bree's cheek and the little girl giggled. She had light green eyes like her father's, a pretty little face like her mother's, and hair the color of golden straw in the summer sun. She was a sight to behold–like an angel being swallowed by a barstool.

"I keep telling her that her mother should have named her Breeze, for that's what she is–a beautiful breeze what blows through the room whenever she comes in."

Bree waited until she finished chewing, then waved her hand at me. "Hello Uncle Finn!"

She went right back to her sandwich and that was that. As soon as they were done, they slid off the stools and raced for the kitchen. Rambunctious was true enough, but lovely as well. Up until that day they'd only known love and affection and peace. From here on out all of that would change. I tried to take a snapshot of it in my mind. Something I could somehow send to them later, to remind them of happier, more carefree days and, well...pie of course.

AND SO IT went for the rest of that week. Callie would drop them at school, do her housework and come to Mary's, where the two of them would work the days away in companionable silence and sometimes a bit of laughter, both of them knowing that every day that went by meant less and less chance the men would return.

I wasn't much use to them, what with my arm all bound up. I spent a good portion of my days sitting by the water, reading the books I bought. Every day I watched the harbor, knowing full well they couldn't come sailing in on a ship that had been found in pieces. I watched anyway.

Most people don't even get a second chance and here I'd been given three. Twice I should have died in the war, maybe more. And now this. I seemed unable to die by normal means, so there must be some reason I'd been spared. If the old woman was right and I was set here for a purpose, I needed to know why.

I didn't really expect to find the answer in those books, but they kept my mind occupied while I waited for some sort of answers to wash up on the shore. Perhaps then I could gather the broken pieces and lay them in the sand and the old woman could read them to me like tea leaves. Maybe she could tell me what went wrong, and what comes next.

The whole town knew of the tragedy and came by at intervals to ask if there was any news. They were careful around the children, not to say anything that might scare them, but the looks on their faces said it all–everything our hearts already knew.

Declan asked about his father and Callie told him their boat hadn't come back yet and we weren't sure where they all were, but that we must pray for their safety, so he did. Every time I saw the lad and he didn't have a piece of pie in front of him, he was mumbling under his breath. It broke my heart.

Bree was like a little porcelain figure, so beautiful and fragile I was afraid she'd crumble into pieces at the news. She seemed to know intuitively that something wasn't right. She didn't talk a lot, but the way she wandered around the pub and stared out the windows, you could see it in her eyes.

I often noticed her watching me. Sometimes I would catch her and start making faces, which always made her laugh. Her laughter wiggled its way into my heart and planted itself amongst the weeds. Like a balm that soothed the raw places, it still hurt, but in a good way. Even though it reminded me of things that would never be, life had to move forward.

There were still so many children who needed the love of a father.

17

B y the third afternoon we'd made a game of making faces at one another, and even Declan got in on it. We were laughing and Callie smiled over from the bar where she was cleaning glasses. I winked and went back to our game. It was the least I could do, keeping them occupied.

Mary called Declan into the kitchen–said she was going to teach him how to make his own pies and he jumped up and ran like a shot. Bree shook her head at the same offer and plopped down next to me in the booth. "Uncle Finn is going to tell me a story."

I looked down at her and then back up at Mary with eyebrows raised. "I am?"

Little Bree looked up at me and nodded with big, pleading eyes. Mary just ushered Declan into the kitchen, smiling all the way.

The little angel climbed up into my lap and sat herself right down. Callie looked over at us and started to cry. She turned away so Bree wouldn't notice, and I just started talking.

"Well then, what story would you like to hear?"

"The one about the little bird."

"The Little Bird, you say?"

"Da tells us the story of the little bird with the beautiful song.

The one that the fisherman followed out over the sea as it sang, and they had all sorts of adventures."

"Well now, that's a clever twist on an old classic." I said.

Callie's voice came from across the bar, barely holding steady as she spoke. "A tradition started by Peter's father, so that when he was out on the sea the children would imagine him having all sorts of adventures until he could follow the song of the bird back home to them."

I looked down at Bree. "And what kinds of adventures do you like to imagine?"

"Declan likes pirates, but I like faeries."

"Well since Declan's making pies, I say faeries it is."

She clapped and settled herself on my lap as I wrapped my one good arm around her middle. I looked up at Callie in surprise. Her mouth turned up as she gave me the go ahead, so I tried to think of what to say.

The original story was one my grandmother told us, with Da translating, of course. It was the story of a monk who fell in love with a certain bird's song and was so intrigued by the beauty of it that he followed it to distant lands. When the monk finally returned to the monastery he found it changed, with the same walls and gardens but new faces, and when he inquired about it, he was told the legend of a monk who'd followed the song of a bird and wandered away two hundred years earlier but had never returned.

The monk realized the story was about him, so he asked the other monk to take his confession, knowing he would die that night. That's just what happened, and he was buried in the monastery graveyard. They say the bird was an angel, and this was God's way of taking a man to heaven who is pure of heart and loves nature.

I swallowed hard. I wasn't sure I liked where this was going. I looked down at Bree's tiny head. "Now I've heard that story before, but I'm not sure I remember it all too well. How about you start it off and we'll tell it together."

"Can I get my doll first?"

"Your doll?"

"I always hold my doll when we tell this story." She slid off my lap and went to fetch it from her bag. It was a rag doll, homemade by the looks of it, and just as adorable as Bree herself, with straw-colored hair and two light green buttons for eyes. She climbed back up on my lap and showed it to me. "See?"

"Well that's a pretty little doll. Did your mum make that for you?"

She nodded with big wide eyes and clutched it to her heart. "Her name is Annabelle."

I flinched physically, as though I'd been shot all over again, leaning my arm on the table and trying to catch my breath.

"Finn, what's the matter?" It was Callie. "Are you all right?"

I looked up at her with wild eyes that had already started to tear. Every muscle tensed. I wanted to run. I wanted to push Bree from my lap and run away from there. Into a bottle. Anywhere.

Bree looked up with doe eyes. "Is it your shoulder, Uncle Finn?"

If only she could see the drawing hidden in ink underneath my shirt. "Aye. A sudden pain come over me is all. It'll pass away in a bit."

"Don't you like her name?"

Perceptive wasn't even close. Uncanny was more like it.

"I do like her name. I like it very much. How did you choose it? Do you have a friend Annabelle at school?"

I looked up at Callie, but she shook her head. "We made the doll last summer before she started school. She woke up one day and said she'd had a dream. There was a baby named Annabelle without a mommy and she wanted to be her mommy, so we made a baby doll for her to take care of."

Last summer? I thought I might be sick. I needed some whiskey in a very bad way, but I couldn't just ask for it whilst telling a children's story. Besides, I hadn't the stomach to sit with her anymore. The shoulder was aching something fierce.

"I have to go upstairs for a moment. Would you excuse me Bree?"

"What about our story?"

"We'll finish it in a little bit. Would that be all right?"

"I guess so."

I grasped my shoulder with my good arm and started toward the stairs.

"Is it your shoulder still?" Callie asked. "Do you want me to call Mary for you? Or the doctor?"

"No. I've some medicine he gave me. It's upstairs is all. Let me just run and fetch some. It'll take a few minutes to kick in, then I'll be back."

"Promise?" Bree stood clutching her doll, expectant.

I didn't know what to say, but what came out of my mouth was, "Of course. I promise."

Upstairs I tore open the new prescription, which was stronger than the one the army gave me, and washed one down with a little whiskey, and then a little more whiskey. As the memories pushed their way into my consciousness, I broke out into a cold sweat and could smell the alcohol coming out of my pores. It was nauseating, this tortuous cycle my life had become.

I brushed my teeth and rinsed my mouth, then stood in the shower for the second time that day, hoping to wash away the stench of it all. I even put on some aftershave, trying to hide the scent of the whiskey from Bree.

I stood in the bathroom looking at my reflection in the mirror. It wasn't even the same person looking back at me. This man looked wild and untamed. Out of control. I took out the trimmer and shaved my shaggy beard close to my face and cleaned up the edges as best I could with my left hand, then took another look. It was better.

I still wasn't able to wrap that arm on my own though. I went downstairs looking for Mary and again I surprised Callie, but this time she looked at my face and then at my body and smiled.

"Better?" I grinned.

"Aye" she said, turning away.

I found Mary in the kitchen with both children, making pies. Annabelle was sitting on the counter next to Bree.

"See, Uncle Finn? Annabelle likes making pies too!"

I swallowed down the lump in my throat as I held the bandage out to Mary, who glanced at the ink on my shoulder as if she'd never noticed it before. "Now there's a strange coincidence you don't see every day. I'll have to hear that story some time."

"Not likely." I turned my head away and let her cover the tattoo over with the wrapping, then help me get my shirt on. "I wasn't always useless, you know."

"You're not useless now either." She said, matter of fact, then rubbed the back of her fingers against my chin. "But I do like the shave." She patted my cheek lovingly. "Now the way I hear it, you owe this little girl a story."

"Ooh! Me too! Me too!" Declan cried.

"What about your pie?" I tousled his hair.

"I can still eat some later, can't I Mary?" He looked up at her as if it were a real question.

Her eyes were shining. "Of course you can! Go on now, have your story."

I hadn't planned on pirates *and* fairies, so I had to think fast.

"We're going to make this story into an adventure, and adventure stories need to be told out of doors. Do you think your mum would let us go sit by the docks? Maybe we can feed the birds while we're there, if Mary's got a stash of crumbs somewhere?"

I looked at Mary, knowing full well she kept her crumbs for just such an occasion. Before I could finish the question at the end of my inflection, they were off, running out to beg Callie for some much-needed time outside on a rare sunny day in the harbor.

Callie buttoned the children into their overcoats, and I pulled mine onto my good arm and hiked it around my shoulder. She came over to me and pulled the edges closed, buttoning it for me. "There now. Surely you'll need that one good hand of yours for holding on to Bree's."

I thought about how Mary was right. Her name did remind you of a breeze.

"And I like seeing more of your face," Callie added. "You've a handsome face and you shouldn't be hiding it behind that enormous bunch of fuzz all the time."

I looked at her for a split second trying to figure out if she was flirting with me. She couldn't be–that wouldn't be right. Luckily, she caught my meaning right away.

"And don't be gettin' any ideas, *Uncle* Finn. This is my thanks for you taking a hand with the children is all. Nothing more."

"Good," I answered, maybe too quickly. Although I didn't mean to wound her, I also didn't want her to think I was something that I wasn't. That *something* being *available*.

The minute I was buttoned into my coat, Bree grabbed onto my good arm and started pulling me out the door.

"Can you manage the bread bag, Declan? I seem to be one arm short and in need of a right-hand man."

Callie laughed, but Declan didn't get the joke. She kissed Bree on the head and waved us out.

"Don't worry," I called back over my shoulder. "I'm sure they'll be hungry for pie soon enough."

ONCE WE FOUND a decent spot to sit, we hung our legs off the docks and let them dangle over top of the water.

"I'll never be able to tell the story exactly the way your da does, so how about we'll make up a new story that's sort of the same and sort of different? What do you say?"

They both agreed that was a fine idea, and Bree pulled Annabelle from inside her coat, to have her sit between us on the docks to listen.

I turned to Declan first. "Now Bree tells me that you hear the story of The Little Bird with pirates in it and her version has faeries, and the way my Nana told it to me has a long journey by land instead of by sea, so what do you say we combine all three stories and make up a whole new adventure?"

"I'll start!" Declan announced.

He began the story, I assume, the way his da would normally tell it, with a fisherman and a boat and a bird with a beautiful song. The bird's song led him out to sea, and along the way he met some pirates and had to fight the brutal men in order to be free to follow the little bird.

I stopped him and let Bree add in some faeries that helped come to his rescue. She said they magically calmed the seas and took him by rainbows to the next stop on his journey, where of course he met a beautiful princess who taught him how to fly.

Turns out I didn't have to add much at all. By the time we were done, Declan had forgotten all about pirates, and the faeries had all but disappeared from the story. Soon they were making up adventures by sea and by land on islands that popped up out of nowhere. All along, the bird sang to the fisherman and he was happy forever after.

Bree shivered in her coat and I put my good arm around her. "Are you cold, sprite? Is it time to go back, then?"

She shook her head and snuggled into my side, squishing Annabelle between us. "Do you think my daddy followed the bird song?" she asked suddenly.

My heart hit the deck. "I don't know. He may have."

Declan started mumbling and moving his lips.

"Would you like to hear the end of the story the way my grandmother told it?"

"Umhmm," Bree said into my coat.

Declan scooted closer and put his head against my shoulder, which was still tender, but I couldn't deny him that small comfort. Here was a boy who missed his father–who wished and prayed for him fervently. I had very little to offer them, except maybe the hope for a few faeries to guide him home. I couldn't tell them about a monk who came back to die and be buried, so like Peter had done, I decided to wing it, so to speak.

"After the man had traveled a great distance, he thought to himself that it seemed to be getting late and he wanted to go home, so he followed his tracks in reverse. When he arrived in the town, he didn't recognize anyone, and when he inquired about it, he found that the journey had taken him longer than he thought, because it was now many years in the future, when his children's children were alive. He realized that God must have taken him to heaven in a special way, and it was time to go back and be with God forever. So, he followed the bird's song one last time, and went back to heaven to be with God."

We were all silent for a time. I didn't know what else to say. Suddenly Declan announced "Hey! We forgot the bread!"

He held up the bag triumphantly, and we tossed handfuls out onto the water, watching as the birds swooped in to grab them. When the bread was gone, we picked ourselves up and went back inside.

I dropped the children off with their mother, all rosy-cheeked and ready for some tea. She offered me a cup, but I declined. I needed to get away for a bit, so I went and found Mary.

"I need to go to Galway on some errands. Might not come back for a day or so."

She looked at me for a moment. "You can drink yourself silly just as easily right here in my bar, you know. I'll even put you to bed myself if need be."

"I need to be alone. I can't be here right now. Not with them." I inclined my head in the direction of the children, who were telling their mother about our adventure story. "That tide is comin' in hard and it's about to crash through their shores. I need some distance or it's going to sweep me back out to sea with it."

"They love you, Finn."

"They've known me three days."

"Aye. And they love you still."

"I'm not their da."

"I know that."

"And I'm not going to be sticking around to take his place neither." She got my meaning. It was plain enough. "Couple more weeks, maybe, but this arm's not going to let me stay much longer. I'll have to go elsewhere, find some work where I'm useful."

"Where? What will you do?"

"Don't know yet. Can't think about that right now."

Mary took a deep breath. "All right."

———

18

G alway turned out to be the perfect distraction. After I saw the chemist, I wandered out onto the street, where there was some sort of festival going on. Food vendors and people jammed the square, and it was just what the doctor ordered. I tried to remember what it was like to just enjoy a carefree festival with some friends, until I realized I didn't have any. I'd either lost or alienated just about every person in my life.

After graduation, all my friends from Oxford went in different directions. Colleges can be great meeting places, but their goal is to be a sending place. They're like large, communal airports–people always coming and going, using university to get them from one stage of life to the next. Sure, there were some relationships that solidified and became lifelong friendships, but since I'd already bolluxed the only real friendship I ever had, the rest seemed pointless.

I stopped at a food stand and got tapped on the shoulder by a cheeky American fellow.

"Hi! Would you mind taking our picture?"

"I'd love to, but..."

He put his hand up to stop me from talking. "Don't worry, this isn't one of those crazy complicated cameras, I promise. It's just point and shoot–like this." He shoved the camera in my hand without really even seeing my face and hurried to gather his group into a memorable pose.

I decided to play a game with him. "Well, I would, but I'm afraid it wouldn't come out–"

"Nonsense! It's fine, just shoot it! Okay everybody. Smile!"

I held the camera down at my side and tried to look pathetic and embarrassed. They all looked up at me, smiling and posing.

The young man stared at me. "Is something wrong?"

"I'm afraid I've only got one arm."

The whole lot of them gasped and looked down at the other arm of my coat hanging empty at my side. It was all I could do to keep from laughing but I'm pretty sure I did a decent job because he ran back over to me and started apologizing profusely. "Oh my God! I am so sorry! I didn't even notice."

"It's all right," I conceded. "Happens all the time."

"Good job D," came from someone in the back. A couple of the girls whimpered as if they'd come upon a stray dog.

"I really am sorry. I'm David." He stuck out his right hand. "And you are?"

"Still...unable to shake hands properly. It's my right arm that's missing, see?" I wiggled my body a bit to make my empty sleeve flap around for affect. "You're not very bright, are you?"

He clapped his hand over his mouth and turned about ten shades of red. His friends slowly backed up and turned away, completely humiliated by his obvious lack of tact. "Oh my God. I am the biggest ass!" He wavered a bit. "And... I am so drunk! I hope to God I don't remember any of this tomorrow."

My mouth broke just a little bit as I stood there, still trying to play along but finding it increasingly difficult.

He caught just a hint of it, before the light bulb fully lit. "You're messing with me, aren't you?"

"I am," I said, pursing my lips together, trying hard not to break into all-out laughter. "I mean, I do have a right arm, just not the full use of it at the moment."

I stuck the fingers of my right hand out through the buttons in my mid-section as proof and David started busting up laughing, at which point I completely lost it. I mean, I had my good hand on his shoulder, holding me up, but he was stumbling so badly he couldn't help me at all.

I tried to get the truth out in between breaths. I hadn't laughed that hard in a good long while. "I'm recovering from surgery. The arm is bound to me chest at the moment."

"Oh my God, I think I just peed myself." David snorted.

The whole lot of them were laughing by this point, and when we all dried our eyes, I stuck out my left hand for a shake, obviously awkward for effect.

"I'm Finn. Pleased to meet you."

"Well Finn? Where I come from, that's called getting Punk'd, and for that I need to buy you a drink! Where should we go?"

I swept my arm around to indicate the entire street, which had several establishments from which to choose. "This is Ireland, mate. You can't fall down without landing on the doorstep of a pub! Take your pick, I'm not fussy."

We made our way into a place that had music spilling out through the front door. There was a live band and plenty of room for dancing and no shortage of people willing to get up and give it a go. Turns out David and his friends were a group of dancers from New York come to tour Ireland and experience Irish dancing. I sat with David at the bar while his friends joined a traditional jig, trying to learn the steps as taught by the locals.

"How long have you been here?" I asked.

"Just a few days. Started in Dublin and have been making our way around. We'll be two nights here then head down the coast through Limerick, Cork and around to Waterford, then Wexford I think, then back to Dublin."

It was exactly the route I'd taken to get here, only in reverse.

"Are you here with a company of dancers or on your own?"

"On our own. The eight of us all know each other from PA. Sorry, school of the Performing Arts, in New York City, and we're all trying to get into an off-Broadway production of Riverdance, so we decided to share expenses and do some authentic research."

"And what do you think of our fair country so far?"

He took a long draught off a Guinness and slurred, "I loke it... veray moch."

"Better stick to dancing, mate. Accents aren't your thing."

I ordered a glass of Jameson's and David slapped both hands on the bar.

"Oh, and I suppose you could do mine better than I could do yours?"

I laid on an extra heavy roll of the brogue and said, "I'm not sure I can do an American accent, never having been there, but I'd be willing to challenge you to a duel at a British accent. What you think?"

"You wouldn't stand a chance," he said with a pretty good Cockney. "I played leads in both Sweeney Todd and Oliver. I think I could give you a pretty good run for it."

"Is Cockney the only one you've got, then? Because there are different accents, you see, depending on where you go in Britain. In and around London you've got a North London and a South London accent, then out in the different counties you've got Cornish, Yorkshire, Derby, Birmingham and Suffolk, just to name a few." Each time I changed a name I changed my intonation just a bit to reflect the slight differences in each region's dialect.

"Okay, smarty pants. I get your point. Does this mean I owe you another round?"

He grinned up at me, already pretty far gone. He looked about ready to fall off the stool as it was. I wasn't sure another round was in the cards for him.

"It's Fancy Pants, if you please, and I believe this one's on me."

He shook his head and sipped on his Guinness, defeated.

"I'm sorry, you're just so much fun to...mess with." I said in perfect British.

"How do you do that?"

"Do what?"

"Switch back and forth like that between an Irish brogue and perfect British?"

"Well, the British are far from perfect, believe me." I toasted him for the hell of it and he drank anyway. "At any rate, I've spent my life splitting my time fairly equally between both countries."

"How so?"

"I was raised here but went to secondary school and college all in England."

"Is that so?"

"It is." I laughed. Why this should be interesting to him I had no idea, but he seemed greatly entertained by my life story.

"And which, if I may ask," he slurred again, but dropped his voice to a whisper, "is the better of the two countries" He leaned so close to me that I had to pull my head back for fear he'd actually kiss me, until he finished with "...for women."

Now *here* was a question I could help with. "Stick with Ireland, mate...all the way." He smiled, happy that he was already in the right place. "British babes are way too much work. These girls here?" I looked around. "They know how to have *fun*!"

"Well then, what are we waiting for?" He started to stand and wobbled a bit.

I shook my head. "You go on, mate. I'm making love to a nice glass of whiskey here."

"Oh, come on!"

"No really, I'm just not interested."

"Are you gay?"

"No." I shook my head and grinned into my glass. "Just emotionally unavailable."

"Who said anything about emotions?" He smirked, as if it was a genuine question.

I laughed. Here was boy after my own heart. Or at least, my former heart. "Well, I can't very well do push-ups with one arm, if you know what I mean."

"Suit yourself," he laughed. "All the more for me!"

I sat at the bar while he and his friends danced, until one of them, a girl named Jessie, pulled me out onto the dance floor and challenged me to a duel of sorts–Irish dance style. She did a few steps, and I followed with one better. She went again, and I bested her again. Soon we were in the middle of a crowd in a step-for-step challenge.

Of course, I had an unfair advantage, having spent my life in pubs dancing with drunk people, so I held my own pretty well, until I stumbled off balance (being one-armed and all) and knocked my bad arm into a post. I cried out in pain and the party was over for me. All the Americans came alongside me and tried to help.

"I'm all right. I just need to lie down for a bit."

"Do you need to go home?"

"I'm not from this area." I grabbed onto my arm. "Actually, haven't acquired a room yet for the night. I was just about to do that when you asked me to take your picture." I grinned.

"Well, you're staying with us," David announced. "And I won't take no for an answer."

We all slept it off in three hotel rooms jammed with the lot of us. Turned out David and I got along really well, and when he was sober, he was really quite intelligent and easy to talk to. He was caring in a way that meant something, if that makes any sense. Although he was a perfect stranger, or maybe because of that, I felt free to tell him about the things I had been through. He actually listened and seemed genuinely concerned.

It wasn't one-sided either. After I told him about the war and Kathleen and the boating accident, he told me about his father's alcoholism and his mother's rejection of his desire to be a dancer, his sister's suicide and how he felt about the people at PA.

"We're all like the family we wish we'd had. We support one another's goals and dreams and we're there for each another, you know?"

I didn't know. I'd never come across someone so open and emotional without being needy–someone who gave through vulnerability. It was exactly what I needed; I just didn't know that until it happened. We sat at the bar in a different pub the next night and talked and drank for hours. By then he knew pretty much my whole life story, from Regan to Oxford and back again.

A tight bond formed quickly between us, similar to the way I felt about the men I served with. Even those I didn't really like, I would have taken a bullet for. And in a way I did. We were all in the fight together. Some lost their lives, others lost their limbs, and the rest of us just went home maimed–either emotionally or physically. It wasn't a perfect situation, but we all got through it the best we could.

"Maybe that's all you're doing now," he said to me over coffee and breakfast the following morning. "Getting through it the best you can."

I scoffed at him. "With pills and booze and the decision to swear off women? That sounds healthy to you, does it?"

He smirked. "Well, not the swearing off women part. For that I think you might actually need rehab." He took a bite of his eggs. "Going cold turkey? Man, you must be hurting. No wonder you drink."

I laughed and it felt good to laugh. He was funny, and we were relaxed together, like old friends must be.

After two days of dancing and partying and sight-seeing and getting to know David and his friends, we parted with an exchange of information, and every single one of them promised to put me up if I came to New York. I promised I'd think about it, but that was about it.

It was time to go back to Mary's, and I knew it. In a way I felt guilty for having lost myself so completely, but the distraction had been necessary. I needed time to process it all in the background before reality took hold and shook us all awake.

As I PREDICTED, it was nearly a full week before they decided to call off the search entirely and announce the men lost to the sea.

Lost as I had wanted to be lost.

And yet I wasn't. I wasn't on the boat the day of the storm, and my dreams had warned me of it. My shoulder made doubly sure I wasn't there.

But why?

The question burned hotter than the whiskey.

No bodies were ever found, but what washed up on shore a few miles away was the floating waterproof utility locker that held their phones and GPS device. It gave us a pretty clear picture of exactly where they were when the storm hit, and the route they'd taken to try to get back.

Peter had recorded some voice messages telling of their exact coordinates should they have any problems. He said the storm came up out of nowhere, faster than it had been predicted and much more severe. Then, in the middle of one of his messages, there was an earth-shattering crack as the boat was struck by lightning. There were frantic cries from James and John who said they were breaking apart and the hull was taking on water.

Peter's voice came back on the recording saying, "Declan and Bree? Daddy loves you and is so proud of you."

More cries for help from James and John in the background.

Then Peter's voice again. "Callie, I love you with all my heart. I'm calling it in now! I'm calling it in now..." The line went to static, and the message died out.

We had been in some pretty rough seas together, the four of us, and those men had cages that weren't easy to rattle. For them to be frantic like that, it must have been bad. I kept putting myself in their places, imagining their thoughts and actions as the boat took on water and broke into pieces.

Peter knew when he recorded that message. He knew how bad it was and how far they were from land, because he took off his St. Christopher's medal and his father's watch and his wedding ring and placed them all in the box for safekeeping.

They brought Callie that waterproof box, and she touched each piece ever so gently before laying them back in there for safekeeping. Someday the watch would be Declan's and the necklace would go to Bree. Callie put Peter's wedding ring on a chain around her neck and seemed strengthened by it somehow, as if she carried his essence with her.

I guess we all have our ways. Some things get put behind us, while others are carried forward. Remembrances. Trinkets of our grief. My wallet held a letter, and in my pocket was a single key.

I watched Callie tuck that ring under her shirt and put on her apron, wondering if she'd watched her mother respond in kind. She knew this grief. She knew what her children were feeling, and yet, this was the life they had chosen. It was the life that they knew.

Every job carried its own brand of danger. We were all soldiers, all of us. Doing what had to be done and keeping safe those we'd vowed to love, serve and protect.

After we heard the news, I went for a long walk up into the hills. I wanted to let Callie and Mary have space for that final grief, and I needed to look out over the harbor and say goodbye. To them, and to this place.

19

When I got back to Mary's, the kids were sitting outside against the house, drawing in the dirt with some sticks.

Bree dropped her stick and ran to me, wrapping her arms around both my legs in a monstrously tight embrace. I reached down and hugged her back and said, "Hello, beautiful."

Declan stopped drawing and looked up at me, very serious. "Daddy's not coming back."

I swallowed. Bree was still attached to my legs. "I know. I'm so sorry."

He thrust the stick in the ground. "I prayed and everything!"

I set Bree aside and bent down to his level, brushing the hair back from his face. He swatted my hand away. I couldn't blame him.

"Aye, but what did you pray for? Safe passage home, no doubt?"

He nodded.

"And how do you know that your prayers aren't just exactly what got them there? Home to heaven, where the three of them will be waiting to greet you again someday. You sent a special angel with those prayers, that guided them home just when they needed it most."

His little face turned up toward me as he realized what I was saying. "You mean, *I* sent the songbird?"

"You just may have. I'll bet those prayers were just exactly what your da needed right when he needed them."

He slammed himself into my chest and threw his arms around my neck and started to cry. I held him as my own tears rolled freely down my cheeks.

I'd spoken words that came out of nowhere. Words he needed to hear. Words I wasn't even sure I believed myself. They were just...there when I opened my mouth.

Mary came out and picked up Bree and carted her inside, letting me have my moment with Declan, unhurried. I sat in the dirt and rocked him as we comforted each other. My grief swallowed me into his until I no longer knew what I was crying for, I only knew I had to let it go somehow.

This was not my family, and yet, I wondered what would become of us all.

There was no way that I could stay. I couldn't fish, one-armed as I was, and rural fishing villages could hardly find employment for Oxford-degreed businessmen with a specialty in computers. Trying to build Mary's bar into something it wasn't would cause it to lose itself, and her along with it. She didn't need tourists. She needed to keep things running the way they had always been run. She needed it, because it would keep her going, and the town needed it, because it was constant and familiar.

Callie would go back to work for Mary, I imagined. Her house would be sold to give them some money to live on, and together they would raise those children. Together they'd get through it. Mary wouldn't have it any other way. She loved those children like they were her own grandchildren, but I didn't really belong there. I knew it and they knew it, and it was just a matter of time before it got awkward.

I took the kids on a walk up into the same hills I'd just come from. I didn't know how to comfort them, but I knew it had helped me to see like an eagle instead of a groundhog, so we sat overlooking the harbor, feeling the wind on our faces.

"When I grow up, I don't want to be a fisherman. I want to be a pilot," Declan said. "Or an astronaut."

"Well most astronauts are pilots first, did you know that?"

His head shook slowly from side to side. "No wonder I like both."

I smiled. "You can be anything you want to be, Declan. You're a smart boy."

"But Da would want me to be a fisherman, because he was a fisherman and his da was a fisherman."

It was one of those moments. The ones where you wish you knew the right thing to say.

I didn't, so I just said what I *thought* was right. "Your da would want you to do what makes you happy. Just because being a fisherman made your da happy, doesn't mean that's what'll make you happy."

He thought about that for a moment. "I suppose you're right. But who will take care of Mommy?"

"Well, you will of course. Once you go to college or learn to be a pilot or an astronaut or whatever it is, then you'll be able to help provide for her. But you have to figure out what you want to be first. She's a big girl, your mom is. She had a job herself before you were born. And she's got Mary and even Bree here to help look after her while you're away at college. That's how families work. They all help each other."

"I want to be a doctor," Bree announced.

"Well then, a doctor you shall be my beautiful Breeze. And wherever you blow, you will make people feel better."

She smiled up at me. "I want to help babies like Annabelle who don't have any mommies or daddies to care for them."

It was still hard, every time she said that name. I couldn't believe she had produced a baby from a dream with the same name as... "I think that sounds very nice."

"There won't be any money for college, you know." Declan concluded somberly. He was wise beyond his years and carried too much weight on his tiny shoulders. "I heard Mom and Mary talking about it."

"What did they say?" I asked.

"Mary told Mom not to worry about it. That God would provide."

"And what do you think?" I said.

"I don't think God cares much about college. He should worry about people, not college."

I let out a great sigh. "Perhaps you're right, Declan. I went to college, and so far I haven't done any of the work I studied about, but I imagine I will eventually. It will become useful to me, because it will help me to help others."

"What do you mean?"

"It's not important right now. Just know this: If you want to be an astronaut, there will be a way for you to become one."

He thought about that long and hard, his face pinched in concentration.

"For instance, did you know that if you join the military, they can train you to be a pilot? And they pay you while you learn, and you don't have to go to college for it."

His eyes got wide. "They will?"

"But you have to be smart and keep up with your studies to do it. They don't let just anyone in, you know."

"I'm smart, you'll see!"

Bree tugged on my jacket. "What about me?"

"What about you, dearie?" I smiled every time I looked at her.

"Can they teach me to be a doctor?"

"You still have to go to college for that. It's a bit more complicated. Besides, the military is no place for a pretty little thing like you. It's dangerous business, going to war."

"Have you ever been to a war?" she asked.

"I have." I brushed off my knees and tweaked the end of Bree's nose. "But someone's getting cold up here. We'd best head down for a cup of Mary's hot chocolate. What do you say?"

"Yes!" they both sang out.

"All right then! Lead the way."

Bree grabbed my hand as Declan wrapped an arm around my waist from the other side.

"I love you, Uncle Finn" Bree called up as she skipped along.

"I love you too, Breeze."

Declan squeezed my waist nice and tight and then let go.

"I love you too, Deck Man."

He laughed at my newly made-up name for him.

"Did you know that they call the bridge of a spaceship a deck also? It's not just boats that have decks."

He shook his head. "They do?"

"An astronaut flies a spaceship, but it's still a ship. It's just a special kind of boat that flies along through the air instead of the water. You see? It's not so different from being a fisherman. You'd just be at the helm of a different kind of vessel."

"And I could fish for rocks and plants on other planets!"

"Aye. I suppose you could."

I could tell he liked that idea very much.

THE STORY of the tragedy was all over the news and when crews came asking for interviews, it was my job to give them the facts and send them away, asking that the privacy of the family be respected. Since I was useless for lifting, I helped occupy the children while family and friends moved the three of them into Mary's place.

Before the funeral, I went back to Galway and took care of a couple of things at the bank. There was no reason those children should suffer, and who knew how long it would take to sell a house in that economy?

I stuffed a fair wad of bills into a large plain envelope and packed it in with my things. I'd have to slip it in the pot when people came through to deliver their condolences so no one would know it was from me.

I also started a small trust account for Declan and Bree, for college. I'd try to put into it once I started working steadily, and maybe by the time they were ready, there'd be something to go on. It was the least I could do. The little Annabelles of this world needed someone to look after them, after all.

My arm was doing better. The week's worth of forced rest and anti-inflammatory medicines helped tremendously, and it really seemed fine as long as I didn't overdo it. Dr. Ryan came by to check on Callie and pulled me aside.

"How's that shoulder?"

"Better by a little. Still locks up something fierce while I'm sleeping. I wake up in agony and have to push it back in a certain way just to release the joint."

"You might want to go back and have the surgeon take a look. They'll fix it again if need be."

That was true enough, but the last thing I wanted was another surgery. "During the day I can have it unbound for a couple hours at a time before it starts getting sore again."

"Well, that's progress then, isn't it? I want you to keep moving it gently when it's unbound, and I'm going to have the chemist give you a sling instead of the wrapping—kind of an intermediary step. It'll be easier to do things yourself. Just rest it in the sling when it's sore, and don't sleep with it bound at all. We need to relax those muscles and get them moving on their own."

"Sure, and Mary will be relieved not to have to wrap me up all the time."

"She loves it, and you and I both know it." He winked at me. "I'm going to write for a muscle relaxant pill as well. I want you to try it at night. Do you need more of the pain medicine?"

"If you don't mind. It really does help me sleep."

"Of course, but be careful with all of this. It can be addictive. Try not to combine both pills until you know how the muscle relaxant affects you." He wrote out another script and gave it to me. "I'll check back with you in another week or so."

I nodded. "Appreciate it, Dr. Ryan."

I didn't tell him I would be leaving after the wake. I'm not sure I realized it myself until that moment, but as I looked around the pub, I just knew.

Maybe it was all those books I'd been reading about seers and magic, but standing there I saw a clear vision of myself dressed in fashionable clothing, sitting in Da's pub in Dublin, only it had been redesigned somehow. Then suddenly I was boarding a plane and flying across the ocean to New York City.

"Finn?"

I turned my head and looked at Dr. Ryan. "What is it?"

There was a look of concern on his face as he studied me. "I was just going to ask you the same question. You looked dazed for a minute there."

I took a deep breath. I wasn't about to tell him I was seeing things. "I was just...looking around, remembering the night I first met Peter and the boys." I shook my head and looked down at my shoes. "Hard to believe, is all."

He placed a fatherly hand on my good shoulder. "I know. It is for all of us. I'll see you tomorrow, Finn."

"See you then."

20

An Irish wake is a beautiful thing, really. They hardly ever lay the body out in the parlor anymore, but in the more remote areas of the country they still follow many of the old traditions. They've mostly done away with the keening, thank goodness, because that part just tears my heart out. All that wailing and misery can't possibly be helpful.

Since there were three of them, it was decided we would celebrate all of them together. James and John had been orphaned at the age of ten–their father by drinking and their mother by cancer, although I wasn't sure which one of them went first. Anyway, they were all one big family now, so it seemed only proper, but that meant the crowds would be huge, and Callie's tiny house and kitchen would have been overwhelmed. Holding the wake at Mary's seemed much more practical.

In place of coffins, we set up pictures of them on a table near the door. The kids made colored drawings and paper streamers to hang across the bar posts for the party. We stopped the clocks and turned the mirrors and I was charged with taking my half-pint helpers and going 'round to buy what was needed. Pipes and tobacco and snuff, extra food items, bread and rolls–things that were light enough for Declan, Bree and I to carry with my one good arm and their miniature versions. They liked helping, and I liked having their company, especially knowing it would be the last I'd see of them.

I wasn't sure how long I would stay after the wake. I didn't want to rock their tiny worlds too much, but I also didn't want them to grow too attached and replace their father with me. It wouldn't be right, for me or for them. I wanted to stay in their lives and planned to come back for regular visits of course, I just couldn't be there for them in the way that they needed. I had to go. I had some things to make right.

I dropped the children off with our packages and slipped out to the city one last time, where I bought a few trinkets and some nice clothes, complete with a tie and jacket. Nothing like that in the closet at Mary's, and I'd lost so much weight, nothing I had back at Da's would've fit me anyway. I wasn't a soldier anymore. Didn't look like I could protect much of anything. Didn't feel like it either. I could barely protect myself.

Still, I got a real haircut and had them take my beard down to a chinstrap. They cleaned up all the edges, and when I looked in the mirror I caught a glimpse of the man I used to be, melded with the one I'd become. While I had no desire to go back to the old me, this new version wasn't much better off. I really looked at the face in the mirror. It was pulled too tight.

Air-hungry.

Ready to shatter.

The only solution was to bring the past and present together and forge it into something stronger. Something that could stand in a strong breeze without blowing over.

After I'd showered and come downstairs, Callie did a double take. I suppose the sight of me with a fresh haircut, nearly clean-shaven, and dressed in a Brooks Brothers suit was a little much, compared to my normal attire. I even put on a splash of cologne, although not for her benefit. It was mostly just to feel a bit like myself again.

She stared at me and didn't speak for several seconds, then

grabbed for the ring around her neck. I looked down, and she looked away.

Mary came out of the kitchen and just about fell over. "Well now, don't you look sharp!" She came over to me and pretended to straighten my tie, though I had tied a perfect Double Windsor. "I always knew there was something special hiding under that beard."

I smiled my charming smile and she ran her hands down the lapels of my suit. "Fancy pants indeed. Did you rob a bank somewhere in your travels that I don't know about?"

"I had some put by," I said simply.

"Aye." She smoothed the folds of her black dress. "And you won't be embarrassed, setting with the likes of me?"

"Never!" I leaned down and kissed her cheek. "Not in a million years."

"Have you decided yet what you're to be doing?" She asked.

I shook my head. "Right now, I'm just trying to breathe in and out."

"Fair enough."

A TRADITIONAL WAKE starts out as a somber sort of morning that turns into an all-day party, often stretching late into the evening. Everyone in the community comes by at one point or another. Usually the older generation comes early in the day. Pipes are smoked, stories get told, laughter and booze all flow together into the evening. It's a celebration of life, and a right jolly send off. This one was no different.

I kept my arm out of the sling for a good part of the day, but by evening the pain got to be too much, so I slipped upstairs and put the thing back on. It was black, luckily, so it blended right into my suit. I also popped a pain pill to take the edge off, then went down to the bar and poured myself a whiskey. I was pouring for a few others with my one good arm when the door opened and in walked my da.

I blinked hard a couple of times, trying to make sure I wasn't seeing things. He spotted me right away, nodded, then proceeded to shake hands with a few of the men standing by the door. He gave his condolences to Callie, who looked confused, then introduced himself to a couple of the others.

I watched all of this with interest, trying to ascertain first, how he'd found me, and second, what the hell he was doing there. Those questions would have to wait, however. I set a glass of Jameson's on the bar and waited for him to come over.

He didn't really have to explain who he was to Mary. She shook his hand, then looked at me, then looked at him. "Well, it's not hard to see where Finn gets his handsome good looks."

He smiled and kissed her hand. "And you might be?"

"Mary Murphy, and this here's my establishment. Finn rents a room from me."

"And it's a fine place you have here Mary. I'm so sorry for your loss."

"Aye."

"If you'll excuse me."

There was food on every available surface, and people packed in between. Da made his way over to me as Mary and Callie looked on from their seats by the door. He pulled me into a hug but was gentle because of the sling.

"Hello Finn."

"Da."

"Shoulder still bothering you?"

"Aye."

I handed him the glass and he thanked me, then sat down at the bar and looked around the room. "You've lost weight. Are you all right?"

"Depends on your definition."

He took a long, slow sip. "Nigel told me about your visit."

I figured that would happen shortly after I left, but it had been months. Surely he hadn't been looking for me all that time?

"And?"

"And nothin'."

"Have you been lookin' for me?"

"Not exactly. Figured you didn't want to be found or you'd have called."

I took a drink and felt the meds kick in. "You figured right. And yet?"

"Saw you on the news."

"The news?"

"About the accident."

"And you thought you'd show up to a funeral for three people you've never met?" I was irritated by his presence, but I watched Callie whisper to Declan and Bree as they pointed at us. At least I still had a father.

He leaned his arms on the bar. "You look like hell."

"Well I feel like hell, so at least I'm consistent." I raised my glass and downed it, and he did the same.

"I'm worried about you. Come to see if we could talk about some things."

"Not tonight."

"No, not tonight. Tonight is about your friends. I assume these were your friends?"

I looked around the room then back at Da. "Aye."

"Do you mind if I stick around?"

"Suit yourself."

Someone started singing, and soon we were lifting our glasses to the three lost men and everyone in the place was singing along, including Da. More shots were poured, and songs were sung about women and the sea.

Everyone knows the Irish songs, and everyone knows what it's like to experience loss. The songs were our tribute, our collective grief, our sending forward. Soon I didn't care that Da was sitting there, in the middle of my other life.

His intrusion had been an unwelcome one, and yet? It was time, and I knew it, and somehow he had known it too. So I let him come in for the night and sit with my friends, and be a part of our grief.

One by one, and sometimes two by two, the villagers left. The older women helped Mary with the bulk of the cleaning and putting food away, and eventually even the old men left after they saw the children asleep in their chairs. I carried Bree up in my one good arm and Da lifted Declan and followed me to their room. Mary sent Callie up to bed as well and started cleaning up the last of the glasses.

When we got downstairs, Mary was wiping down the bar. "So, Mr. McCarthy, have you need of a room tonight?"

"I have indeed."

"I've one left open, if you're so inclined."

"Much obliged, ma'am."

"Last on the left, top o' the stairs next to Finn, if that's all right with the both of you."

"I don't mind if he doesn't," Da replied.

I looked between the two of them. I certainly didn't want to be rude. "Fine by me."

Da grinned. "I'll just fetch my bag from the car then."

He left, and I went to wash out my glass.

"Go on up to bed now, Finn. I'll take care of the rest of this and get your da settled. It's going to be another long day tomorrow, and I've a sense you've no mind for discussing the deep things tonight." She inclined her head back toward the stairs. "Now's your chance."

I leaned over and kissed her on the cheek. "Thanks Mary."

Only a true friend drives the getaway car.

21

The next day we were going to church. I usually took a pain pill each morning to start my day and try to loosen things up, though I hated the idea of being off my wits in church. Something seemed so wrong with that, but I'd gotten to where I couldn't do without it, so I guessed God would have to understand. In fact, my arm had been feeling quite a bit better. It was my heart that still protested the movement.

I hadn't been to church in quite some time. I wasn't sure exactly where God and I stood on a lot of things, but I went out of respect for the dead. I crossed myself and knelt in all the right places, feeling sufficiently numb the entire time. Then, just as the priest was giving a sermon on death, I broke.

I don't mean that I broke down and cried. I mean something shattered in the core of my being and I got up and bolted out of that church. I left my jacket on the pew and everyone sitting there and literally ran out the back door. I ran with no regard to the pain in that shoulder. I ran up into the hills as far as I could. I ran until I didn't have any breath left. And then I started to scream.

As the church bells rang out, I dropped to my knees and let fierce cries marry with the clanging of the bells. I screamed and I wept until I had no more voice and no more tears. I screamed inside my soul and I swore angry words to a God who made no sense–a God who took parents from children and children from parents.

I sat there for a long time, just letting the wind blow across my tear-stained cheeks. The air seemed to come alive, as if it were picking up my tears and pulling them down to the harbor. The sea had a mesmerizing power, and a wisdom born of eternity. Its waves had crashed every shore throughout time, pushing its waters in and pulling them back out. Some things it kept, like the bodies of the lost. Some things it gave back, like pieces of broken vessels and boxes of remembrance. The sea was like a great collector of sorrow. All those salty tears–the cries of the lost, for the lost, deposited for safe keeping. For eternity.

Maybe it was my tears that needed to get lost at sea, not me. Maybe they needed to go and mingle with the others, so I could go forward. I imagined the air sparkling like Bree's eyes as it wafted out over the water, gently laying what was left of my grief to rest.

Or maybe I was high on painkillers and the whiskey I'd washed them down with and I was having hallucinations.

Either way, I felt better after a while, so I made my way back down to the church. Everyone had left and the priest was up near the altar when I went in to retrieve my suit jacket.

He turned around as I came in. "They took your coat with them. I imagine you'll find it back at Mary's place."

"Oh." I dropped into a pew. "Do you mind if I sit a while?"

"Of course not." He busied himself with other tasks for a few moments before coming over. "May I sit with you?"

I silently acknowledged him as he sat down next to me. He didn't rush my process. He literally just sat with me for a while.

Eventually it was me who broke the silence. "I think I need you to take my confession."

He patted my hand. "Why don't we just talk first? Tell me what's weighing so heavy on your heart."

There was a large crucifix hanging behind the altar, with purple and gold embroidered cloth draped over every possible surface. Paired with the heavy aroma of incense, it was like being in the palace of a king. I felt dwarfed by the enormity of time's passage along those cold stone walls that had stood for centuries, through war and famine. They had seen the acknowledgment of every emotion that had ever existed. Like the sea, this little church seemed timeless and eternal.

"I don't understand life or death." I smiled down at my shoes. Perhaps I should tell him something he didn't already know. I tried again. "For a long time, I didn't care about either one. Now it's like a switch got turned and I care too much. Everything's out of balance, and I can't seem to turn that switch back off."

He chuckled in the way that old men sometimes do. "I don't think that switch is meant to be in the off position. Are you saying it's possible to care too much then?"

"When it shipwrecks your life–sorry, no disrespect intended– then yes."

The priest looked so peaceful, as if nothing I could say would shock or overwhelm him, and I envied that level of calm. I wondered how many things he'd taken into confidence in his sixty or so years as a priest. He was an old man now who, if it hadn't been for the collar, looked more like a grandfather than anything else.

As he touched my hand, I could sense a pervading peace, as if I could tell him every stray thought and horrible pain, and it would all just dissolve as soon as it reached his skin. I knew that wasn't what absolution was about, but I wanted it all the same. I'd carried my burdens like a soldier's pack for so long, and I was so tired. I wanted all those feelings and all that pain to just go away.

We sat in those stiff wooden pews and I unloaded my pack, bit by bit. I told him all about the man I'd been before the army. I told him about Kathleen and the baby. I even told him that I tried to marry her, as if that made me a better person somehow. It didn't, of course, but that was beside the point.

I told him about my injuries, the painkillers, the whiskey...about disappearing from my life and ending up in this village, meeting Peter and the boys, and how much I'd grown to love those two wee ones whose hearts would be forever altered by the loss of their da. I even told him about running up into the hills and my theory that the sea was filled with the tears of the world come together into one place.

He smiled. He listened.

I sat in that open pew of a confessional with a curtain drawn across my heart and unburdened myself. These were modern times in an ancient church, and he knew perfectly well what I was looking for. He also seemed to sense that the words of ritual prayers and the rosary weren't a normal part of my life. He bypassed what I thought I wanted, and gave me instead what I really needed: the truth.

"There are a great many questions that come to a man in his life. Sometimes he learns the answers, and sometimes he doesn't. I've been listening to peoples' stories for fifty-seven years. Would you like to know what I've learnt in all that time?"

My nod was a formality.

"Time is the real gift."

"Pardon?"

"To be given life is a great gift indeed. But we are never guaranteed a lifetime, not in our human way of understanding it anyway. Life and death are merely two points on the same line. But time? Time is the real gift. Each day, each hour, is something to be counted and cherished."

I looked up at him with eyes that threatened to let loose their tears again, but the old priest wasn't afraid of my tears. He just kept talking.

"Some people live relatively short lives and accomplish great things. Others have a hundred years or more and accomplish nothing. It's not how much time we're given that brings value to our lives, it's what we do with the time we have. Finn my boy, every man's journey is filled with its own brand of explosions and losses, but we're all faced with the same choice. Time is your gift, and only you can choose how to spend it. Time has to be chosen."

As he finished speaking, I began to tremble, as if all the painkillers and whiskey had been screamed out of me and I needed a fresh infusion to keep from shaking. He grabbed onto my hands and it stopped immediately, replaced by an electric calm that buzzed through my entire body and put my senses on full alert. Then he looked into my eyes and spoke again.

"Time will run out. It runs out for every man, every woman, and even every child. We don't get to control that." He looked down his nose over the top of his glasses at me. "Nor should we want to." He finished sternly. "You have to choose to let go of your grief and move on."

"That feels somehow disrespectful to the dead."

"My boy, the dead have already moved on. And if you could ask any one of them, they wouldn't want you to live like a dead man, when you had the chance to be fully alive."

I thought about what he said. He was probably right, but it was just so hard to wrap my brain around. Maybe I just needed more time. I thanked him and started to stand, but he pulled me back down.

"Not so fast."

He led me in a prayer anyway and granted my absolution. He had to. He was a priest who was bound by duty, and I respected him for it. The traditions of the church didn't technically allow for a confession to take place in this manner, but he was either too old or too wise to care. I shook his hand, thanked him, and left the church.

Even though I hadn't been a practicing Catholic since my early teen years, there were certain things that never left your soul, and on the off chance that I needed such a thing, I was glad now to have it. Living this simple lifestyle, so much closer to nature's ways, brought me back to basics in a way that confused my sense of progress and big cities and technology. It was like I'd torn a page from an ancient book and somehow needed to bring its wisdom with me into the next part of my life. I pocketed his words and walked back to Mary's.

22

W hen I entered the pub, folks were already eating and talking and laughing. Out of respect I suppose, no one mentioned my hasty departure from the church. Only Da came over and pulled me into an embrace. "Have some lunch, then we're going for a walk, you and I."

A tiny tidal wave wrapped itself around my legs and I swept Bree up into my arms, holding her close to my chest for a moment.

"You smell nice!" She took a big whiff of my chest.

"Well thank you! So do you!" I kissed the top of her head and set her back down. "How's my girl?"

"Where did you go?" She looked up at me.

I squatted down. "When I left the church, you mean?"

She nodded, wide-eyed. Surely no one she had ever known would leave church in the middle of a service like that.

"God wanted to talk to me in private, so I hurried out to meet him."

"He did?"

"Aye. He did."

She blinked a few times. "What did he say?"

"Well, if I told you it wouldn't be private, would it?" I tapped her nose gently with my pointer finger and she smiled.

"Sometimes I tell Annabelle things I don't want anyone else to know."

I squeezed her hand. "It's good to have someone to tell your secrets to."

Da was watching the scene with amazement. I don't think he'd ever seen me around children, and if he did, I was probably repulsed by them. That is, the old me would have been.

After Bree wandered away Declan came over and tugged on my pants. I lifted him straight up with both hands and set him on the bar. Never even felt a twinge in that shoulder.

"Deck-man! How are you today?"

"I'm good. I liked what the priest said."

He was a thoughtful boy, and an intuitive one at that, but I wasn't going into it a second time. "Have you met my da?"

Declan looked over at him and nodded, excited to show me what he was wriggling out of his pocket. "He gave me this!"

"A bag of marbles, is it? Do you know how to play?"

"Yes! We play at school all the time, but I've never had my own set before."

"Brilliant! You'll be the talk of the schoolyard!"

"And he gave Bree a special apron that's just her size too, so she can help Mary make pies!"

"Did he now?"

I looked over and could see the emotion behind his eyes. Da felt the same as I did about these children, and he'd only been there for a day. Maybe he was more ready to be a grandfather than even I had thought. I hadn't considered how his knowledge of Kathleen and the baby's death had affected him. Was he sad? Did he grieve for a person he'd never met? A grandchild he would never know?

Declan nodded enthusiastically as Da lifted him down off the bar. "What do you say you and I go outside and play a few rounds while Finn eats his lunch? Would you like that?"

Declan just about yanked Da's arm out of its socket as they made their way out the door. Just then a plate showed up in front of me, already laden with food, and a pint of Guinness as well.

Mary smiled up at me. "You'll need your strength to deal with that one."

"You mean Declan or Da?" I winked at her.

She took up her towel and started wiping the bar. "Your da and I had quite the talk last night after you went to bed."

"Did you now?" I dug into my food and waited for the story, which was sure to be forthcoming, knowing Mary.

"He means to take you back with him," she said, matter-of-fact.

"I know." I wiped my mouth and put the napkin back in my lap. Something about being dressed in a suit brought the manners straight to the surface. "And I don't mean to put up a fight."

She seemed shocked that I already knew his intentions and was resigned to them. "Loves you something fierce, that man."

"Aye." I stared at my plate and felt like a toddler, needing to finish all my vegetables before being carted off to bed.

I knew I needed to figure myself out, and staying there, in that village, with those wee ones, wasn't going to help me do anything but sink even lower into denial. Da was strong. Willing. And as much as he'd given me my space, there was a time and a place to step back in and that time was now. I wasn't angry, not really. Truth be known, I was somewhat relieved.

"He uh...told me a few things, your da did." She smirked at me.

"Oh, this should be good." I stabbed a piece of meat and waited. "Go ahead, what have you learned?"

She lowered her voice, as if she didn't want to leak my secret to anyone else in the pub. "Like you've not just one but two master's degrees. And from Oxford, no less."

"It's truth, I can't deny it." I took a sip of my beer. "Does that make you love me any less?"

She slapped my good arm.

"Now what else?"

Mary huffed. "That you're one of the smartest men he's ever known."

"Well now, that's a lie if ever I heard one." I grinned. "You'd best consider the source before you go believing everything you hear."

Mary put her arms up on the bar. "What I want to know, Finn McCarthy with the Oxford education, is what have you've been doing here, working on a fishing boat all these months?"

"I told you that the first day I walked in." I took a bite of my stew. "I haven't lied to you. I've been hiding from my demons."

"Well I think they finally caught up with you."

I nodded and chewed with my mouth shut tight, then washed the bite down with some Guinness. "Don't worry. I set 'em free up in the hills today. They won't be coming 'round to bother you after I'm gone."

"And how is it you talk like the Irish with that British upbringing?"

"Who said I was brought up British? I only went to school there."

"And a fancy boarding school at that."

"Aye, but those are international. Would you like to hear my Indian accent? How about South African? Spanish?"

She pushed on my arm as I went through a litany of different accents I'd learned to imitate over the years. "Stop it now!"

"I'm just trying to make a point." I was grinning but Mary's face was serious.

"So am I. You're going to break those wee hearts when you leave, you know that." Her voice was trembling, and although she inclined her head toward Bree, anyone could see it wasn't the kids she was referring to.

I reached for her hand. "I'll miss you too, Mary." She quickly wiped a stray tear from her eye. "But you and I both know I have to do it, and the sooner the better. I don't belong here."

"I know." She started wiping again. That bar was clean enough to lick food off of, but she was a nervous wiper.

I still had hold of one of her hands, and waited until she looked me in the eye. "What else did he tell you Mary?"

"Just a few...other things." She wouldn't look at me.

"About the women, no doubt." All she had to do was look at me and I knew he'd told her about Kathleen and the baby.

I tried to steady my emotions.

"I'm so sorry." Her eyes were wet, and her hand squeezed mine tightly, but I stiffened reflexively and pulled away.

"So am I." I took a long drink off that Guinness and finished it. "Can I have a bit o' Jameson's?"

"Certainly." She pulled down a glass and poured, hesitating before sliding it toward me. "You know, Finn, I see you with those children, and I can't help but think...the day is gonna come for you. And when it does, you're going to be a wonderful father."

"I'm not so sure about that, but I can tell you this much. If you ever see me bringing a girl around to meet you, she'll be the one."

"I'll be on the lookout."

"Just don't hold your breath."

I'd finished the whiskey by the time Da came back in with Declan. The wind had pinked their cheeks and he asked Mary for a cup of coffee. I decided to join him, and we took a booth in the back, where, surprisingly, no one bothered us. Rather than go back out into the cold for that walk, he just started talking right there. It was fine by me. My shoulder wasn't too fond of the cold weather.

I was too big to lecture, not that an Irishman ever stops trying, but I was curious what exactly he wanted to discuss.

He held the steaming cup in his hands and took his time getting around to it. "I've been thinking about what you said."

"What I said? When?"

"Few months back. About the place in Dublin."

"Oh?"

He nodded. "I was there last week. Took a fresh look at the place in comparison to some of the other bars in the city and I think you're right. It's in a great location, and with the right changes, it could be a real moneymaker. All I need now is someone with the right kind of vision and business sense who's willing to do what it takes. Are you lookin' for a project, maybe?"

I studied him for a moment. "As an employee? Or a partner?"

"Well that all depends."

"On what?"

He produced both bottles of my painkillers. "You're going to have to stop taking these."

My mouth dropped open. "Where did you get those? Were you going through my things?" I tried to grab them but he stuffed them away in his pocket, then looked around to make sure no one saw.

"Now this is why I wanted to go for a walk. I'm not lookin' to out you, I just want to come to terms. Either you quit the pills or the deal's off."

"What deal?" I could feel my anger rising. I didn't appreciate being bullied, least of all by my own father.

"How much money have you got?"

Less than I used to, after setting up the trust for Bree and Declan, but still it was plenty. "Enough, why?"

"The deal is, we both put in half the money it takes to renovate and get the right kind of advertising, but you can call all the shots. You do the hiring, make the staff changes you think are necessary, and after three months on your system we see where we're at with the bottom line. Then we split the profits, fifty-fifty. If all goes well, I want to take your ideas to New York City. I've got a line on some warehouse space in a great location for an urban bar. Money I've got. It's the vision I'm lacking, and I need someone I can trust. What say you?"

"I say...why would you trust someone you know is addicted to alcohol and painkillers to run a pub?"

"Because I know you, Finn. I don't believe you're really addicted. I think you're just hurting, and that's ok for a time, but time has a way of working things through. I've had this nagging sense to come and find you for a few weeks now, but I didn't know where you'd gone."

"I'm surprised Nigel's wife didn't rat me out."

"She did, in a way, but I talked with them months ago, and neither of them knew where you were headed, so I just decided to wait it out. Imagine my surprise when I saw you on the news, looking nothing like your former self. I took it as a sign. It's time to come home now, son. It's time to rebuild."

He wasn't being condescending, he was being sincere. Just like the priest had said, I knew I had a choice to make.

I took a mental inventory of my shoulder and didn't feel one bit of pain. It had been like that all day, as a matter of fact. Ever since the screaming episode and my visit with the priest. I'd lifted Declan without so much as a whimper, and even now, as I moved it...

And then, there it was. The vision, from when I was talking with Dr. Ryan. A trendy new look to Da's bar in Dublin, and me flying to New York, with the old woman's voice in my head.

Follow it. It will lead you away from the bloodshed and the tears.

23

I had very little left to lose, and was more than intrigued by this idea of second sight. I wanted to ask Da about it. Perhaps once we got back to Dublin. "All right, it's a deal. But I can't promise it won't get ugly."

"I look in the mirror every single day. Ugly doesn't scare me."

I laughed as we shook hands. I even used my right hand and there was no pain whatsoever. If, by some stretch of the imagination, I was being given a second chance, I'd do well not to blow it. "When do we leave?"

"Whenever you're ready."

"How about tomorrow?"

His gaze flickered around the room, no doubt wondering how I was going to leave these fine people. To be honest, I didn't know either, but it had to be done.

He crossed his arms and leaned back. "Tomorrow it is."

While we finished our coffee, my brain was on rapid fire. I was still angry with him for searching my room. I wasn't a child anymore, and to be honest, I wasn't sure I could make it without the pills, but I knew I could always get more if I really needed them. My prescriptions were on file with the army, and I could go back to Birmingham if necessary. It wasn't such a bad risk. And whiskey would always do in a pinch–something I'd never be in short supply of running a pub in downtown Dublin.

Da went to clear our cups and got pulled into a conversation with some of the men at the bar.

I noticed Callie sitting by herself on the other side of the room and smiled gently. I'd hardly had any interaction with her since the double-take. I felt a little more comfortable with my jacket off and my shirtsleeves rolled up. I guess I was more approachable too, because she came over and looked down at the spot Da had vacated.

"Were you two finished? Do you mind if I sit down?"

"Not at all." For some reason, the British accent always came out around women.

She tilted her head. "Peter told me you were good with accents. Was that on purpose?"

I think I may have blushed a little. "No, not really. Sorry. My mistake."

"I...wanted to thank you for being so kind to Declan and Bree. They just love you."

"Well, the feeling's mutual, I assure you." I felt around the table for something to swirl, but my cup had been cleared. I looked down, embarrassed. "Seems I'm a cup short."

"I was just about to have a little brandy. Will you join me?"

I thought about the girl back at Da's pub in Dublin and tried not to laugh at the memory. There were just too many things that weren't worth trying to explain. "Sure."

She slipped two snifters off the rack and reached back behind the bar to pull up what looked like a private stash.

"Now what's this?"

"It's apple brandy. Made right here in Ireland–a bit south of here, in Mallow."

"Yes, I've been there."

She nodded, slightly nervous. I wasn't exactly sure why I made her nervous, but I could make a decent guess. She poured us each a bit. "A little different from a Guinness or whiskey, but special in its own way."

Change the subject, Finn. "And what are we celebrating?"

She sat rubbing her finger around the rim of her glass. "I was really worried about how we'd manage without Peter's income until the house sells, but the townspeople have been very generous." She looked up at me, her eyes full of tears. "Someone even left an envelope full of money in the pot yesterday."

"Is that so?" That was my cue to swirl my glass.

"You wouldn't know anything about that, would you?"

I shook my head and added a small shrug. "Why would I know anything?"

She wasn't going to let me off the hook. Just sat there staring me down, waiting for me to break. "Seems there's a lot about you none of us knew."

Great. Mary'd been blabbing about the Oxford bit. "And what is it Mary's told you?"

"Believe it or not, Mary hasn't said a word, although I've tried to get it out of her."

"Then on what, exactly, are you basing your suspicions?"

"Oh, I don't know. Maybe it's the fact that in the space of a single day you managed to slip away and come back looking like a totally different person, in a suit that costs more than some of us make in a month. You've obviously been incognito. What interests me is why? It's not like the life of a shaggy-bearded fisherman with calloused hands is a natural draw for most people. Especially rich people."

She raised her eyebrows to prove her point. "And you can dress and look like this kind of a man and yet you haven't taken a girl? That doesn't make sense either."

She looked me over, then looked over toward Da. "And now your da shows up and he's got money to burn as well, apparently, as he's already showered my children with gifts and candy and he barely knows them. So yeah, I'd have to say I'm suspicious."

I wrapped my hands around my glass and leaned my elbows on the table. "I'm not *dangerous*, if that's what you're worried about."

"I never said you were."

"Listen, I haven't had near enough to drink, nor do I have the heart to give the whole story again, but you can tell Mary I said it was all right to tell you, after I'm gone."

"Gone?"

I hadn't meant to say it like that. I looked down at my glass and swirled the brandy, then put it to my lips briefly. "I'll be leaving with my da come morning. He needs me to help him with some business in Dublin."

"Just like that?"

I exhaled slowly, trying to steady my voice. "It's time."

She didn't respond.

"Look." I grabbed her hands and it startled her. It startled me too. I hadn't meant to fluster her, but I could see that I had, so I dropped them. "Sorry, it's just–I can't be a fisherman anymore. Not without them." I tipped my head toward the table by the door that held photos and memorabilia of Peter, James and John. "And not with my shoulder the way it is."

"What happened to your shoulder? Originally, I mean?"

I sighed. She was going to weasel it out of me drop by drop. "A bomb. In Afghanistan."

She still looked confused.

"I served in the British Army. They had to rebuild my shoulder last year, and I was discharged, due to my injuries."

"Oh! I'm so sorry. That must have been terrible." She stared at my shoulder with a look of concern. "But the accent makes more sense now, doesn't it?"

She chuckled and I laughed along with her. "My mother is British, actually."

"So why on earth were you trying to be a fisherman if you've got a rebuilt shoulder?"

"Now you're starting to sound like Dr. Ryan." I smiled and lifted my glass to her.

She watched me for a moment then chose to drop it. "Listen, I don't need to know your whole life story, but what I am currently interested in is the state of those two little hearts over there. This isn't going to be easy for them."

"Harder now, but easier later."

She nodded in agreement. If it was going to happen, it should be soon. Especially since I could see her trying to hide her own disappointment. It would have been all too easy to work my way into her heart. And her bed as well.

"When all this ends tomorrow, you'll need to start getting back into a routine with your lives. Best I'm not a part of that. I can't be what they need." I shook my head. "I can't really be what anyone needs right now. There are some things I need to get straight, so I'm going to go before I cause any...unintentional collateral damage."

She bristled. "Is that some kind of military term for a broken heart? Because that's what it still is, you know. When you're seven and five–it's not called collateral damage. They're human beings, Finn. And I hope you're prepared for more tears."

I wasn't, actually. Didn't know if I could take seeing more tears in little Bree's eyes. "I'm sorry."

She shook her head. "It's nothing but life. We all have to get used to it sooner or later." Obviously frustrated, she slid out of the booth and took the brandy with her. "I'll talk to them first and then send them over so they can say goodbye. They'll be off to bed soon. They're still exhausted from yesterday."

When I looked over at Bree she gave a yawn as big as her head. She clutched Annabelle and started to slump forward. "Can I ask a favor?"

"You can ask."

"Can I tell them a bedtime story tonight, and say goodbye that way?"

"If you like." She softened her stance and laid a hand across my arm. "You're a good man, Finn. One of these days you'll make some lucky girl a fine husband, and I hope one day to meet her."

I tipped the last of the apple brandy up as she walked away. "As do I."

24

I watched as Callie made her way over to Declan and Bree. She whispered something to them and waved in my direction. They both perked up and ran for the stairs to get ready for bed. Within minutes they were back down in their pajamas, pulling me up the stairs, one on each hand. Callie laughed and Mary smiled and everyone else in the bar called out a goodnight as we headed up the stairs.

Da dropped his head and looked away. He knew this wasn't going to be easy.

They hopped up into the bed they shared, and I sat on top of the covers, between them. They each snuggled under one of my arms. Declan was on my right, and he asked if it hurt me to have him on that side, sweet boy that he was.

"No. Not a bit." I smiled. And it was true.

Callie hadn't told them I was leaving. She left that bit of news up to me. The question was, how should I break it to them? I waited but no grand ideas came to mind. "Shall we have a story then?"

"Yes, please!" Declan sang out.

Bree didn't speak, she just buried her head in the side of my chest. I was afraid she would fall asleep before I got through the story, so I decided to tell them first and get the hard parts over with.

"First, I need to tell you both something."

They looked up. "What is it?" Declan asked.

"My da's here because he needs me to come home with him for a while—to Dublin. He needs some help with his business, and he's asked me to be the one to help him."

"What kind of business?" Bree asked.

"He owns a pub, like this one—like Mary's."

"Can't he get someone else to help him?" Declan's forehead knitted together into a scowl.

"Well, I'm the only one who knows exactly what needs to be done."

"How many sleeps will you be gone?" Bree wanted to know.

I looked down into her angelic little face and my heart deflated just a little. "That's just the thing, Breeze, I'm not sure. It may be quite a long time."

"How long is that?" Declan wondered. "Forever?"

"No, not forever. I'll come back and visit you."

Bree slid out from under me and sat up so she could study my face. She sat there blinking at me for the longest time, like she was trying to understand something that wasn't comprehensible. Finally, she said, "Visit? So you won't come back to live here at Mary's anymore?"

"No. I'm sorry. Da needs me to do this, and I want to help him if I can. You understand that, don't you Declan?"

Declan frowned, but then he nodded. He seemed to understand that a boy helps his father when his father asks.

"And the two of you and your mom are here to help Mary with this place, so then everybody has a job to do, and everyone is helping everyone else, you see?"

Bree wrapped herself around my middle. "But I don't want you to go away."

I kissed the top of her head. "I know, Breeze, and I will miss the two of you very much, but if you like, we can write letters and you can send me pictures while I'm gone. Would you like that?"

She loved to draw. I knew she would like that idea. She smiled up at me.

"And you, my little man, you're going to need to take care of these girls while I'm gone. Can you do that?"

He shrugged a little. "I guess so."

"And you need to do very well in school, remember that! If you're to be a pilot or an astronaut you must know your studies very well."

"I will."

I hugged them both to me, so proud of their strength in the face of uncertainty. If only some of it could rub off on me.

"I have to leave in the morning, early, before you'll be up for school yet, so that's why I wanted to tuck you in tonight."

"Can we still have a story?" Declan asked.

"Yes of course!"

Declan looked straight at me. "I love you Uncle Finn."

"Me too!" Bree added.

"I love you too. Both of you. And I want you to be good for your mum and Mary. Mind them and don't give them too much trouble, okay?" I tickled them both.

They giggled and squirmed and settled back in. Bree yawned again. She wouldn't be awake for much longer.

"Once there was a young prince and a princess–a brother and a sister, just like the two of you. They went for an adventure, exploring all the meadows along the edge of their kingdom, until finally they came to a large grassy hill where it was said that the kings and queens of the past had all been laid to rest. They climbed to the top of the grassy knoll to listen to the sound of the wind and the birds and to watch the clouds make pictures in the sky.

"Soon they fell fast asleep, and in their dreams they met those kings and queens from distant lands. They went to court and feasted with the kings of old and were taught wisdom by the sages and bravery by the knights. They were even given gifts to take on the next part of their journey.

"When they awoke on that same grassy knoll, the gifts they had been given in their dreams had been brought forth and were lying next to them. They each had a special trinket to take with them, to be reminded of their dreams, and that anything is possible."

When I finished the story, Declan and Bree were warm and heavy against my chest. I sat there with them for a long time, just listening to their breathing and trying to make memory of the gift I would have to take forward on my journey. A gift of their presence. Their lives in mine.

I laid their precious heads down on their pillows along with the trinkets I'd bought for them, then stood on shaking legs. I raked my hands back through my hair, trying to make sense of it all. This was a big loss for tiny hearts, but they had each other. And Callie. And Mary. And the townspeople. I knew they would be well-loved and well-tended, but for the briefest moment I had to convince myself all over again that I wasn't their answer.

WHEN I WALKED out into the hallway, Callie was sitting on the floor with her knees pulled up to her chest, swigging brandy right out of the bottle. She kept tipping the bottle up and taking small sips, which was probably all she could manage with something so sweet. It might have been amusing, if it wasn't so pathetic.

"That was nice," She whispered.

Apparently, she'd been listening the whole time.

"Okay, maybe it's time we got you to bed as well." I'd never seen her drunk, but if there ever was a time, today she was allowed.

"How can you be both men?" she slurred.

"What do you mean?" I tried to take the bottle, but she wouldn't let me.

"When you're with them, you're like–a normal person–like, an incredible dad. And then, you're just...*you* the rest of the time!"

I blinked, laughing out loud. The first lesson in holding your liquor was *not* allowing your filter to be compromised. This girl had obviously never taken lessons.

"Well, there's a bit of refreshing honesty." I tried to pull her up, but she refused to let me help her, so I sat down next to her instead. "Do you want to talk about it?"

"What's there to talk about? My husband is *dead*. And I've two children to raise alone, and my parents are both dead, and why do you have to be so infuriatingly handsome anyway?"

I raised my eyebrows. It was worse than I thought. "Come on now." I pulled her up again and this time she didn't fight me. "This is going to hurt in the morning."

Her arms went slack around my neck. "Yes. It is."

When her face hit my chest, she started to weep with gentle sobs that shook her whole body against mine. It was heartbreaking, and I didn't think I had enough left in me to do the job justice. I didn't mean to hold her like that. I hadn't had a woman pressed against me in so long...

My body responded unexpectedly, and I put her back from me a bit. "Hey now, let's get you tucked in as well, shall we?"

I picked her up in one fell swoop and carried her into her room, not an ounce of pain in that shoulder. When I set her down, her arms were still around my neck for balance.

"Finn?"

"What?"

She grabbed my face and kissed me. I started to kiss her back, then stopped just as suddenly. I wasn't prepared for that, but I knew enough to stop the freight train. It didn't feel right, not at all, and again I set her away from me. Now I knew how Regan must have felt.

"Callie? Let's get you into bed."

She stumbled a bit. "I'll bet you say that to all the girls."

"What girls? You said yourself I don't have any girls."

"Aye, but I can tell. You've been with your share of women."

I helped her lay down on the bed and took her shoes off for her. "And your point is?"

"I don't have a point." Her head dropped heavily onto the pillow. "I don't have anything anymore."

I knelt down next to the bed. "Now that is not true. You have those two beautiful children in there, and they need their mother.

You have to promise me you'll be strong for them. Don't give up, Callie."

She stared at me for a long time. There was a question in her eyes, but her mouth didn't move.

"What is it, love?"

"I know it doesn't mean anything to you, but...would you kiss me? Just the one time, and gently, like a man kisses a woman goodnight. Peter always kissed me goodnight, and I just want to feel that, one more time..."

I reached down and cupped her face in one hand and kissed her lips, gently, like she asked. Her eyes stayed closed and the corners of her mouth turned up into a little smile. I pulled the blanket up round her shoulders and turned out the light, leaving her to sleep.

After that, I was absolutely drained. I never even went back downstairs, but collapsed on my bed. I dreamt of a black-haired girl I'd never met, and woke early the next morning with a settled sort of feeling, ready to go. Da helped me pack my things into his car before coming in for a light breakfast. Callie and the little ones were still asleep, and that was just as well, as far as I was concerned. Saying goodbye once had been hard enough.

MARY SPOKE VERY few words as we ate her boxty and sipped piping hot coffee from warm mugs that begged me to stay in the familiar. When we were finished, we pushed up from the table and I started to clear my dishes.

"Don't worry about that, Finn. I'll get it later."

I stood in front of her, not knowing what to say. Words were inadequate, of course. We hugged, and she begged me to stay in touch, which in that part of the world meant stopping by for a visit now and then. I told her I'd try my best. Da thanked her for taking such good care of me, and we started for the car.

I'd just got my fingers on the handle when the pub door flew open and there stood Bree, with Declan close on her heels. The wind whipped her nightgown around her legs and Mary came running out with blankets to wrap the children in. Bree just stood there, looking at me, clutching Annabelle to her chest.

"What is it, Breeze?"

"You're going to follow the bird's song, aren't you Uncle Finn?"

Our story. Not last night's, but rather the first, from when we'd met. While we were still waiting for the news. "Yes Breeze, I am."

"And will it take you far away to distant lands?"

I thought about the vision where I was boarding a plane for New York City. "I don't know yet, Breeze, but it might."

"But you'll come back before you die, right?"

How could I promise her that? Her own da had said goodbye to her one morning and was never coming back. I walked over and picked up the big bundle of blanket and child. "If I do, will you remember me, even if it's been a very long time?"

She giggled, as if that was the silliest thing anyone had ever said. "Of course I will!"

Nothing had ever sounded more beautiful to my ears than that little girl's laughter. "And will you tell Annabelle stories for me? At night, before bed?"

Her eyes twinkled with delight as she nodded.

I set her down and looked over at the boy, standing there in his pajamas, looking for all the world like he wanted to kick our tires flat. I squatted down in front of him. "I'm going to need some of those prayers of yours–the ones that send the angels to show me which way to go. Can you do that for me?"

He blinked hard a few times.

"I'm going to need those angels," I spoke softly to him.

He threw his arms around me and held on tight, nodding his head into my neck. "I will."

"I love you, Deck-man."

"Goodbye, Uncle Finn."

25

The first part of the ride to Dublin was relatively silent. Da and I knew each other well enough to let the other alone. It had been an emotional few days, and I didn't have any pills to dull the pain. I'd finished the last few swigs off the whiskey in my room before coming down that morning, but a whole cask of Jameson's probably wouldn't have been enough to dull the throbbing in my heart.

When we got to Athlone we stopped for a bite.

"I have to ask you something, Finn."

"What's that?"

"When I told you I wanted to take you back with me, you didn't even put up a fight. Even when I took away your pills. Why?"

It was a bit of a risk, but I began to tell him about all the strange things that had been happening to me since I left Nigel's place, starting with the strange glow drawing me to the harbor and some of the dreams I'd been having. I even told him about the old woman in the black dress with the blue shawl near the docks in Galway who spoke strange words to me, then disappeared.

"She told me I had the sight but not the wisdom."

"She told you that?"

"Aye. Then she was gone, and I was standing in front of a bookstore that was painted the exact same color as her shawl, and I felt drawn to go in. When I did, a man I'd never met handed me a book he said I'd been waiting for."

"What was the book?"

"It was about seers and magic and druids. In the book, it talks about the gift of sight. One of the chapters was actually called *The Second Sight*. Do you know about it?"

He nodded but didn't elaborate.

"She said I couldn't let it die with me. That it had to carry on. Then she told me if I learned to follow it, it would lead me away from the bloodshed and the tears."

I told him about the vision I had while I was talking to Dr. Ryan, of me dressed in different clothing, sitting in his bar in Dublin, but how it looked different than I remembered it, and in the next part of the vision I was boarding a plane to New York City.

"That's how I knew I was supposed to go with you. That my time there was finished."

He listened quietly while I spoke.

"I even saw Kathleen's death before it happened, but most of the time I don't remember the dream until I'm there living it, like a déjà vu. Sometimes I remember a dream in the morning, right when I wake up, but then it's like it dissolves out of my memory, until it starts happening for real."

"How long has this been going on?"

"On and off for a lot of years, I guess. Used to happen when I was a kid all the time, but I thought it happened to everyone. When I realized it didn't, I kept quiet about it. Then when I got older and started going to school in England, I got so interested in football and girls I stopped dreaming for a while, so I forgot about it. Started up again toward the end at Oxford. Am I...crazy?"

"No, you're not crazy. You've a gift, my boy, 'tis all. I've had my suspicions for some time, but I didn't know for sure until now."

"You knew?" I stared at him. "Why didn't you tell me about this?"

"I just told you–I didn't know for *sure*. Besides, your mum didn't like all that talk about faeries and second sight. She doesn't believe in it and didn't want me filling yours and Eiran's head with nonsense, as she put it."

"But it's...not nonsense, is it?"

"My mother–your grandmother–hails from an ancient family line of those who were gifted with the sight. Sometimes every generation has one, but sometimes it skips a generation or two. Hard to say when it's going to pop up."

"You mean, you have it too?"

"Not so much with dreams and visions, no. I just sense things about people, especially people I'm close to."

"You mean, like whether they're a good person or not? That happens to me too."

"Aye, but also what they're struggling with. I can tell when they're in trouble." He looked pointedly at me.

"That's why you made a search for the pills."

"Aye."

"And why you left me alone for all this time."

He didn't respond.

It all started to line up and make sense in my brain. "And how you knew it was time to come and find me."

"You catch on quick, for an Oxford man." He winked and took a bite of his sandwich.

"All these years you've been knowing things about my life without telling me?"

"Now what good would it have done for me to tell you things you needed to learn on your own?"

My eyes narrowed a bit. "What else do you know?"

"Listen my boy, I know less than you think. Just more than you thought."

"Well, that's comforting."

"It's not like fortune-telling. I can't *make* it happen. It just...does, sometimes. I've learned to live with it. You will too."

That much was true, at least. My dreams and *visions*, if that's what they really were, came about without much warning. "You make it sound inevitable."

"It is what it is."

"What does that even mean?"

"It means, my boy, that you were born with these gifts, and they can't be returned. You can either learn to live with them and appreciate them for what they are, or you can reject and ignore them, but they will continue to exist, whether you choose to acknowledge them or not."

"What did you mean when you said an ancient line?"

He smiled. "Would you like to find out more about it?"

"How?"

"You could always pay Nana a visit."

"Only if you translate." I grinned.

"You probably remember more than you think."

My eyes narrowed. "Mmhmm."

As we drove, we talked about all kinds of things. He asked me about Kathleen and for the first time I was able to recount the fun and beautiful things about her. I told him about ordering her a steak when she was a vegetarian, thinking I was all that, and how she shut me down hard. He laughed and laughed and said sincerely that he wished he could have met her.

The rest of the ride we talked all about the pub–the one in Dublin he was looking to turn around. We'd had some vague conversations about business in the past, but I told him that as a profit-sharing partner, I'd have to know everything. I wanted to see the books, get a sense of their budget and pay allowances, the kitchen expenses, advertising...everything.

"I don't think you understand."

"What's that?"

"I'll be there with you for about two weeks, but then I'm going to America. I've got some possibilities there I need to pursue, and I'm giving you the place in Dublin to run. Completely. I said you'd call all the shots, and I meant it. It's a full-time job and then some."

"Who's been running it up until now?"

"I have, for the most part. All the other pubs have their own managers, and I just oversee them, but Dublin was my baby. That's why I named it Finn's Place." He grinned. "It's only right that it should fall to you."

"You're going off to explore New York City without me then?"

He laughed. "You'll come to New York, eventually. But Ireland will always be home."

I thought about England, and the fact that he was only half right.

"You can stay at my place, if that suits you. Then when I go off to the States I've someone to watch the house for me."

It sounded like a decent plan. Even if Dublin wasn't my favorite city on the planet, I could hardly pass up the opportunity. Especially since I knew beyond a doubt that I could turn that pub around. The old timers wouldn't be happy with me, but they'd have to get over that.

I planned to keep some traditional foods on the menu, maybe designate areas where some of the old flavor and character remained while making room for the new. After spending all those months in the quiet of the countryside and by the sea, I wasn't sure how I'd respond to city life, but I was about to find out.

First though, we were going to see Nana.

She and my grandfather had moved away from Connemara, which was near Galway, when Da started secondary school. I remembered her taking me to Galway as a child, and it gave me the shivers. It was interesting that when my life tanked, I'd felt drawn to that area specifically, and now I felt drawn to her.

26

W e drove north and east and ended just outside Navan, where Nana lived. Driving down the narrow roads, Da looked nostalgic, if not a bit apprehensive.

"Do you remember this place?"

As I looked around, it was like opening the door from black and white to technicolor. Memories flashed in and out of my consciousness–playing and riding bikes and running in the fields with Eiran, laying on our backs in the grass and looking up at the clouds until we fell asleep.

My grandmother had a small farm on the outskirts of the town with a few animals and a garden, which she still worked in every day.

Even though she was in her sixties, she wasn't an old woman, by any means. She was vibrant and active and...well, strange, as I've said before. As we drove slowly up the dirt and stone driveway, there were piles of rocks in different places in the fields, just like Eiran had described. I remembered Nana walking around the piles and praying.

Or at least, it looked like she was praying.

When we pulled in, she was sitting on the porch. Da greeted her first, and she immediately pulled me into an embrace that was a little longer than comfortable, then set me back away from her, tilted her head, and looked at me for a few minutes without saying anything at all. Then she addressed my father in Irish. She said something along the lines of, "Looks like you got there just in time."

I bristled. "What's that supposed to mean? In time for what?"

A smile crossed her face as she realized I understood her. I think she wanted to test my ability, because she went off then on a long, rambling explanation of how she'd known for three days we would be coming, and then grabbed onto my hand, ending with "*Brón orm as ucht do thrioblóid.*" *I'm sorry for your loss.*

"My loss? How do you know about that?"

"Three friends, all at once." She sighed. "So tragic."

"You must have seen it on the news?"

"I don't have a television," she replied, still in Irish.

She understood my English–she was just stubborn, and wholly determined to maintain her language. The village she lived in was a Gaeltacht, once of the few scattered places around Ireland in which Irish was still the primary spoken language.

Although my ability to speak the language was still fairly limited, I understood almost everything she said. How did that happen? It was like a switch got thrown in my brain somehow. Her words flowed in and made sense without the usual intermediary translation step. Maybe it was the military? We'd studied basic linguistics in the Intelligence Corps, and I'd messed around with the boys on the ship a bit, but this was different. It felt...strangely normal.

I shook my head, trying to clear it of the fog that seemed to have settled over my thoughts since we arrived. I looked at the chair opposite her and she said, "*Suí síos, le do thoil.*" *Sit, please.*

I did as she asked and Da looked at me in amazement. He said to her, "*Conas ab fhéidir é sin a tharla?*" *How is that possible?*

She responded without hesitation. "*Fág anseo liom é. Beidh chuile rud soléir i gceann tamaill.*" *Leave him here with me. Everything will become clear in time.*

"Please don't talk about me as if I'm not here."

Da shook his head and looked at me. "How are you doing that?"

"I don't know."

She asked Da to go and collect some vegetables from the far garden, and something about gathering specific herbs, for we would have a stew for dinner. He nodded and obeyed without argument, which was interesting to watch. I hadn't really seen them interact as mother and son before, at least not since I became an adult. One thing was perfectly clear. She was not a woman to be trifled with.

Da went inside and changed into some work clothes, then went out the back door with a basket on one arm and some tools in the other. Meanwhile Nana and I just sat.

I noticed that her chair was a rocker, while mine was stationary. It was hardly fair, as she sat rocking back and forth, rhythmically creaking the floorboards in a simple, hypnotic cadence. It was as if she circled me with her perusal. I felt her presence as if it flew at me from all angles, sometimes coming in close and then backing off in the distance. She took a slow, deep breath in, as if she was determining the essence of my smell. Every nerve ending felt raw and exposed. I could feel her pulling events out of the annals of my life. I didn't dare say a word but tried to relax and just let myself enter into this strange form of non-verbal communication.

Finally, she stopped rocking. "I can help you with your questions."

I didn't have to ask how she knew my questions.

"But you have to be willing to walk the path."

"What path?"

She took her time in responding.

"You have three journeys ahead of you. The first you have already been on. It is a dying of everything within you, until the next path opens."

She only spoke Irish and I only spoke English and yet we understood each other perfectly well. The intellectual side of my brain that had been studying quantum physics collided with the part of my spirit that reached out to her for an unexplainable miracle.

"What path?" I asked.

"I don't doubt your questions are many. You have been trained by the world of academia and are sorely lacking in your understanding of the ways of our people. I will speak to your father about that. It was his responsibility to teach you, but no matter, I suppose. You're here now, and as I said, I've been expecting you."

"What do you mean, you've been expecting me? Did Da call and tell you we were coming?"

"I don't have a telephone."

"You don't have a telephone? Who doesn't have a telephone?" As a child I would have never spoken to an elder this way, but as a grown man who had seen his share of pain and sorrow, I felt I had a right to question the strangeness of her ways. I wasn't going to swallow whatever she gave me, bones and all. It would need to be dissected, and I only planned on eating the meat.

She ignored my indignation. "Your pain preceded you. I felt it coming three days ago."

"I don't understand."

She laughed softly. "You think I'm a crazy old woman. You always have. But you needn't be afraid of me, Finnegan. I've waited a long time to tell you these things."

"Tell me what things?"

"Twenty-six years, if I'm not mistaken."

"What do you mean you felt it coming? And why is it I can understand everything you're saying?"

"Because it is time for you to understand."

"When the student is ready, the teacher will come." It was a quote I had learned at Oxford.

"That's a very wise saying."

"It wasn't me, it was Buddha."

Her eyes bore into me. "Just because I don't have a television or a telephone, do not mistake me for an uneducated woman. I know who said it."

"I'm sorry. I didn't mean to-"

She started to rock again, slowly and with her eyes closed. "This world has been spinning for a very long time, Finnegan. There are no new truths. Only those that have yet to be realized and understood."

"Truth and myth share a very thin line." It was difficult to keep the sarcasm out of my voice.

"At times, yes. But you mustn't misjudge the truth based on its vehicle."

"It's vehicle?"

"Let me ask you. Do you think every story the news stations carry is true?"

"No. I don't. I think it's impossible to get at the truth without looking at it from multiple sides."

"Good." She smiled. "Remember that in the coming days."

"What's that supposed to mean?"

"Only that *truth* has been carried on the wings of story for generations."

I thought about the stories I had told to Bree and Declan. Ancient stories, full of symbolism and metaphor, adjusted to their situation, told in simple ways that made sense to their tiny hearts and minds.

"You must see past the obvious to discover freedom."

"Freedom from what?"

Her eyes opened and the fire that flashed in them caught me off guard. "From knowing."

My brain was twisting on itself. I didn't want to learn any more lessons. What I wanted was a drink. I licked my lips and looked out across the land, trying to think about something else.

"You don't really want a drink, you know. What you're thirsting for doesn't come from a bottle, and it doesn't come from the chemist either."

She was starting to freak me out. "How did you do that?"

"Do what?"

"How do you know those things?"

"I hear them. Sense them. See them. Dream about them. It comes in different ways at different times. But besides that, you reek of it."

I looked down at my shoes. Was this what the old woman was talking about?

"Tell me about her."

My head flew up. "What?"

"The old woman in the blue shawl. I saw her in a vision the other day. She was holding your hand. What did she say to you?"

I remained silent. I'd told no one but Da about the old woman and that was only a couple of hours ago. This couldn't be true, and yet my heart was threatening to beat right out of my chest.

"It's all right, Finn. I've been shown these things for a reason. To help you to see that this is real. It is not a figment of your imagination, even though your Oxford training would like you to think otherwise."

I wanted a drink. Badly. My hands started to shake, and I grabbed onto one with the other to try to steady them.

"On the shelf above the sink in the kitchen, you'll find what you're looking for. Then come back and we'll talk some more."

I rose slowly, staring at her as I walked past. She looked like a normal person from the outside, but she wasn't normal. Not at all. And it was slightly terrifying to think that I might be on the same sort of collision course with my own destiny.

27

I went into the kitchen and found the shelf she had indicated. On it stood three bottles of Jameson's and nothing else. I pulled one down, found a glass and poured myself a healthy dose which I downed to steady the shakes, then poured some more before walking back outside.

Mentally I was scratching my head. What did she mean she had known for three days? There was no other liquor in sight. When had she bought the Jameson's? And why three whole bottles?

Maybe there was a reason Da kept us away from her all this time.

I sat back in that flat chair on her porch and sipped while she talked and rocked. She told me about our ancestors and their druid roots. The way they could feel and sense and know things based on their connection to the energies found in all living things.

She told me I was different, with the same gifts that she carried. That my effect on people was stronger than I thought, and that was why the women flocked to me and...allowed my advances. It was very strange, and a little embarrassing, talking to my grandmother about these kinds of things, but she acted like it was perfectly normal.

"You make it sound like those women had no choice–like they were under some kind of a spell."

"Not a spell. But they were attracted to more than just your good looks and rugged charm. They were drawn to something inside you. Something even you didn't know was there."

"Might've been nice if someone had shared this with me a little earlier. Maybe I would have been a little more careful."

"Would you?"

"What do you think I am?" I was shocked by her candor, although looking back I don't see why I should have been.

Still, she wasn't ruffled by my anger. "I think you're a man who very much enjoyed his conquests these last several years and wasn't ready to learn the truth."

"You keep saying that. What truth?" I slammed back the rest of my drink.

"There are three bottles there on the shelf, Finnegan. You may drink them, but when they're gone, you're done, so measure them carefully."

She was talking about the withdrawal. How long did she think I would be staying there?

"You mustn't fear your memories, my boy. They are the fragments that make up who you are, and they must be ordered and unified if you're to come home to yourself."

I felt that same electric buzz as when Da had spoken to me at the hospital in Birmingham. The same one I felt with the priest after the funeral, but she wasn't even touching me.

"You want to run from them, but instead you must piece them together into the fabric of who you are. It is the only way you will *ever* be free."

This idea of freedom. She kept dangling it in front of me. I wanted to pretend I didn't know what she was talking about. I wanted to toss her off as a crazy old woman, but my spirit knew better. I craved the things she spoke about in a place that was deeper than the whisky or the pills.

Just then Da came around the corner of the house with an armload of vegetables and the herbs she'd requested. Nana stood abruptly.

"That's enough sitting. We should cook together. Three generations, sharing a meal. Won't that be nice?"

I'd never cooked with Da before. We'd been eating pub food for as long as I could remember. It was always just made by whoever was in the kitchen that day. Mum was a terrible cook, but she at least took us to nicer restaurants and demanded table manners and use of the proper fork. Being at Mary's, I'd learned a few things so I could handle myself in the kitchen, and Da was surprisingly adept, as if he'd fallen back into a different life. A life with her. I kept trying to imagine what their life had been like together, mother and son. It surprised me that I hadn't ever considered it before.

Nana put us to work chopping vegetables and some meat she'd stewed the day before. We put it all into the pot and sat together at her table. She told me stories of Da and his football prowess and how the English scouts had come looking for him because stories had been told about him playing for the club teams in Dublin.

"He would never have been recruited to the better teams if we stayed in Connemara. He was meant to play."

Although her current lifestyle was far removed from organized sports and city life, I tried to imagine a younger version of her, sitting on the sidelines, cheering him on. Suddenly she wasn't a crazy old woman, but a proud mother, whose child had achieved greatness, and she had helped see to it. Da never said a word. He just sat there, eating and listening, unwilling or perhaps unable to refute her testimony.

The food was fantastic, and I was ravenous. I filled my belly with meat and gravy and carrots and leeks, and it was the most satisfying meal I'd ever had. After dinner she pulled down some brandy from the back of a cupboard.

"Shall we?"

We sat in her living room and shared snifters of brandy, laughing as she told more stories of when Da was a boy. Then I asked her to tell us about when she was young.

"I was raised in a village by the sea. Our land overlooked the waters of the ocean. Most of the men in my family were farmers or fisherman. My mother wove tapestries and made cloth. When we weren't working, we sang and danced and told the stories of old. We listened to the earth and the wind and the water." Nana stared absently, across space and time, into another world. "The sea will always be my first love. It guided our seasons and our lives."

"So why did you come so far inland? Why leave the sea, I mean?"

"Because the earth was calling." She said it with such simple conviction I almost felt silly.

I looked at Da. He shook his head as if to say *don't ask* so I left it alone. The brandy was strong, and my head began to swim. I'd only had a little whiskey and the one snifter of brandy, but it felt as if I'd been drinking all night long. I was suddenly warm and sleepy, and wondered if I was the only one feeling it. Da seemed fine, and Nana watched me with interest. Maybe I was coming down with something.

"I think I'm going to head to bed, if that's all right." I wasn't even sure if we'd been planning to spend the night. All I knew was, I needed to lay down before I passed out. I went to stand and could barely accomplish it.

Da came over and steadied my arm. "Are you ill?"

"I'm not sure."

"He's fine Colin, let him alone," Nana said.

Da immediately let go of my arm, and I found it strange, once again, that he obeyed her so completely.

I started down the hall and heard the two of them talking, still in Irish. "You need to take it slowly with him, Mama. He's been through a lot."

"There is no other way," Nana replied. "You will leave him here with me and come back in two weeks' time."

"Aye."

"You've done the right thing, Colin. He needs to know."

"I wanted to wait–until he was ready."

"The handle is on the inside of the door."

Their conversation trailed off as I undressed and got ready for bed. Da spoke Irish perfectly, and yet I never knew. Sure, I knew he'd grown up around it, but I didn't think he'd remember it after all these years. It seems there was a lot I'd never known.

My eyes were heavy...so heavy.

28

I swear I began to dream before my head hit the pillow. I dreamt of medieval battles and ancient ruins being conquered and plundered. I dreamt of knights on horseback with gleaming swords–entire battle sequences where damsels were rescued, and celebrations were made around roaring fires. I dreamt of sacrifices and promises, marriages, births, funerals...

I woke up exhausted, as if I'd only slept five minutes, and yet the sun was already halfway up the sky. Nana wasn't in the kitchen, but the coffee was made with a few biscuits and some ham on a plate. I drank the coffee and ate my meal quietly, listening.

The windows were open and the sounds coming through them were full of light and life, like a great symphony of bird's song and pig's grunt. The wind carried strange smells and noises I'd never heard, and they assaulted my senses one by one as if each were fighting for center stage. I became aware of every animal, every blade of grass being blown into the next, and a light breeze that at times carried the aroma of wildflowers past my nose. Everything was heightened.

There was a note from Da explaining that he had gone to Dublin and would be back in a couple of weeks, and that if I really wanted to know the truth I should stay and listen. So, he had left me after all. Not that I was afraid of my own grandmother, I just found it interesting that he followed her instructions without asking me what I wanted. I suppose he figured I was a grown man and could make my own decisions, but was he? Or was it something deeper?

I found Nana in the garden, weeding carrots.

"What did you mean when you said the handle was on the inside of the door?"

She looked up at me and smiled. "Sit."

I did as she asked.

"Pull. Here."

I pulled where she asked, and up came a beautiful orange carrot. I looked at it, then looked at her. "It's a carrot. What does that have to do with the handle?"

"The beauty was on the inside, pushing up through the darkness." She put her hand on mine. "The bushy greens on the top were the clue it was ready to be revealed."

"You realize you don't make sense, right?" I dusted the carrot off on my shirt and took a bite. "It's good though. Thanks for the snack."

I started to get up, but she put her hand onto mine. "I'm not finished yet."

"Why did you send Da away?"

"Because you and I needed to spend some time together."

"I barely know you."

"Exactly my point." She smiled.

"Would you like me to do something else for you? While you pull carrots?"

"Do you see this fence that surrounds my property?"

"Aye."

"It's twenty-two acres I've got, with cows and pigs and a couple of horses. I need someone to walk the boundaries and check the fencing–make sure there are no areas that need mending. Can you do that?"

"You want me to walk the fence line?"

"Aye."

I stood up and brushed off my pants. "And what would you like me to do if I find an area that needs to be fixed?"

"There's a bucket in the barn–you can carry it with you. It holds a hammer, some nails, a few strands of wire, that kind of thing. It's not too difficult, once you get the hang of it."

"Anything else while I'm out there?"

"You'll be plenty busy. Might want to bring a bit of water and some bread along. You'll get mighty thirsty."

What did she think I was, a child? It was twenty-two acres for God's sake. It's not like I was walking to Dublin.

I grabbed the tool bucket and headed off, frustrated by her veiled requests.

The fence wove up and down hills that were majestic in their beauty. I tried to enjoy the scenery, but there were actually a lot of small repairs that required attention. Between the army and working on Peter's boat, I'd done a fair bit of everything, so it's not like it was difficult work. However, I'd only finished about five acres' worth of fence line by the time my stomach started growling at me. I was thirsty too, damn it.

I cut back across the fields and headed for the barn, where I found a small metal tin covered in cloth and a pitcher of water. In it were a few chunks of bread and cheese, and the water was ice cold. A flask stood ready to be filled so I wrapped the last of the bread and took it all with me. I had a few hours of daylight left and intended to finish the job. My shoulder was surprisingly quiet the whole time, which I found strange. I wanted the painkillers for other reasons, but not because I had any actual pain.

If I went slowly on the Jameson's I might be able to make it last until Da got back, but even that was questionable. I'd have to take just enough to ward off the shakes each time. Hell, I didn't even know if I wanted to be sober, but something about being in this place was defining, like the fence that formed the property line. It seems strange to say it this way in the retelling, but inside those borders, I felt safe.

I know this because a strange feeling came over me when I

walked outside the fence. There was a line of demarcation I didn't understand. I only knew I felt better, and more at peace when I examined the fence from the inside looking out. Maybe that's what she meant about the handle and the door.

There were a couple of cows that hung around while I worked. No matter how far I walked, they seemed to always be grazing nearby.

"So, what do *you* think I'm doing here? Besides mending fences?" I asked one of them.

It looked at me, chewed, looked at me, and chewed some more.

"That's about what I thought too."

By the time I finished the sun was setting, and I was hoping there was dinner to be had. Man could live on bread and water, but it wouldn't be a pleasant existence. I put the tools in the barn and used the outdoor sink to get most of the dirt off my hands before going inside.

"I need a shower," I announced.

"You'll find everything you need in the bathroom."

It was a crude affair, with a claw foot tub set under an ancient looking shower head and a curtain pulled around all of it. I stood under the water until all the dirt was washed away, then filled the tub with what looked like some homemade shampoo and sat in the hot, aromatic waters until every pore felt open and relaxed. I tried to remember the last time I had a real bath–and then I did.

It was there. In that very tub.

Nana used to make Eiran and I "bathe the day away" as Da would translate it. The few times we stayed with her, it was this very tub we sat in, played in. And the smell of those herbs brought it all back to me. Regardless of what I did or didn't learn from Nana, I was in fact, reconnecting with a forgotten part of my history. An undiscovered, unremembered past.

When the water was finally cool again, I drained it away, wiped out the tub, and gathered my dirty clothing. Walking out into the hallway in just a towel, I caught a glimpse in the mirror. An image flashed of a girl standing there, but when I looked a second time, it was gone. I started to shake and knew it was past time for that glass of whiskey I'd been dreaming about all afternoon.

29

The kitchen smelled of roasted pork and colcannon. Nana's colcannon beat every pub version I had ever tried. Or maybe I was just starving. At any rate the freshly dug potatoes and kale mashed together with scallions and butter and fresh cream sent my taste buds to heaven. It even beat Mary's food, and that was a tough prize to win. I started reaching for seconds almost immediately. Nana looked at my thinly muscled arms and seemed genuinely happy to watch me eat.

Over dinner she began to tell me more about 'our people'. She told me legends of the ancient Celts and how men used to wrap themselves in the hides of animals and sleep by the riverbanks to see what dreams would come. She said it was common practice to retreat to a solitary place to meditate and receive visions. I was only half-listening. The food was so good it was as if it was feeding and strengthening my actual bones. I could feel things shifting in my body as I sat there, craving it all and taking it in, body, soul, and spirit.

"Did you have any sort of visions while you were walking the property today?"

Was that why she sent me out there? To see if I would have a vision? I wasn't about to tell her about the dark-haired girl in my dream the night I left Mary's place–the same one I'd just seen in the mirror–so I decided to play it safe.

"No, but I did notice something strange about your fence line. What was that? Some kind of a spell?"

She seemed to know what I was referring to without having to question me any further. "Not a spell, just a boundary line. A blessing, of sorts. You can feel it because of your gifts. I imagine you've had similar sorts of feelings before. You probably just dismissed them."

"You think I should pay more attention to them?"

"Your connection to the earth exists whether you pay attention to it or not. It's up to you if you want to fine tune it and listen more closely."

"What's the advantage to listening? Are you telling me the rocks talk? The trees? The cows?"

"No, the cows don't talk, at least not to me, but they are awfully good listeners, I've found." She winked at me with that knowing smirk of hers, as if she knew I'd been talking to the cows. Her head moved up and down like the rhythm of her rocking chair as she closed her eyes and listened.

"Now go and get your glass of whiskey and tell me about your time in Galway."

I did as I was told, without question, as Da had done the day before. Perhaps this was the kind of respect and obedience she demanded, but perhaps it was something more. She wielded an authority that seemed to reach beyond common courtesy or even elderly respect. I came back with the whiskey and sat down.

"See now? All day without a pill, and this is the first whiskey you've had. You were too busy to worry about it."

It was strange letting her speak to me about these things. I felt I barely knew her and yet here she was walking me down this delicate line. "That's not true. I thought about it all day long, waiting to be able to come in and have some."

"That's just priorities, my boy. Some would say a hard day's work deserves a bit of drink at the end of it. You don't *need* it, Finn. Not really."

"But you don't approve."

"I neither approve nor disapprove. Your relationship with that bottle doesn't matter to me."

"Relationship?" I laughed out loud. "I don't have a *relationship* with it."

"What would you call it?"

"A mutual admiration," I announced, sipping happily with a grin on my face. I thought I was being clever.

Nana didn't seem to agree. Her face became very still, eyes fixed on some point out past the porch, past the edges of reality perhaps. "I know what attracts you to the bottle, but I wonder, what does the bottle see in you?"

Suddenly the thick brown liquid seemed to congeal across my tongue until its thickness filled my throat. I panicked, thinking something had gone wrong. I'd been poisoned, I'd...

"I'll tell you what it sees." She continued. "It sees an opportunity to choke the life out of you. To send you to your death before you ever discover your destiny, and if it can't quite kill you, then it will keep you distracted and wallowing until you no longer care that it exists."

"That what exists?"

"The path to your destiny."

"What destiny?"

"How should I know?"

"Because you seem to know everything else."

She smiled and shook her head slowly. "Your destiny is your own quest. I only know what it's not."

"What it's not?" I repeated. "I'm afraid I'm terribly lost."

"Not to worry." She smiled. "You won't be lost forever."

"No, I mean I don't understand what you're talking about."

"I know exactly what you mean."

I took a long sip off the whiskey and felt a strong desire for more, but in my head, I saw it as a thick, black smoke circling my body and wrapping me up until I couldn't breathe anything but smoke. I started to cough involuntarily and watched some of that black smoke come out of my mouth.

I blinked a few times, trying to determine whether or not it was real, but there was no evidence of dissipating smoke in the room, only a vague sense of dread as I polled my senses for an accounting of what had just transpired. Was this withdrawal? Had I been drugged? It was like I could hear Nana's voice in my head, but when I looked over at her, her mouth wasn't moving.

In my mind she was explaining the difference between metaphor and symbolism. We had a whole conversation about the difference between metaphor and literal visions, some of which are for teaching and some which needed to be followed to the letter, like a déjà vu. I tried to remember some of the things I'd seen and pick apart reality from dreams and visions, but it was no use.

I knew this much: that black smoke was my desire for the whiskey, and it really was clouding my vision and choking the life out of me.

I was trembling again. Badly. Whiskey was not the enemy. Control was. The perception of need. Still I sipped it down little by little, forcing it past the constriction in my throat. I didn't care what my mind said about it. My body and my mind were colliding, and I couldn't stop it from breaking apart.

Like a dream sequence images started floating past me. Wood and propellers and masts and sails littered the water. Lifeboats filled with people I'd loved and some that I hadn't cared about at all– wreckages of past relationships. Most of them dead, some of them gruesomely bloodied. All of them floating aimlessly out to sea. Jasper, Connor, scores of women I'd slept with, some that I'd dated for a while. Peter, James, John, Kathleen, Annabelle. Mum, Da, Eiran, Grams, even Nana, only her boat was tethered to mine.

And in the last boat was Regan.

One of her beautiful green eyes was black and blue, and her gut was bruised too, like she'd been sucker-punched. I started to cry.

· · ·

NANA PUT her hand on mine to steady it. Immediately I felt her peace and drew from it, trying to pull it all the way through my body. "What you need, my boy, is to let it go."

I looked up at her, my jaw so tight my whole face shook with the effort. "Please make it stop."

"A little at a time maybe, but you have to let it go. Once you've released its hold on you, you'll be able to drink it without an issue."

"Impossible."

"No, it's not. You've simply forgotten how to feel."

"I'm afraid you're wrong. Feeling *is* the problem."

She shook her head. "We feel things all the time. Feelings are normal, everyday things. It's when we let those feelings drive our actions out of balance that we have a problem."

I shook my head vehemently, disagreeing completely. "I feel too much. That's the problem. I need to feel less."

Her hand was still on mine. She squeezed me suddenly and when I looked up, her eyes were like steel. "Open the door, Finn. Stop pushing them deeper in. Open the door from the inside and let them go free."

"How? How am I supposed to do that!"

I was yelling at this point. I wanted what she talked about, but I had no idea how to get it. This cat and mouse game she was playing, trying to get me to discover it on my own, was driving me crazy.

She faced me and took both of my hands in hers. It was like completing some kind of a circuit. Every hair follicle felt energized.

"I want you to visualize an actual door," she said. "Behind it are all the screams and cries, all the anger, all the feelings you've deemed unacceptable. There's a long hallway leading from that door up and out the top of your head. Let them go. Open the door." She held tightly to both of my hands. "I won't let you fall."

Immediately I started to weep. I watched that door swing open in my mind, and I wept inconsolable tears. Worse than my screams on the hilltop. Deeper than anything I'd ever known. It was like some kind of a trance. At times I barely felt Nana's hands, could hardly hear my own cries as I was swept up into these feelings of grief and sadness and anger and longing. I watched whole scenes of my life play out in slow motion and wondered briefly if I was actually dying–if my grief could be physically killing me.

Regan, Kathleen, Peter, James and John, Declan and Bree, even things I'd held against Da and Mum came cycling through as my emotions swirled. I watched as a vision of Kathleen and the baby circled in my mind. She was holding her, and they both looked perfectly content. They floated up the hallway and away from me, toward heaven I supposed. Kathleen waved as they went, and I felt myself relax a little. They were together, and Kathleen was taking care of her.

I thought about the men in my unit, the horrors of war, the dead soldiers, and my guilt over being kept alive so many times now.

Then Nana's voice entered my consciousness. "You're alive for a reason. Walk in it. Accept it. Move on."

She was right, of course. Although I felt completely unworthy of the opportunity, I was in fact, still alive. I could regret it or live it, like the priest said. None of those soldiers, not even Kathleen would want to see me throw away my second chance on self-destruction. It was weakness, nothing more, and I wasn't born to be weak. I'd been strong my whole life, up until recently. I saw the whiskey bottle shaped like a crutch and in my vision, I broke it in half.

"You will not control me!" I yelled.

I'm still not sure if I said it out loud or if it was just in my head, but as soon as I said the words, I watched that circling smoke start to dissipate completely. The last thing I saw before I opened my eyes was the faintest whisper of gray still wafting around my head, and then it was gone.

It was quiet in the house. Everything was still.

Nana looked at me and smiled. "You've done well, Finnegan. How do you feel?"

I blinked a few times, trying to take a mental inventory. "I'm not sure. Good, I think."

She took a deep breath and dropped my hands. "That's quite enough for one day, wouldn't you say?"

I scanned the room, trying to find a clock. What time was it? "How long have we been..."

"About an hour." She shrugged. "Tomorrow we'll talk some more."

She got up and left me sitting there wondering what the hell had just happened. I wanted to call her back–to have her explain to me what in the world was going on, but then the whole experience began to fade like that thick gray smoke. I felt drained and yet somehow lighter and more energized, as if that soldier's pack full of heavy emotions had been lifted and I'd been relieved of my duty.

For the second night in a row I collapsed onto the bed, nearly unconscious by the time my head hit the pillow. When I woke up the next morning, I barely remembered a thing from the night before. I found Nana making breakfast, and she poured me some coffee as we sat down at the small table in her kitchen.

I knew she still wanted me to tell her about the woman with the blue shawl, so I did. I explained the entire scenario just as I'd explained to Da, from the first vision that drew me to the harbor up through the dream about the boat.

"Let me see your books," she said when I was finished.

"My books?"

"Yes. From the book store."

I went and retrieved the small stack with the now well-worn pages and hoped for the best.

To my surprise she didn't dislike the one on quantum physics, nor any of them really. She said they were all a part of the search, and that the spiritual journey had nothing to fear from science. The more science discovers, the more it actually proves what the spirit has led us to believe all along.

For an old woman with no telephone, no television, and no computer, she was surprisingly well versed in quarks and particles of light, which she said were the energy and life force of the universe.

"Call it what you will," she explained, "but everything you see is made of that light, at its tiniest base of a form. I like to call that light–that energy–*God*. You may call it whatever you like."

I couldn't figure out if she was crazy or brilliant. "Are you even Catholic?"

She laughed. "God has been around a lot longer than Catholicism."

"You know, you have an uncanny ability to answer a question without actually answering it."

"If you really listen, you'll find that I answer every question and then some."

"And this whole time I've been here, you won't speak English, but you understand it perfectly well."

"You understand me, I understand you...Why should either of us change our tongue?"

For the rest of that morning she talked to me about the history of the Celtic people–stories handed down by oral tradition, from generation to generation. She told me that my gift was neither common nor rare, but that if I allowed it to guide me, it would show me things that would move me closer to the path.

Then she poured me a glass of whiskey.

"What's that for?"

"Although your mind is becoming free, your body still depends on it. You will have to sip it now and again or the pain will be terrible."

"It hasn't been that long Nana. Only a few months. I can't have become so terribly dependent."

"And yet, you shake when you shouldn't. Trust me. Drink."

I did as I was told, but the whiskey tasted like–I don't know–medicine. "What did you put in this?"

"You watched me pour it from the bottle. I didn't put anything in it."

"But it tastes...different."

"It's your need that has changed, and it's affecting your perception of the taste."

"That's bollocks."

She laughed. "It is what it is, my boy."

Still, she was right, as usual. The cool liquid dropped into my stomach and calmed me somehow, and I hated that it did that. Once I had seen the need for what it was, I was shocked and appalled, not to mention embarrassed.

Was that how people had seen me these last months? As a weak, nothing of a man that drowned his sorrows in a bottle of amber grace? Was that the man I longed to be? There was no honor in weakness; no courage in burying oneself alive.

I slammed back the rest of my drink, determined to be done with it, but along with it the tentacles of numbing ease wrapped around me, tempting me back into oblivion. "I have to go." I stood abruptly. "I have to go for a walk. A long one."

Nana watched me struggling against my need. "Would you like to take some bread and water this time?"

I smirked at her. "Very funny."

"I'm quite serious. I packed you a small lunch. You'll find it in a bucket on the back porch."

"How did you know I'd need a lunch?"

"I didn't." She smiled. "I guessed."

"You guessed."

"All of life is really just a guess. That's what makes it fun." She sat back and closed her eyes. "I'm going to take a little nap while you're gone."

I grabbed a jacket and headed out the back door, only to find the lunch she spoke of sitting right there next to my shoes. This was seriously one of the stranger experiences of my life. I wished someone else had been there to testify to it, but there was only me, inside my own mind and thoughts, stringing pieces together and trying to create a complete picture from broken shards.

I walked out past the fence line and kept walking until I couldn't walk anymore. Then I sat down and ate the lunch Nana packed for me. I listened to the breeze for a while, then walked back.

Nothing huge happened on that walk, but it kept me busy and

away from that bottle. Kind of like the fence line experience. I got back around dinnertime, tired and thirsty. Again.

Nana set the bottle down in front of me along with an empty glass. It was so strange, the way she challenged me with it. I took the glass, poured some and slammed it back. I poured some more and slammed it back again. She just stood there, looking at me.

"How much is enough, Nana?" I didn't mean to yell, but the words came out louder than I anticipated.

"You tell me." She replied. Her face was calm and motionless; her body relaxed as she stood in front of me.

I slammed one more shot and realized I didn't want anymore. My stomach felt sick and I went to the bathroom and lost its contents. Then I went to bed without supper.

30

For three days I sweated and my stomach ached. It felt like dying, and yet she left the bottle for me in case I wanted to curb it somehow.

I didn't.

In a last-ditch effort to martyr myself for my own stupidity, I chose the suffering over the easy way down the mountain. I wanted to know and remember the pain of withdrawal so I could look back on it with the kind of disdain that never wants to go there again. The wanting for the whiskey was still there, of course, I just fought back against the want. It was touch and go for a while. At one point I even tried to gulp down just one mouthful to ease the torment, but I ended up spitting it right back out.

Nana sang around the house as she puttered–hauntingly beautiful melodies with very few words. I floated away on them numerous times, only to come back to reality and the pain of a pounding head, drenched in sweat. Honestly? I could deal with all of the physical symptoms. I still remembered my time in the infirmary at basic training. It wasn't pretty, but I knew I'd survive.

It was the nightmares I wasn't prepared for. I would wake up screaming, and when I told Nana about them, she made me some kind of tea that put me into a dreamless sleep. She may have been crazy, but I was in love with her herbs.

On day three I was able to hold down some broth. By day four I was so anxious I wandered around the yard talking to the chickens. Days five and six depression set in. I laid in bed the whole of both days realizing over and over again what a wretched human being I was. She wanted me to feel? No problem. I had more feelings than I knew what to do with.

I refused to eat anything of substance. Nana just kept bringing me tea and crackers and told me to sleep it off.

In the in-between times, when I was 'quiet and reflective' (as she referred to my debilitating depression), she sat by my bed and told me stories. Some were legends, like the ones I'd adapted for Declan and Bree. Others were stories about our family's ancestors–about the different gifts and talents each possessed and how they used them for good or for evil, depending on their choices.

"Nothing happens without a choice, Finnegan. You may say that others have chosen for you or that God has run you out of options, but that's not the case. Circumstances just are. It's like the weather. You wake up, you look outside, and you dress accordingly. Sometimes you have to change your plans due to the weather but it's nothing to get mad about, because that would be silly. You don't control the weather; you just adapt to it."

She held onto my hand. "You cannot blame your drinking or the pills on the death of your friends, your wife, or your child. You always have a choice, no matter what. How you react, and how you live your life, is yours and yours alone."

I said nothing. Her words repeated themselves in my mind until they stuck to the edges.

"Every one of these experiences are seeds that have been sown into the essence of your being. You must spend the time needed to harvest those memories, then plant them in the past, where they can do you some good."

Maybe it was the Irish, and some of it was getting lost in translation, but I swear sometimes the woman made no sense at all. I didn't want those memories to be planted. I wanted to yank them out by their roots and burn them and then scatter the dust far, far away from my consciousness.

It was the thoughts of Regan that hurt unexpectedly. So many things I'd done and said and none of it could be taken back. There was only one thing I didn't want to take back. One incredible night that had tipped the entire stack of dominos. Because of her I could never go back to the way I'd been, and it drove me mad. It drove me away from her.

Eventually the stomach pain subsided. All the pain subsided, actually. My head stopped aching, and I'd sweated so much putrid, toxic waste out of my pores I half expected to look in the mirror and see a completely different person.

Alas, I was the same, shaggy-bearded, too-skinny, used-to-be-good-looking guy I'd been the week before. Pity. One would think that after such a major life catharsis you'd have something decent to show for it. Instead I looked like I'd been sitting on death's porch, without enough energy to even stand up and knock on the door.

Nana refused to make a big deal about it. "Finn my boy, it's all temporary. Don't worry about things that don't matter to God."

She would say things like that as if they were a matter of course, but how was I supposed to know what mattered to God and what didn't? I'd spent my entire adult life riding the fine line between the Catholic and Anglican churches. Even still, I'd basically ignored both their teachings in favor of a "do what's right in the eyes of Finn" theology that had been working just fine up until the last year or so. I wasn't ready to concede that my negligence should warrant a change of heart.

Still, there were things that didn't make sense–undeniable, experiential type things. Things that didn't stand a chance when pitted against the scientific method. I had no idea how to reconcile them, but they happened all the same. All of it led me there, and surely for a reason, but it was like my head was in a constant fog, and I couldn't line all the pieces up in the right order.

Nana sensed this, and she didn't try to push me. She didn't care if

I believed in God, or anything else for that matter. She seemed to be at something deeper, but if there was anything deeper than God, I couldn't exactly fathom it. The whole thing had me on edge, questioning everything I'd ever known or even thought I'd known.

I asked if she was going to teach me the specifics of how I was supposed to work within these dreams and visions, but she just shook her head. "The path will teach you much better than I can."

"How can you say that? You have so much wisdom to give."

"I found my wisdom along my own path, just as you'll find yours. I can only teach you the basics."

Worse than a joke with no punch line, I was left trying to figure everything out on my own. All her stories were like riddles. We had some nice times together though, toward the end. We worked side-by-side in the gardens and she helped me plant two small trees, one at each of the far ends of her property.

The one on the west end represented my losses, and as we sat on the porch that night, we watched the sun go down on them. Each night I would have to choose to put them to bed, she explained. The tree to the east represented my future. The sun would rise each morning and it would get the day's first light, the warmest rays, and the best chance at survival. I would say good morning to a new day and face it with as much courage as I dared.

THERE ARE THOSE TIMES, I suppose, that represent an epiphany in our lives. Times when everything suddenly makes sense in a way it never did previously. I wish I could say that about my time with Nana. Instead it was like watching a crippled man struggle to pull himself down a very long and frustrating road.

DA CAME BACK at the end of two weeks, just like he promised, and the first thing he noticed was two full bottles of Jameson's still on the shelf. He looked me up and down. "You're all right then?"

I nodded once.

"Ready to go to work?"

"Aye."

"Finn, why don't you go out and bring me some of the herbs from the far garden? The ones I use to make your tea. I want to send some with you."

I grabbed a bucket and some scissors and immediately headed out the back door, realizing with some amusement that I'd become my father. Still, I whistled as I went out among the piles of stones and gathered the herbs she requested.

In my time with Nana I found that I loved working in the earth almost as much as I loved being on the sea. I'd tapped this part of me that connected with nature–with life itself as a force to be reckoned with, and yet it was time to move forward. To say goodbye to this peaceful land that had become my sanctuary.

I decided to build two small cairns of my own, on the far ends of the property, underneath the trees I planted. I sat down next to each pile of rocks and did my best to pray. Beside the first, I prayed that I could properly let go of my past. Beside the second I prayed that I could embrace life on the other side of my grief.

I was a different man than when I'd come, grounded in a way I'd never known was possible. Whether this was Nana's doing or some magic in this place, or God himself, remained to be seen.

When I returned, she and Da were sharing a cup of tea out on the porch. Nana looked strangely satisfied as she took the bucket from me, as if she knew what I'd been up to. I shook my head and went to pack up the last of my things, not knowing if I would ever understand her. I'd learned so much under her tutelage, but there was so much more to be gained, not the least of it being all the weight I'd lost. Still, the next part had to be on my own, and we both knew it.

As I gathered my pack and the few personal items I'd brought with me, I caught my reflection in the mirror. My face was still pale and drawn tight across my cheekbones, and my shirt hung from my limbs like it was drying on a thin bit of clothesline. Weight could be regained, I decided, and wisdom had been worth it. Suddenly the bedroom I'd sweated and labored in these last two weeks felt like a coffin, and leaving it was my second chance at a life worth living.

I was ready to put my skills to work, and even though I was going off to build a better bar, I didn't fear being around the alcohol—maybe because I didn't fear being around myself. I think Da was right all along. It wasn't the alcohol or the pills that were the problem, I was just lost and looking for an anchor.

Nana had been right all along. I'd found exactly what I needed there, in that place, but it didn't come from her—not directly. Somehow, I discovered a well of grace I hadn't known existed, and it seeped into my bones, filling the cavities with strength and the freedom to embrace it all without remorse or recompense.

Grams had been right too. Knowing who I was and where I'd come from proved invaluable, and it changed everything. Grams had given me the English side: it was the Irish half that was lacking.

I'd come full circle now and felt much more complete—a wholeness born of joys and losses. Both had driven me to the edge of myself, and it was from there that I had the best view. The door handle really did open from the inside.

Leaving now, I knew I could never be lost again. So many wondrous things had happened in that place. Deep things that spoke to my inner man. Things that defied logic.

Purging things.

Healing things.

I felt truly alive, possibly for the first time ever, so I happily said goodbye to the coffin, and hello to the rest of my life, but I don't think I'll ever feel a beautiful breeze without thinking of that precious little girl.

Driving back to Dublin with Da, it seemed as if I'd lived another man's life. I don't know how else to describe it really, except it felt like coming out of a very deep sleep. Slowly the colors came back into focus, the sounds dialed into a new frequency. My heart still knew a sorrow that might never go away, but instead of a foreign object I needed to drown or fight off or run from, it was assimilated into the fabric of my being. It just...was.

They say a fox can only ever run halfway into the forest, because after that, he's running out again. As Nana's house got smaller in the rearview window, I felt like that fox.

While I knew for certain I wasn't out of the woods, I was definitely headed for the edge of the undergrowth. Light was on the other side.

31

D ublin was exactly as I'd left it. I don't know what I expected really, but when Da parked the car, I had trouble getting out.

"What is it?" he asked.

I looked up and down the busy street. No one knew I'd been gone or what I'd been through, and none of them cared either. They were my experiences. My crosses to bury in the backyard of my own house. I knew I had to step forward; I just couldn't get my feet to do it.

I turned back toward him. "What if it doesn't work?"

"What if what doesn't work?"

"This plan. This–sobering life I need to start leading now."

"It's not like that." He came around to my side of the car. "It's not *just starting*, don't you see? Your life's been sailing along without you for the last little while, 'tis true. But now's time to take back the helm and steer a bit."

I thought of Peter at the helm of his own boat with James and John working by his side and me just along for the ride. They'd been lost at sea, and I hadn't. Kathleen, our child, Jasper, Connor, all those soldiers lost to the war and me still standing at the end of it all. Honoring them with a happy life seemed like betrayal, and yet, I had to put their memories away if I was going to survive. I couldn't live inside their stories anymore.

Da put a hand on my shoulder, bringing me back to the present. "What do you say? Shall we go put a Dublin landmark back on the map?"

"Aye." I nodded firmly.

Da was good to have around in a pinch.

WHEN WE WALKED into Finn's Place, Brandy turned a few shades of red seeing the two of us together. I barely remembered our first meeting and hoped I hadn't led her on. I had little enough strength and stamina as it was. Even my eyes felt weak. The whole atmosphere had me off my guard.

We ordered a couple of sandwiches, but when she brought over a bottle of Jameson's, I shook my head and asked for water instead. Her eyebrows went up, but she did as I asked.

At a booth in the back, I sketched out my ideas for remodeling the place, and Da was almost as excited as I was. The mirrors and new lighting were things we could do ourselves, and he knew a good carpenter who could refinish the bar top and the floors. I showed him my ideas for redesigning the menus, the new logo, and the website branding, then made a list of menu items to add to the usual pub fare.

"Some places are all about the tourists," I explained. "All the locals know it, and they stay away. They prefer to come to quiet little unassuming places like this that the tourists don't know about."

"Or don't care about," Da nodded. I knew he wasn't much for tourists, but we both knew they were a good bit of the business revenue in this part of Dublin.

"I don't want a place that attracts tourists either. What I want is a trendy place all the *locals* will flock to, and because of that the tourists might show up as well, but our main business has to be the local crowd. Maybe get some of the radio programmes to broadcast from here live, bring in local bands and comedians–that sort of thing. If we make this a place Dublin can be proud of, then the rest will follow naturally."

Da considered that for a bit. "I like it."

"I thought you would." I winked at him.

"It doesn't matter if I like it though."

"Say again?"

He put his elbows up on the table and leaned in. "I told you this was your project. I want you to build it your way. In the end it's the numbers that will do the talking."

It wasn't so much of a challenge as it was a gift. Da scribbled a few figures as we talked, and his estimate of what it would cost, not including advertising, turned out to be surprisingly accurate. We decided to get to work the very next day.

We worked on the renovations at night and in the mornings, and opened the bar for business as usual in the evenings. We only had to close it for two days to set the clear coat on the refinished floors and bar top.

The tables and chairs arrived on schedule, as did all the linens, which of course made the old dishes look hideously ugly, so I sent Brandy to pick out new ones. She also chose the uniforms: crisp white shirts over navy blue pants with maroon aprons and visors.

Her handwriting was much better than mine, so I had her make up the chalkboards over the bar. We scheduled nightly drink specials and menu items, and once the awning and outdoor seating was in place, there was nothing left to do but invite the press.

Apparently renovating an historic building in downtown Dublin was a fairly big deal, because the Irish Times did a piece, and then several other small papers came to take interviews and snap photos. Even the local news station covered us, putting me on camera and catching us on a particularly busy night. It was a perfect setup for the local radio DJ, who'd gotten a tip from one of the reporters and asked if he could do his show from the bar during one of our local talent nights.

After that the floodgates opened. People came to check it out because of all the media attention but stayed for the food and the atmosphere. I cleared an area in the back corner and set up a small stage for musicians, making sure there was a really good sound system to blast it out to the streets.

I ate there.

I slept there.

Hell, I barely left at all except for occasional showers at Da's place and trips to the market for fresh flowers and the like. The revenue was pouring in. Da made back his investment in no time, and true to his word, spent most of his time in New York City.

At the end of each night I had one drink with the staff, usually vodka, as I'd sworn off of Jameson's. We would go over the day's ups and downs and talk together, like a small family. I gave each employee a tiny share of the profits, paid weekly in their checks, like an extra bonus.

They loved that the harder they worked to bring in business and make the customers happy, the more they personally profited in the end. It didn't cost us much in the big scheme of things, and every person in every job got the same share of the profits. No one was better or worse, more or less important to the whole effort. We were a true team–kind of like Gaelic Football. Even the old-timers seemed to like the changes. I would talk to them as the renovations were going on, asking for input and incorporating some of their suggestions. The place was doing great.

Da and I split what was left, and I was making a tidy sum as well, so I promoted Brandy to manager. She thrived in her new role and turned out to be a great organizer, but she watched me the same way Callie had watched me, with interest and longing. Putting her to bed drunk would not have been so easy, personal vow or not, so I had to be extra careful.

Brandy did the ordering and inventory and handled all the scheduling, so slowly I turned the day to day operations over to her as well. In the evenings I maintained a heavy presence, talking with customers and interacting with the staff, but my days were spent developing the technology for the CGI idea.

While I was waiting on the patent, I started a marketing plan and built a website. Professor Smythe stayed true to his word and invested in the project. We partnered financially and pitched the technology to a few film producers he knew, and one of them agreed to beta test it on a project he was filming in France.

Once they were in post-production, I left things in Brandy's capable hands for a few days and went to consult on the project and train the team. They loved the interface and decided to use it for the entire film. Professor Smythe and I were both invited back for the premiere.

Although the French are entirely too fond of wine, it was the women I found the greater temptation. Celeste was a beautiful, long-legged brunette with olive skin, soft lips, and skilled hands. She introduced me to a Hollywood producer at a party in a penthouse suite in Paris. She tried to get me drunk on old French wine and lured me into one of the bedrooms under thinly veiled pretenses.

It had been so long, and it would have been so easy. It started out like a well-choreographed routine, but then the trigger got pulled. No sooner did I have her in my arms than I was back in the dust in Helmand, holding Kathleen's head in my hands.

The fire died like it had been doused with a hose. I used what limited French I could summon from the drunken recesses of my mind to apologize and left the party. The next morning, I hightailed it back to Dublin. Some things had been fixed, and others had worked themselves out over time, but that part of me was still broken. There was no doubt about it.

AT THE END of six months, Finn's Place was *the* hot spot in Dublin. Things were going along so well, in fact, that we were ready to reproduce it in New York City. My ideas needed big city mass and word of mouth. It was a bit daunting, given the size and scope of New York and a culture I wasn't familiar with, but Da assured me we weren't opening another American bar.

The locals already had their favorite haunts, and small Irish pubs were a dime a dozen. He wanted to appeal to the melting pot and cater to the European community in Manhattan, hoping its international appeal would also attract the Americans by offering something different than they were used to. He was essentially taking the premise of my ideas for Dublin and turning it upside down for New York.

"Now where did you get such a fantastic idea?" I smiled. "Seriously, that is a brilliant marketing scheme."

"Learned it from an equally brilliant chap I know." Da clapped a hand on my back, taking care to avoid my bad shoulder.

"And what shall we call this brilliant joint venture?" I wondered.

"How about Finn's?"

"Again? Already been done, I'm afraid."

"All right then, how about we just use your full name? *Finnegan's*. It's not an everyday name, but it works. Sufficiently European without being inaccessible. And it keeps a bit o' the Irish in it as well."

"I like it! Perhaps you've missed your calling," I teased, elbowing him softly.

He smiled proudly.

"You can name it anything you like, you know. We don't have to name it after me." I offered.

"Yes. We do."

I smiled awkwardly back. Apparently, the subject was closed, although I'm not sure why. It was like that with Da sometimes. He just knew what he wanted and that was that. There was no use in arguing. I felt humbled by the gesture, and rather small.

We decided that Finnegan's would put a European flair on the idea of a New York night club. No food–just drinks, dancing and atmosphere. I emailed David, and he was super excited, insisting that I stay with him while the idea was getting off the ground. He also promised to talk it up amongst all the Broadway actors and dancers he knew.

With any luck we'd have another hit on our hands, but it would be a lot harder this time. Even with our commitment to a European club idea, in New York we'd be starting from scratch. At least in

Ireland we knew the culture. Da said we needed to forget about the American culture and just stick to building what we know. He felt certain it would work, and as I've said before, Da had great instincts when it came to business.

We were set to leave the following week. I was feeling good about things in general. I could have a drink or even two without anything getting out of hand. Even the near-miss of a one-night stand in France with Celeste hadn't caused me to tip overboard and go on a bender, and my head felt clearer than it had been in months. It was time. I took a few days off and went to see Regan.

32

W e hadn't spoken a word since the night I left her standing on her stoop. I tried to remember the bloke who did and said those awful things, but he was long gone, and I couldn't go to America without telling her how sorry I was. She deserved to hear the whole story–to be allowed to ask questions, and I needed to be able to answer those questions soberly.

I considered just showing up at her flat, but decided it was probably better to call first, just to be sure. Sure enough, she chose not to return my call, but instead emailed a response, saying it was fine for me to come, but if I wanted to speak to her alone, we should meet somewhere other than her flat. I couldn't really blame her, after the way I'd behaved, so we arranged a dinner out and I flew to London.

When she walked into the restaurant, I felt supercharged. I was seated at a table toward the back and watched all the heads in the place turn as she walked through the door. She was oblivious, scanning the restaurant purposefully until she found me. The waiter took her coat, but I got up to seat her myself, and kissed her cheek lightly in greeting.

"It's good to see you," I started. "You're looking well."

"As are you." She looked me over. "What's the occasion?"

I glanced at my sport coat and trousers. It wasn't like I was wearing a tie. "What do you mean?"

"You're all dressed up."

"I'm just trying to make my best impression."

"Well you'll do that with your words, if that's the case."

"Don't worry. I plan to." I was suddenly glad for the sport coat. It helped take the chill off. I smiled and sipped my water.

Regan didn't fail to notice the decided lack of alcohol on the table. "Did you just arrive? Where's your drink?"

"Would you like something? Bottle of white wine perhaps?"

"Perfect."

I signaled the waiter who brought the chilled, waiting bottle. The glasses were promptly filled, and the bottle left in an ice bucket next to the table. She looked almost annoyed at my presumption. I guess I hadn't learned much from Kathleen after all.

"So. You called this meeting. What's up?" She sipped carefully.

"I was hoping it could be less of a meeting and more of a dinner between old friends."

"Well then, I guess we should get the business part out of the way first."

She had every right to be upset, but I hadn't expected such an icy reception. I looked at her in all sincerity. "I'm so sorry."

She put both elbows up on the table and leaned forward. "And what exactly are you sorry for?"

"Would you like me to make a list?" I tried my charming smile but the heat from her face melted it almost immediately.

"Why not let me? Let's see...Perhaps you're sorry for getting so drunk that you came on to a *married woman*? Or maybe it's the complete silence you've kept since then, seeing as you haven't bothered to call, write, or otherwise let me even know you were alive!"

"I can explain-"

"But I think-" She stopped me mid-sentence, held one finger in the air, drank the rest of her wine, then left me hanging while she poured herself a second glass. "Perhaps what I'm most curious about is whether you're sorry you *slept* with me, or sorry that you told me—which is it?"

"I'm sorry about all of it." I swallowed, feeling the red creep up my neck. "Except for the sleeping with you part, if we're being honest."

I too downed the rest of my wine. If there was a night for a little overindulgence, this would certainly qualify. I didn't know how else to get through the rest of the conversation.

"I'd like that," she replied.

"You'd like what?"

"Honesty."

"Well, I'm here to give it to you."

"I'm all ears." She sat back, arms across her chest, challenging me with her eyes.

I'd gone over it a thousand times in my head but sitting in front of her confused all my circuits. Being around her had always been like that for me.

"After I left that night, you wouldn't have wanted to hear from me, believe me."

"What I would have *liked* is an explanation of what the hell you were talking about." Her arms were still crossed, and her eyes blazed with a fire I'd seldom witnessed in her.

"I know, I shouldn't have left you standing there like that."

"You threw it in my face!" She leaned forward again. "Knowledge so intimate it was bound to crush me, and yet you brought the hammer down without remorse and left me there wondering just what the hell you were talking about! Then you topped it off with eighteen *months* of deafening silence."

She was right, and I had no excuse. None.

"Do you have any idea how I've struggled since then to figure it out, only to finally have a dream about you one night that was so real I woke up embarrassed? Do you enjoy toying with a person like that?"

I looked at her in all seriousness. "In the dream, was it the night of my twenty-first birthday, by any chance?"

She went white. "That was *real*?"

So she did remember. At least a little. I nodded slowly.

She put her face in her hands. "Oh God. Oh my God!"

When her hands dropped to the table, I grabbed onto them. She looked up at me with tears in her eyes. I'd always hated seeing her cry and this time was no different. Her hands were trembling, and I knew it was as real for her that night as it was for me. She may have blocked it out initially, but eventually the memories came back.

"When did you know? The whole time?"

She shook her head violently. "Not until you said those things, and then it ate away at me and about drove me batty!"

I held her hands tighter to keep her from hysterics. She started to calm down and we sat there just looking at each other, my heart throbbing in my ears.

She took a deep breath and blew it out. "When I dreamed about it, it was so real, I thought it had to be a memory."

"I guess the truth has a way of coming out eventually."

"Why didn't you tell me before?"

I shrugged. "I wasn't going to tell you at all. I thought it would be easier that way."

"Easier for whom?"

"For me, of course. Selfishness is what I do best, remember?"

"Selfish?" She pulled her hands away, color creeping into her cheeks. "That's not how I remember it."

I blinked back surprise. I guess she was more present that night than either of us realized. It may have been the only time I'd ever given myself to a woman like that, but I'd given all I had, and it was comforting to know she had seen that side of me.

"After you got out of the hospital you never mentioned it, so I assumed you blocked it out. I thought if you knew, it would change everything between us, and I never wanted that. Besides, after all that teasing and me pursuing you all those years, if you knew you were the one that started it that night-"

"What did you say?"

My eyebrows went up. "Do you think that *low* of me? Did you think I took advantage of you? Really? After all we've been through, I have always respected your boundaries."

"Yes, but–"

"But nothing. And I'm not saying this to soothe my pride."

Her eyes narrowed. Clearly, she was unconvinced.

"Do you want to hear what you said? Maybe that will jog your memory."

"You still remember what I said?"

I hadn't rehearsed this part, but it needed to be said. If nothing else she needed to know what that night had meant to me. "Look, I know you're a married woman now, but you weren't then. You may not even understand this, based on your perception of the kind of man I am, but spending that one night with you changed my whole world. It was the single most amazing night of my life to date, and considering the number of women I've been with, I'd say you should just take the compliment."

I sat back and took a breath, wiping a hand over my face. "I can recount every moment of that night. Every word. Every touch. And it has haunted my every relationship since."

She was crying then. Real full tears rolling down her face. "Tell me what I said."

I swallowed. There was really no turning back now. "You said, *You're a grown man now Finn. I think it's time I showed you what I meant.*"

Her face fell and she stared at me through those gray-green pools, and that was the clincher. I knew then that she really did remember, but I kept going anyway, just to prove my point.

"You slipped my jacket off and pulled my shirt out of my trousers." I took a deep breath, reliving it. "We made love for hours. I don't know how many times. It all ran together."

"Stop."

"No, listen! I have to explain this."

She took another long drink and drained her wine glass, then nodded at me to continue.

"All those years, you'd been babbling on about finding someone you wanted to get lost in. Someone who you were friends with first, and the sex was just an extension of the intimacy that already existed."

She shook her head. "I can't believe you were listening all that time."

I smiled sadly. "I'm more than you think I am."

She grabbed my hand. "No, that's where you've got it wrong, Finn. You are everything I've always known you to be. I just saw it first."

I pulled my hand away. I'd never get through the rest of my speech with her touching me like that. "That night proved to me that my way was indeed...inferior. Making love to you was almost *spiritual* in nature. All our collective faults, all our weaknesses laid bare and yet there we were, in the most intimate of acts, sharing love and friendship in a way I'd never experienced before." I took a drink. "Or since."

She sat there shaking her head.

"I don't know how else to explain it, except that being with you was like coming home again."

"But—"

"Don't worry! I know, all right? I know we're not meant for one another. I know you've known that from the start, it just...took me a little longer to come around." I smiled weakly. "But what you gave me was hope. Hope that perhaps I could someday find that kind of love on my own."

"Finn, I had no idea. I'm so sorry."

I ignored her apology. After all, what did she have to apologize for? "After that, everything else seemed empty."

"Is that why you left?" She blinked several times. "Is that why you joined the service? Did you have a death wish?"

"Not a death wish. I just needed a life that wasn't full of excess. My entire life I had everything I wanted except the one thing that was most important. I guess I went searching for a way to strip away everything that was unnecessary."

"And did you find it?"

"In a way, yes."

"So Sandhurst was out. That makes more sense now."

I just nodded. We'd been through some of this already. "When Kathleen got pregnant, I realized I was marrying someone I didn't love. Although the sex was great, and we had a lot of fun together it wasn't...intimate. And I lost that hope."

We were quiet for a while, just letting it sink in around us.

She sat back against her chair, her shoulders sagging as the tension finally melted away from our relationship. "What happened after you left me that night? Where have you been since then?"

"I think we'll need some food in our stomachs for that one. Are you ready to order?"

We made small talk about her work and family until our food came, and then I told her about my journey. The painkillers and the drink, the pubs and the bus ride, the old woman and the visions. I even told her about Peter, James, and John.

Sometimes she held my hands as we talked, especially when we got to the part about Declan and Bree, but it wasn't romantic. We were back to being two friends with an incredible amount of personal history, sharing a meal and sharing our lives.

"How is it you came back from that? I mean, how does one even recover from that level of addiction. How is it you're even drinking right now?"

We talked about Nana and the second sight. About the way Nana spoke to me and brought me through the sickness and pain of withdrawal.

"She sounds like an amazing woman, crazy or not."

"I think we're all a little crazy." I laughed. "Some of us are just more honest about it than others."

Her laugh was warm and real, and she still took my breath away. I took a mental snapshot of that moment and filed it away. A beautiful image of the only person in the world who knew all there was to know about me.

"I'm going to New York to start a new bar with Da. We renovated his pub in Dublin, and it's been a big success. We're going to try a similar thing in New York City, with dancing though–more like a nightclub."

She pushed her plate away and stared at me. "I'm so proud of you Finn. You're like, a completely different man." She smirked. "And I must say, you're rather attractive this way. Why, if I wasn't a married woman..."

"Well, isn't that just my luck!" I laughed, throwing my napkin at the table for effect. "After all these years, *now* you find me attractive?"

"No, you were pretty hard to resist even when you were an arsehole."

"Thanks. Thanks a lot."

"I mean that in the best way possible."

"I'm sure you do."

She tilted her head. "I love the bit of hair along your jawline. What do they call that? A chinstrap, isn't it?"

"Yes, and you're making me self-conscious."

"How ever do you fight them off now?"

"Who? The women?"

She nodded. "I recall saving you quite a few times, but there were plenty more you didn't want to be saved from."

I shrugged. "I'm not looking for a one-night stand anymore." I poured the last of the second bottle into her glass. "You probably won't believe me when I tell you this, but I haven't been with a woman since Kathleen died."

She nearly choked on her wine. "What?"

"It's true." I pushed my plate away and ordered dessert and coffee.

"Well, I'll be damned."

I wiped a hand along my eyebrows. My tolerance wasn't what it used to be, and an entire bottle of wine was messing with my head. I blinked a couple of times.

"And a lightweight at that! Who would believe me if I told them?" She laughed.

"Not me."

"Me either." Regan smiled. "But I do like you this way. Promise me we'll keep in touch from now on. I don't care if you're in New York. Computer geniuses were built for just such occasions. I'm not kidding. Promise me!"

I looked across the table, surprised and grateful. I hadn't expected her forgiveness, much less an offer to reinstate our friendship.

"Done." I smiled, grateful.

"And Finn?" She smiled back. "I do remember that night. It was beautiful, and I'm not ashamed of it. I've always loved you. And I'll always be your friend."

SETTLED COMFORTABLY INTO FIRST CLASS, on my way to New York, the old woman's voice was in my head once again.

 "You have the sight, but not the wisdom."

I wondered what she would say to me now. The gift hadn't changed. I still had no control over it, but I hoped there was more wisdom than there'd been before.

 Follow it. It will lead you away from the bloodshed and the tears.

THIS PATH HAD TAKEN me the long way around my stubborn heart, but looking back, I'm not so sure I could have learned it any other way. So far, my dreams and visions had been right on track. With any luck, maybe someday they would lead me to a woman I needed more than life or breath, and in her arms, although I might be lost, I'd finally find home again.

EPILOGUE

"You're going to love it. I promise!"

"That's what you said about hot dogs, but I never want to eat one of those again either."

"Dude. Stop. This is Yankee Stadium, and baseball is an iconic American tradition. Can't you feel the excitement? I mean, look at all these people!"

"It's lovely. Really."

Finn's mind was elsewhere. Back at the bar, back in Ireland. Anywhere but at a baseball game in a city which seemed to allude him. He knew he was there for a reason, but the last several months he'd been unsuccessful in figuring out why. He couldn't keep his thoughts fixed on the stadium or the people or even the beer he was holding, which was, in fact, a terribly watered-down affair in a flimsy plastic cup that could scarcely be gripped without crushing it and sloshing the beer all over.

He must have made a terrible face when he tasted it the second time, because David looked over and laughed, then flagged down the nearest concessions waiter and switched Finn's drink out for a Coke.

"There. Is that better? Still iconic, still solidly American."

"But considerably more drinkable." Finn laughed and shook his head.

"You haven't been outside the bar in weeks. It's time you had some fun."

"All right then. Explain the game to me."

It wasn't a difficult concept. The rules were simple, and they had fairly decent seats from which to watch the action, but the game was long and only somewhat interesting. Not like Gaelic Football. Here, the players barely ever even made contact! He would have left if it hadn't been for David's obvious excitement. That, and the fact that he didn't actually have anything else to do besides paperwork and inventory.

When it was over, they made their way out with the crowd. There was a girl with dark hair walking just up ahead. All at once the hair on Finn's neck stood up, as if the air pressure had changed and it was about to storm. He looked up, but there wasn't a cloud in the sky. A strong arm pushed him from behind and the man cursed, telling him to keep moving. Finn stumbled forward a few steps then went sideways, and his hand gripped that stupid plastic cup even tighter, launching his Coke all over the shirt of the dark-haired girl. She stopped suddenly and so did time.

With the napkin he was still holding in his other hand, he reached out reflexively to try to help. To try to erase this horrible stain that was quickly soaking into her shirt.

It was then that the world went momentarily black as his face exploded with pain. His eyes watered up as he bent over, massaging his nose. She was shaking her hand out and yelling something, but all he could see through the film of tears covering his eyes was her face coming into focus.

It was her.

REVIEWS / NEWSLETTER

Leave a Review

Thanks for reading *Finn Again*! Your support makes it possible for this independent author to continue creating.

If you liked what you read, please **leave an honest review**! Your feedback really is invaluable.

Newsletter

I send out a newsletter with updates once a month, and they're packed full of news, updates, and **unpublished writing that you, my subscribers get first!**

I don't sell or give your email to any third parties, nor do I use them for any other purposes.

Just updates. You have my word.

Sign up here:

http://createdtofly.com/**newsletter**/

ABOUT THE AUTHOR

Lynda Meyers is an award-winning author, nurse, yoga instructor, reiki master, motorcycle enthusiast and world traveler. She has written fiction, non-fiction and poetry for newspapers and magazines and currently makes her home in the upper left corner of the United States.

For more information, visit: www.createdtofly.com

ACKNOWLEDGMENTS

 This is the part where I get to say that it takes a village, which happens to be true...

The people in my life for whom my heart overflows, who have supported me wholeheartedly and without wavering already know who they are. If I've done my part, they don't need to see it written on a page to know it's true. I don't know much, but these things I do know:

> *I have lived fully.*
> *Loved extravagantly.*
> *Been granted grace beyond measure.*
> *And learned, beyond a shadow of a doubt, that without*
> *   deep, authentic relationships nothing means anything.*

Special thanks, however, to my incredible children, without whom the light of my life would go out.

And to Wendel, who brought light back into the dark places.

Also to Wendy and Megan, whose oceanside birthing suite allowed this labor of love the perfect transition into life.

LYNDA
MEYERS

the
truth
about
truly

The companion novel to *Finn Again*

THE TRUTH ABOUT TRULY

BY: LYNDA MEYERS

She was the girl of his dreams.

It was a chance meeting, but Finn knew her at a glance. The likeness was unmistakable. Even her smell was familiar.

The problem was, Truly wasn't looking for love.

When Truly loved someone, it was a death sentence—and she wasn't going to have that on her conscience. Not again. Love and death were partners in crime, and she couldn't risk doing any more time.

Finn wasn't willing to give up. He'd cheated death twice in Afghanistan. Three times if you count nearly drowning in whiskey and painkillers. He'd been through scores of women, but had loved only once—until now.

His dreams didn't lie: this girl was his destiny. He needed to woo her. He needed to win her heart—*if he could just manage to stay alive.*

She wasn't looking for a knight in shining armor.

He wasn't looking for a beauty to rescue.

But one fateful night changed all that. For both of them.

EXCERPT: THE TRUTH ABOUT TRULY

"Life is short. Break the rules. Forgive quickly. Love truly. Laugh uncontrollably, and never regret anything that makes you smile."
M.T.

Prologue

FINN

Baseball, as I'm sure you're aware, is generally considered a singularly American tradition. However, for us Brits and the Irish alike, we've been playing games with balls and sticks and running 'round bases for centuries. In fact, if you want to get technical, even the name "base-ball" was first coined in an English poem from the mid 1700s.

At any rate, it wasn't like I hated the game, or even hated America, which, at that point in our fledgling relationship had treated me quite well. I just–didn't want to be there, really. Crowds weren't exactly my thing, although if you take into account that I was running one of the more successful new nightclubs in Manhattan, I admit it seems a bit backwards.

I'd gone to Yankee Stadium with my friend David, who literally yanked me out of my office at the club and assured me a good time. I don't know how to tell you what happened when he told me where we were going. I just knew I had to go with him.

I guess I should back up a bit.

Three weeks earlier I'd been at my apartment, asleep, when an entire dream sequence blew through my mind. You know those dreams that feel so real that they creep inside you and make you wonder if you're crazy? That kind of a dream. This one was so real I could smell it.

It was about a girl with dark hair and fair skin and a gorgeous smile. Here's where it gets a bit dodgy: I'd seen her face twice before, and yet we'd never met. Once in a previous dream, and then again in a vision I had at Nana's when I was back in Ireland. Both times I'd been under extreme stress. The first was after an accident at sea that left three of my friends dead. The second was while I was having withdrawals from booze and painkillers.

But that's another story.

This particular dream brought her closer than ever. I opened the door to my apartment there she was, in a long trench coat and navy-blue high heels and this pair of legs that went on forever. I could feel my heart begin to race as soon as I saw her. We were familiar, she and I, but I knew somehow that we had never made love. She commented on my apartment as if she'd never seen it before.

I slipped the coat off her shoulders and her scent overwhelmed me. I still don't know what it was she was wearing. I've smelled a lot of women's perfumes before and this was unlike anything I knew. Of course, it was a dream, so perhaps that particular scent doesn't actually exist. Or maybe it isn't a perfume at all. Maybe it's just *her* scent. At any rate, it's stuck in my nose and even now the mere thought of it makes me catch my breath.

In the dream I poured us some wine and we danced in the

middle of my living room. I ran my fingers across the skin on her shoulders and down one arm, then followed with my mouth. If it's possible, she tasted even better than she smelled.

I was caught completely in her atmosphere. The colors faded away. The apartment faded away. I picked her up and carried her to my bed, but it was all very dream-like, as if we were encased in light. All I could see was her face. Her eyes. Her body underneath me. Something clicked into place when we kissed, like I was diving inside her and exploring from the inside out.

We made love for hours. Or at least, what seemed like hours in the dream. When the room came back into focus it was daylight and she was in my arms, and I knew only one thing: I never wanted to let her go.

The dream had been gnawing at the corners of my mind, just far enough outside of reality to dismiss it, but real enough that I could feel the electricity course through my skin when I remembered the details. This was a woman from my dream world, and yet she was so real to me I could have sworn she existed in this world as well. It was a strange sort of existence that often felt like accessing both realms at once.

The Celts have a name for this. They call it walking between the worlds. I didn't know if that's what I was doing, I only knew that my experiences over the past several years had raised a lot of questions that didn't have traditional answers.

But for now, back to the original story.

David and I were at Yankee Stadium. He was trying to cheer me up, I think. Not that I was depressed. More of a flat preoccupation with the business side of my life and absolutely no desire whatsoever to explore the life and culture of New York.

Ok, maybe I was a little depressed.

We got there and he ordered me a beer and a hot dog. He said these were the things you did at baseball games in America, so I went along with it, even though it was terrible and I ended up giving my hot dog to him to finish.

The beer wasn't much better. It was terribly flavorless and served in a plastic cup that a toddler could crush with one hand. Ridiculous, I know.

"You're going to love this. I promise." He said, taking a bite of my hot dog. "Look at all these people!"

The stadium in Dublin was about this size, and I'd been to football games there. Fans are fans, and these fans seemed as loyal to their teams as any other sport. Honestly, I was bored already. No offense to the sport itself or its fans.

"It's lovely, really."

I took another sip of that beer he'd given me and I must have made an awful face, because David snatched my beer from me and flagged down the nearest concessions waiter.

"He'll have a Coke please."

I laughed at his obvious annoyance but took a sip of the Coke and gave him an exaggerated smile.

"There, is that better? Coca-Cola. Still iconic, still solidly American." David chopped at the air with his hand.

"But considerably more drinkable." I laughed.

"You haven't been outside the bar in weeks. It's time you had some fun."

"Alright then. Explain the game to me." I set my drink down and prepared to concentrate as David went over the rules.

I tried to get into the game, but honestly all I could think about was the paperwork and inventory that needed to be done back at the bar. After the hot dog failure, David made me try an Italian Sausage with peppers and onions and a giant pretzel with mustard. I'm not a huge fan of mustard, so the pretzel was just so-so, but the sausage was fairly fabulous. The smell of it brought me back to Mary's place on the coast in Ireland. Mary owned a pub where I spent quite a bit of time. She was good people, Mary was.

A couple of kids sitting in front of us were arguing, the little girl clutching her doll as she pouted, and suddenly there in my mind were Declan and Bree, two precious wee ones that lived at Mary's place now. Like I said, that's a whole other story, but it felt more like a whole other lifetime.

The crowd kept cheering and David kept talking, but I was elsewhere. At the seventh inning stretch I got up to use the bathroom and as I walked through the crowds I caught a whiff of that scent. The one from my dream.

The girl. It was real?

I spun around, looking for her, but caught myself and chuckled. I was imagining things. I had to be. There were just too many memories today. Too much to pain that had to be put back away. The people in New York were fascinating to watch, though. I almost enjoyed that part of things more than the game itself, so I leaned against a post for a while, taking it all in. I still couldn't shake that feeling. Something was up, I just couldn't figure out what it was. Eventually, I made my way back down to our seats.

"Jesus, I thought maybe you fell in!" David said through a mouthful of pretzel.

"*Another* pretzel?"

"Yeah, I love these things. You want some?" He held it out to me but I shook my head and ordered another Coke. I would need to stay up if I wanted to finish that inventory.

When the game finished, we started threading our way through the crowd. I was still carrying my Coke, and a handful of napkins from our various food items. It was honestly very difficult to walk holding that flimsy cup and I was looking around for nearest trash bin to dispose of it when I got that strange electrical feeling I get sometimes when I know I'm supposed to pay attention.

My eyes searched for the source of the disturbance and I noticed two women walking a few paces ahead of us, one blond and the other brunette. That smell. That perfume. It couldn't be. When I looked at them again, the hair stood up on the back of my neck, as if the air pressure had changed and it was about to storm. I looked up, but there wasn't a cloud in the sky.

I must have slowed down way too much, because the guy behind me gave me a hard shove and told me to keep moving, which launched me forward into the shoulder of the girl. I tried to grip that cup as I stumbled and merely succeeded in squeezing its contents all over her shirt.

She stopped suddenly and so did time, as I reached over with the napkins in my other hand and tried desperately to dry her off. Her shirt was ruined, and I felt simply horrible.

Out of nowhere her fist came up and socked me right in the face. The world went black for just a moment, and luckily David caught me before I hit the ground, because—well, that would've been embarrassing. My eyes were watering so badly, all I could see was her shaking her hand out in front of me, yelling furiously. Finally her face came into focus and everything froze.

It was her. The girl from my dreams. But that was...impossible, right?

I blinked a few times, still massaging my nose, dumbfounded. She kept on yelling at me, as did her friend. David elbowed me and I began to apologize, but it didn't seem to help. A crowd was gathering around us and soon a security officer was standing there asking what the trouble was.

"This a-hole grabbed my breast, that's what the problem is!"

"I did not!" I insisted, trying to calm my voice. "Someone ran into me and my drink went flying. I was merely trying to help. I was just trying to clean off your shirt. I did *not* mean to touch you inappropriately."

The officer looked at me, massaging my nose and started laughing. "You punched him?"

"Yeah. I did," she answered. Her body language said she wouldn't mind doing it again.

"Good for you," the officer nodded, then turned to me and said some word I'd never heard before but I'm assuming it wasn't very nice. "You shoulda known better."

The officer dismissed us and walked away and so did the crowd. We were all standing there and the girl's friend started laughing.

Loudly. So did David. Some mate he was. The girl looked down at her shirt and looked up at me and her face broke into a gorgeous smile. I knew that smile. I still couldn't get over the fact that I knew that smile.

I stuck out my hand. "I'm Finn, and I'm extremely sorry I've ruined your shirt. Please, allow me to buy you a new one."

"I just punched you in the face." She looked down at her hand and splayed the fingers in and out a few times. "And you want to buy me a new shirt?"

Her eyebrows went up and she was shaking her head, still smiling. I couldn't stop staring at her. She was breathtaking.

"It's...the least I could do, really. I'm dreadfully sorry."

"No, it's ok. Truly."

She took my hand and shook it. "If you're sure," I tried to smile. "I don't think I caught your name." God, I wanted to know her name. I was fascinated and intrigued and aroused all at the same time. I tried to keep my eyes trained on her face, but the whole picture was simply beautiful. I tried not to imagine her in a trench coat and a pair of navy-blue heels.

"Truly" she said again. We were still shaking hands.

"Oh, I see. You'd rather not give me your name." My eyes fell and so did my hopes. Standing before me was, quite literally, the girl of my dreams, and I'd completely blown it and she didn't want anything to do with me. "I completely understand. It's...not a problem."

Her hand dropped away, and as she let go the smell of her perfume filled my senses. I breathed it in, and her head tilted slightly as she watched me.

"Her name is Truly," her friend added, with emphasis on the word *name*. "It's short for Trulane, but she hates it when people call her that, so if you don't want to get punched again, I'd stick with Truly."

The girl's eyes went wide. "That is a bold-faced lie!" She looked at me apologetically. "I don't normally punch people either. I'm really sorry. Is your nose alright?"

I wiggled it a bit, checking all the parts. "No harm done, but I must say, you've got quite the right hook for a girl. I've gotten less of a spin by some of the blokes I went to school with."

Her eyes narrowed a bit. "Yeah, well. I guess it was a reflex. Let's just call it good. We have to get going."

She grabbed onto her friend's arm, but her friend wasn't moving. She was looking at David, who was returning the favor.

"Yes. Of course," I offered. "Unless..." She waited. I wanted to know more. I needed to find out who she was. This chance, it was... one in a million. The odds were astronomical. Unless...

"...You'd at least let me buy you a cup of coffee?" That was what people in America liked to do, wasn't it? But maybe she didn't like coffee. I started throwing out other options "Or tea. Or...cocoa." It was no use. I dropped my head in defeat. I was making a fool of myself. "I obviously have no idea what you like to drink."

She was pulling her shirt out of her pants, looking down at the stains. "Well, I think I've had plenty of Coke, so something warm might be nice."

She looked back up and smiled at me again. That beautiful smile. I realized with some surprise that I couldn't hear any of the other people in the stadium. No one else existed. It was like I was in a time warp or a dream sequence, and yet, I knew it was real. And I wanted desperately to take the next step, whatever it might be.

"May we give you a ride?" I asked, as politely as I could. I wanted so much to be a gentleman after having been such a fool.

She and her friend looked at each other. Her friend, who's name turned out to be Kate, said to David "We were just going to take the subway."

"I'm going to need to change," Truly stated, wringing some of the wetness out of her shirt. It was stuck to her body beautifully, outlining the delicate lines of her collarbones and making me remember everything I loved about women.

"Perhaps we could share a cab," I offered. "We could drop by your place so you could change and then continue on?"

She was staring at me and I found myself reliving parts of my dream that I hadn't previously remembered. I swallowed with some difficulty, waiting for her answer.

"Ok" she smiled. "Why not. Kate?"

"You know me, sweetie. I'm always down."

David winked at me and we set off in the direction of the front gates. Hailing a cab isn't quite so difficult as one might imagine in the company of a woman wearing a wet t-shirt.

Chapter One

"Why not go out on a limb? That's where the fruit is."
M.T.

TRULY

Looking back, I can't say that I saw any of this coming. I didn't understand my own story, even when I was right in the middle of it. I wonder if it's like that for most people. It's true that Finn changed my life, but it was already changing - I just didn't know it at the time.

Finn came into my life when I just about had things all sewn up. I was working on my first novel and had a regular stream of freelance gigs in multiple magazines with decent circulation. I'd even published a few special interest pieces in The Times. I had a good relationship with one of the editors over there and he was considering bringing me in on a more regular basis. He liked my no-nonsense way of looking at life, and said New Yorkers seemed to like it too. I mean, let's face it—living in New York can be challenging. The only way to get through it is with good planning and a regular routine.

I'd written a piece about organizing stuff in your closet, followed up with one on organizing your financial stuff, then spread out to include menu stuff, trip stuff, "social media and other time sucking stuff". People were eating it up. They wanted to dub me "The Stuff

Girl." This worked for me. I liked having a place for everything and everything in its place.

It wasn't until Kate and I were in the back of that cab and I was looking into his beautiful eyes that I'd even considered the idea of veering off the path. I'm not even sure it was a conscious decision. He invited me out for coffee and for some reason I still can't explain, I said yes. There are a lot of things I can't explain when it comes to Finn.

That night the guys waited while we stopped by my apartment so that I could change my shirt. The minute we hit the steps, Kate was grilling me.

"You know I'm always up for a challenge, but you? I've known you three years and you've never done anything even remotely close to this! What's going on with you?"

"I really couldn't tell you." The hard New York edge was off of my voice and I was suddenly pensive and almost shy. "There was something in his eyes." I shrugged. "Something in my heart said yes."

"Yes, he's a stalker? Yes, you want to marry him? What does *yes* mean?"

"Yes, we should have coffee! Yes, I should forgive him for ruining my shirt. I don't know Kate, ok? Let's just see where this goes."

She leaned against the door in the hallway as I fumbled with my keys, repeating my words. "Let's just see where this goes?" Just inside the door she turned me to face the small mirror on the wall. "See this face? This girl?"

I looked. Really looked. "Yes. I see her."

"This is not a girl who says things like *Let's just see where this goes.* This is a girl who dots i's and crosses t's. A girl who makes lists and weighs pros and cons." She turned me back toward the door. "A girl with six different kinds of locks on her apartment to ward off stalkers and all but the sickest of thieves with death wishes. Who *are* you?"

She smiled at me then, and I knew she was just teasing. "Hey, I'm just saying is all."

I shook my head and walked to the bedroom, searching the left side of my closet, way back to two-thousand and one, and found the perfect shirt. It was a pale-pink, peasant number with some tiny polka dots in the piping.

"Pink?" Kate says to me. "In the whole time I've known you I have never *once* seen you in pink."

"I know." I winked at her. "Just trying to keep you on your toes."

"Truly you are an enigma."

"Thank you." I nodded and held the door open. "Shall we?"

Kate just kept shaking her head as she followed me out.

"And by the way, I only have three locks – not six," I reminded her.

"Whatever."

———

Down in the cab Finn had been lounging with his arm across the back bench, but he sat up straight and scooted right over when he realized we were at the window. His friend David jumped out and let the two of us in before squeezing next to Kate. Four in the back of a cab is cozy at best.

Kate and David were talking and laughing in no time. I, on the other hand, had no clue what I was doing there, so I figured we should start with the basics. I asked Finn what he did for a living.

"Well, when I'm not accidentally fondling perfect strangers, I run a company that develops new technology for film making. You know, CGI and what not. Dabble in some other ideas."

Dabble? Who said dabble anymore? "Oh. Really?"

"Did you think maybe I was a contract killer or a serial rapist then?"

"You have a very dry sense of humor." I replied.

"So I've been told. I don't mean to put you off though. Do I somehow not look the part of a computer geek?"

He was ridiculously handsome, and when he smiled, only one side of his mouth hooked up, kind of like a lazy eye but farther down. "Maybe it's the accent. I can't really place it. English or Irish?"

"Both actually." He grinned at me and laid it on extra thick, changing voices mid-stream and then melding them together at the end. "Me mum is a brit and me da is an Irishman. I'm afraid I favor them both at times."

"It's a bit confusing but...charming nonetheless." I smiled at him and could have sworn some sort of light twinkled in his eyes.

"And you? What is it you do?" He turned serious to match my earlier line of questioning. I couldn't tell if he was being polite or mocking me.

"Well, when I'm not being inappropriately fondled by half-breed Irishmen, I'm a writer."

"Oh!" He feigned a concerned look and leaned toward me a little. "Does that mean my less than gentlemanly conduct will be ensconced in the pages of a brilliant novel someday?"

"I'm not sure yet. Let's just see where this goes."

Kate eyed me again. She was right of course. I kept saying that. Why on earth did I keep saying that? I'm not a fly by the seat of your pants girl–what was I even doing?

A sigh escaped my lips and Finn looked over. "Bored already?"

"No, just arguing with myself."

His mouth curved up part way. "I hope you're winning."

"Always." He was staring at me. I hate it when people stare at me. "Let's go to a club!" I blurted.

Judging from the look on Kate's face, I'd already lost sight of the edge of the cliff. She looked at me as if I'd grown fur and an extra set of limbs.

Finn looked over at David with a raise of his eyebrows. "Who knew that unintentional abuse could bring about such sweet rewards?"

I leaned forward, shaking my head, and was about to give the cab driver an address when Finn scribbled something on a piece of paper and handed it up. The driver read what was written on it and nodded with a smirk of approval on his face.

We pulled up in front of an unassuming door with a couple of Greek Gods for bouncers and a line around the block. I sighed audibly. I had neither the time nor the inclination to spend an extra couple of hours waiting in the freezing cold. And I definitely wasn't dressed for it. Finn peeked at the line and smiled at me again.

"Shall we?"

This was turning out to be a colossal mistake. I tried to make eye contact with Kate, but she was already getting out of the cab. I knew that look—like we'd just stepped into Saks. I followed her eyes, but didn't see anything unusual. Just a bunch of freezing cold, well-dressed posers waiting to become yet another sardine in the can. I stood by the curb but didn't want to let go of the door. My instincts told me to just get back in the cab and say goodnight, but then a warm, gentle hand was on the small of my back, leading me toward the sidewalk.

Finn smiled at the Gods and they parted the waters. The ropes were unhooked and we walked through to the warmth of a techno-pop haze. The music was loud but not quite deafening. There was plenty of comfortable seating and the dance floor was spacious. Several bar areas spanned the two floors of converted warehouse and it actually seemed pretty well organized. Still a bar, but almost...civilized.

Suddenly I had a new idea for a piece for The Times. I started scanning the layout, making mental notes and pulling out a pad and pen for good measure. I quickly sketched out a couple of the seating ideas and drew a rough layout of the main floor.

"Hey, what's this place called?" I looked up at Finn, all business, and he started to laugh.

He looked down at my drawing and back at me, puzzled. "Planning a party? Good luck. I heard you've got to book this place a year in advance and the owner's a real hard-ass."

"A party?" I shook my head, frustrated. "No, of course not!" I dismissed him. How absurd. Why would I want to plan a party at a place like this? Dissatisfied, I turned to his friend David. "I need the name of this place."

I followed David's grin and it landed on a matching face to my right. "It's called Finnegan's."

The bulb now fully lit above my head, I proceeded to close my mouth and try to act unimpressed. I nodded in Finn's direction. "Is there any other *dabbling* I should know about? Diamond mines, oil refineries, that kind of thing?"

He looked like a schoolboy–embarrassed almost, although it was hard to tell if he was blushing in the dim light. It was adorable and I found my eyes trailing down to his lips as the one side of his mouth curved up. I blinked, shaking my head and forcing my eyes away from his face.

He laughed softly and hooked a finger under my chin so I'd look at him again. "Can I get you a drink?"

I composed myself quickly. He'd ignored my question about the dabbling, so I moved on. Who knows how many women he'd brought here like this, trying to impress them with his Moses act. He waited patiently for my response.

"Well, I don't know. What's good here? Do they have any specialties?"

Finn watched me with interest. I watched right back. He hesitated, then answered. "As far as I know there's not a drink on the planet they can't make. You name it, they've got it."

"Really! Well, color me happy! Let's see if they can make me my favorite."

I threaded my way through the crowd to the nearest bar. Finn was right on my heels. The bartender was an experienced looking fellow, about twice Finn's age with a sort of blonding gray hair but similar blue eyes that smiled at me before his mouth ever started its ascent. Finn leaned sideways on the bar and watched me, awaiting his victory lap.

I slid effortlessly onto a black leather stool and leaned both arms on the deep, polished mahogany. "Caipirinha please."

The man nodded and pulled out a fresh lime, which he cut into several wedges, adding them to a hefty-sized rocks glass with a couple teaspoons of sugar. After mashing them together for a couple of minutes he pulled the telltale red, black and yellow bottle of 51 Pirassununga from a shelf behind him and poured some out, shaking it with a good dose of ice before pouring it over the fruit mixture.

The way Finn watched me made me feel warm and wanted, invited to participate fully in his experience of life. He was laughing again.

"What's so funny?" I looked around for Kate, but she and David had made their way to one of the dance floors and I was alone with Finn and the two hundred or so other blurs that surrounded his face.

"I don't know. Just didn't peg you for a girl who'd spent time in Rio."

I took a sip of my drink and found it perfect. The slow burn that always followed the sweet, tangy smoothness made its way down my esophagus and somehow landed south of where it belonged. I didn't like where this was going.

The bartender tilted his head slightly as he looked at me. "How is it?"

"Oh! It's great! Thank you!" I started to reach into my purse for a twenty but he shook his head. I looked at him, then at Finn.

"Shall we go find a seat?" A glass of clear liquid had made its appearance on the bar next to Finn and he scooped it up in one fluid motion.

"Ok. Sure." I nodded.

Finn tapped the top of the bar twice and grinned at the bartender. "Thanks, da."

There was that hand on my lower back again. I was beginning to feel like the proverbial sheep being led to slaughter. "Da? Nice, Finn. Nice."

He laughed heartily then. "I thought you'd like that one."

We slid into a comfortable booth. "So this is your dad's place then?"

"It's a joint venture."

"Oh yeah? Who started out smoking the joint?"

Finn laughed out loud. "He provides the money, and I provide the planning and *urban design* that makes it a hit."

I looked around again and remembered the article idea. He'd planned this out? It was really well done. Definitely a hit.

"How long do you make people wait out there in the cold?"

He glanced toward the door. "As long as it takes to keep critical mass but not overwhelm it. People like to know it's popular, but they want to be able to breathe as well."

I hooked my thumb toward the doors. "And that's where Venus and Apollo come in?"

He grinned at me. "Yes. Exactly." His arm was still up on the back of the seat, and I liked that it was above me, even if we weren't touching. His other arm was up too. It wasn't like he was trying to put his arm around me, but I found myself wishing he would. I shook my head again. This was completely absurd. Where was Kate when I needed her? I scanned the dance floor but she was nowhere to be found.

Finn tipped his head sideways and studied me. "Who's winning now?"

I looked over. "What? Winning what?"

"The argument you keep having with yourself."

I sat up a little straighter. "I am. I told you, I always win these arguments. I don't stand a chance against myself."

His eyes narrowed and he took a sip of his drink. "So, how is it you came to be fond of Cachaca? Are you sure you've never been to Brazil?"

"Only in my mind." I took another sip, but he still wasn't tracking with me. "Ever read John Updike?"

He shook his head.

"He wrote a book called *Brazil* back in 1995. Kind of a Tristan and Isolde story line."

"Well, see now? I hadn't pegged you for a romantic either."

Ok, so that made me a boring homebody who watched psychological thrillers?

He took a slow, deep breath in and I watched his chest rise and fall. He was very purposeful when he spoke. "What does the book have to do with Cachaca?"

"I don't know, it was the beverage of choice in the story, so I tried it once and I really liked it. It felt exotic to me, even though in Brazil it's a poor man's drink." I took a long sip of my Caipirinha and this time the burn went to my head.

He watched me with some amount of amused concern. "You know, they say Cachaca is like Tequila in some ways. Too much can cloud your judgment."

I nodded. "So I've heard." Finn wasn't the only one who kept things close to his chest. He didn't need to know my history. I was feeling self-conscious, and more than a little angry with Kate for deserting me.

"I like your shirt."

I shot Finn a look. "Excuse me?"

"Your shirt. It's much better than the other one."

"You mean the ruined one?"

His eyes rolled back and his head followed. He did seem genuinely sorry. "Are you certain you won't let me reimburse you for it?"

"Positive."

"Pink. Hmm."

I shook my head. "What is it with you and this shirt thing?"

His head pulled back as if I'd pushed into his personal space. "I just didn't peg you for a pink girl."

It was my turn to raise my eyebrows. I wondered if he knew he was actually going backwards in the point-making game?

"But I like it. It creates this...fascinating contrast." He rolled his hand in a circle as if to frame my head.

I looked down at my shirt. It was pale pink against my winter-white skin, which at this point in my fluorescent light existence was almost translucent.

"I'm sorry, did you say contrast?" I had to raise my voice a bit because the music had ramped up.

Just then David and Kate plopped down, obviously exhausted. She looked over at Finn. "Your friend's a great dancer! I haven't had this much fun in ages!"

Finn smiled and raised his voice to match the increase in volume. "David dances professionally."

It was Kate's turn to be surprised. "Really! Where?"

David shrugged. "Mostly off Broadway. Trying to break in still."

Kate nodded, satisfied. She'd studied at the School of Performing Arts, but never really ventured out past graduation, and hadn't gotten picked up by a dance company. Instead she taught at one of the modern dance studios on the Upper East Side and helped with choreography at the high school in her neighborhood.

"Well, Kate graduated from PA!" I offered with a grin. She kicked me under the table.

"No kidding!" David leaned forward and they ascended into their own little version of dancer's heaven, leaving Finn and I sitting there, staring at one another.

"Can I get you another?" He was staring at my empty glass.

My eyes were already having a little trouble staying focused. I knew I'd lose my cool if I had another and we ended up alone together, but at the time I didn't really care.

"You bet."

"Well, aren't you a brave one?"

"And what is it you're drinking over there? Water?"

"Vodka. And I'll join you in a second round if you don't mind."

I smiled. "I think I'd mind if you didn't."

He was gone in a flash and David followed his lead after getting Kate's order. As soon as they were out of sight, Kate was right in my face.

"What the hell are you drinking?" She picked up my glass and sniffed it. "Oh, no you don't. What are you, crazy? You never order that crap anymore. Don't you remember the last time you drank that poison?"

"Of course I do." I could tell I had a dumb smile on my face already. Kate looked over at the bar. Finn and David were talking to Finn's father. "He is fine. I'll give you that."

As I was watching he looked over at me. Neither of us smiled or made any overt gestures, yet our faces entered into an entire conversation. He just stared and I couldn't break my gaze loose. I couldn't figure out if he was playing me or if I'd somehow entered a parallel universe. Maybe he was right. Maybe he would need to be ensconced in a brilliant narrative someday.

The two of them walked back toward us with drinks in hand, but if I didn't get up and move a bit I'd be sorry when it came time to drink that second round. Before Finn reached the booth I slid out and took the two glasses from his hands, setting them down on the table behind me.

I grabbed his hands, and they were both cold. He must drink his vodka chilled. "Do you dance?"

"Not if I can help it, but I'm willing to embarrass myself if you are."

I pulled him toward the dance floor. "Who said I was going to embarrass myself?"

Before we could weave our way through the crowd the song slowed down and I eyed him suspiciously, scanning the room for the DJ's box. "Did you do that?"

He smiled smugly. "Do what?" In one fluid motion he dropped one of my hands and wrapped his securely around my waist, spinning me toward him until we were face to face. His hand was warm again, surprisingly warm, and I was thankful for whoever dimmed the lights on the dance floor, certain that my cheeks now matched the color of my shirt.

I too had danced much of my life, but the way he moved me around made me feel like an extension of his arms and legs. We flowed easily together, like two rivers into the same ocean.

If this was foreshadowing, I was in for an awfully long fall.

It's important to note here that I wasn't looking for a relationship. At that moment I can honestly say it was pretty close to the farthest thing from my mind. Kate was right. The last time I had Cachaca I'd ended the night with a guy that turned out to be the biggest mistake of my life. Fast-forward two years, including the nine months I spent in therapy, and I was just getting my life back on track. I didn't need a distraction, but then again, I'd forgotten what it felt like to be held by someone who wanted to match his rhythm with mine.

The idea was tempting. The guy was quicksand.

Read this book...

STEEL JOURNEYS, BOOK 1:

THE ROAD TO PATAGONIA

Join Abby Steel on a series of breathtaking international adventures with Steel Journeys - an all-female motorcycle touring company where she calls all the shots. From huts to hotels, it's never the same adventure twice.

To some people, home might be wherever you lay your helmet, but for Abby Steel, home was wherever she laid her ass. Today it's a Harley. Tomorrow it might be a BMW or a Triumph or a Honda. Home was whatever bike fit the terrain. Home was wide open spaces tucked under an expansive sky.

Home was the road.

It took a lot of miles to work through the hurts of her past, but she's finally built a business she can be proud of. Women from all walks of life come to join in her adventures, for all sorts of reasons. Equal parts badass and life coach, Abby genuinely cares about the women on her tours, and they respect her for it.

The Road to Patagonia finds Abby back home in California on a break between trips, when an unexpected visitor threatens to bring all the blocks tumbling down.

STEEL JOURNEYS: THE ROAD TO PATAGONIA

EXCERPT

Abby Steel hadn't seen the inside of her own apartment in over three years. There hadn't been any need to come home really, so she just... didn't. Life on the road kept her busy and building her own business had taken way more time and energy than she'd anticipated.

She looked at the compulsively clean apartment and was thankful, once again, that her sister came and dusted the surfaces once a month. It wasn't as if she'd left it dirty, but time and dust had a way of accumulating in equal and inevitable measure. Lauren had also been nice enough to retrieve her mail from the post office when it no longer fit in her box, getting rid of all the junk mail and opening anything that seemed important. There wasn't much. Abby had very few bills outside the business, most of which were handled remotely.

At this point, she was thankful for familiar surroundings and the chance to recharge. Three years was a long time to be away. It was time to reconnect with her roots and what was left of her family. Riding back from Alaska, many miles had been spent dreaming about long showers and luxurious baths with unlimited hot water. The grime that had built up under her fingernails would need to be soaked and scrubbed, her hair untangled and brushed—things life on the road rarely allowed for.

It would be good to see Lauren and her nieces in the flesh, instead of over video chat. She was excited to share stories of her adventures and show off her pictures, but seeing them would have to wait until she had energy for endless questions from curious little girls. She sat down in one of the comfortable side chairs in the living room with a glass of water and a stack of mail, but barely got through half of it before falling asleep.

When she woke up, the sun had dipped below the horizon, shrouding the apartment in a kind of eerie glow that reminded her of sunsets on the Spanish plains just outside Sevilla. She closed her eyes and let the scene linger in her mind, colors bursting across the open sky with the sweltering summer heat billowing up inside her leather jacket. Riding there had been nothing short of magical. A lot of places felt that way.

It was the magic that kept her on the road. Each new place had its own set of challenges, its own set of charms. The challenges faded, but the charms remained, decorating her memories and dangling from her heart.

For Abby, the constant drifting from place to place created an unusual sort of routine that was comforting in its uncertainty. Lauren thought it was crazy, never knowing where she was going to sleep or what dangers might lurk around the corner, but one person's danger is another person's thrill. She and Lauren, they were wired differently, that's all.

California's Napa Valley had been home for thirty-three years, but she left the small-town of Calistoga with an insatiable need not just to see, but to fully experience all the world had to offer. By that time, she'd already seen most of the US, and a good portion of Canada, but those had all been shorter trips—three weeks at most.

Culture shock becomes something of a nonissue when you're constantly changing cultures. Eventually, the life she'd left in California was no longer the ruler by which she measured all of her other experiences. Instead, her old life became just one of many other foreign concepts, all blended together in a beautiful mélange.

Living abroad had changed so many of her perspectives that her old worldview seemed distorted by comparison.

Leaving the confines of the continental United States and choosing to travel the world turned out to be a polarizing decision. Three years later, she felt like a completely different version of herself.

Being back in her apartment, surrounded by all the furniture and artwork she'd left behind was its own sort of culture shock. They were her belongings, of course, but all the things she thought she would miss had eventually faded into the background. They'd been replaced by people, places, smells, and tastes of a life too vibrant and varied to be contained within four walls.

The life she had built before was there on the walls and in the furniture, blended into the color scheme. They defined a person she wasn't sure existed anymore. A part of her recognized it, was even comforted by the deep familiarity, but an even bigger part wondered if it was possible to go back in time. Time seemed to have gone on without her.

Maybe coming home wasn't a matter of choosing now or then, but rather, allowing the new to inform the old, and the old to make space for the new. If her life was a tree, like the sadhu in India had told her, then she could never hope to become a different tree. The new experiences would instead have to be grafted onto the trunk, eventually growing together into a unique expression of life.

Steel Journeys was a company she had founded all on her own, most of the seed money coming from her inheritance. Lauren had used her half to build a house in the suburbs and was raising two beautiful daughters. Abby chose to pay off debt, buy a condo, and set off on the adventure of a lifetime. She'd spent the past three years researching the best roads, the best views, and the best options for lodging in dozens of countries, taking copious notes and pictures, giving out business cards, and forming business relationships.

Cataloging it all had been a labor of love, born of passion and drive. Each new place had its own rugged truths waiting to be discovered. She filled several paper journals with notes and sketches, cross-referenced with digital galleries.

She couldn't recall precisely when the idea for the business hit her—it was somewhere between Bangkok and Ho Chi Minh City. Like a reformed smoker she suddenly, desperately wanted other women like her to experience the freedom she had seen, felt, heard, smelled, and tasted. That was the dream—to form a women's motorcycle touring company and take it global.

"What, the entirety of the United States isn't enough for you?" Lauren had asked.

The answer was simple. It wasn't enough. It would never be enough. Wanderlust was embedded deep in her DNA—so deep, in fact, that she wasn't sure where it ended and she began.

Lauren was happy being a soccer mom and living in the suburbs. She was a card-carrying member of the PTA. The only cards Abby carried were a Visa and her gun permit. She didn't carry her gun internationally, of course, but traveling solo had taught her a thing or two about self-protection. Tucked into remote corners of the globe, far from big cities and police patrols, the rules were different. Street smarts were learned, and she had learned plenty.

It *was* a long time to be away, but for Abby, home was a concept, not a place. To some people, home might be wherever you laid your helmet, but for Abby, home was wherever she laid her ass. Home was her saddle, which for the last three years had been a Harley, and before that a BMW, a Triumph, and a custom café racer she'd rebuilt with her dad. Home was the wind in her face and wide-open spaces tucked under an expansive sky.

Home was the road.

This homecoming—this apartment—was one more stop along the way. It was the obligatory reset point on a map filled with push-pins. Except, of course, this room was tastefully decorated, with a comfortable bed, down blankets, and the best sheets money could buy. That bed was calling to her, and the rest would have to wait.

She woke the next morning with dirt on the sheets and little balls of dirt surrounding her jeans, which were hastily removed and crumpled up in the corner like a one-night stand. Perhaps a shower might have been the better choice before bed, but it was still a hundred times cleaner than most of the places she'd lived recently. Dirt was a part of life, and the only thing it damaged was a person's sense of expectation. She put it out of her mind and padded toward the bathroom.

The requisite extra-long shower, complete with a double scrubbing of her hair, ears, fingernails, and feet took longer than strictly necessary. Lauren was expecting her, but after three years, what was another thirty minutes? When she felt reasonably satisfied with her results, she filled the bathtub with lavender-scented Epsom salts and soaked, with the sun streaming through the glass block window.

As she soaked, she listened to pan flutes and meditation music that reminded her of some of the temples and monasteries she'd visited in India. She only spent a few weeks there, barely scratching the surface of just one region, and there was still so much to see and explore. Indian people were very kind to her, and she admired their deep spirituality. It was definitely on her *must-return* list.

She emerged from the bath and pulled a long, clean, white T-shirt and some yoga pants out of the closet. "Well hey there, guys! I haven't seen you in forever!" She paused for a moment, staring at the sheer volume of clothing neatly arrayed before her and shook her head. After surviving for so long on two perpetually wrinkled shirts and one tank top, it all seemed so extra.

Still, it felt amazing not to be wearing jeans or leathers, and *not* sweating into a helmet for a couple of hours was a delicious thought. Most of the time she wore her thick brown hair up or braided to keep it out of her face. She decided to blow it out a little and let the ends curl up naturally with some leave-in conditioner. She'd barely noticed how long it had become. Upon closer inspection, it was desperately in need of a trim, but split ends would have to wait.

Life's sense of urgency was something that had mellowed over the miles. Time was slower in other parts of the world. Life was about the experience. Relationships. Good conversations. Being present in the now was something she was still working on, but an area where she'd seen a hell of a lot of improvement.

It was satisfying to think that some measure of growth and change and wisdom had come over time. Everything had fallen into place, and she was finally doing exactly what she wanted with her life. When she opened the back door to let in some fresh air, even the birds sounded happy. The way the morning was going, nothing could harsh her mellow.

Except maybe her ex-boyfriend showing up at her door.

Read this book...

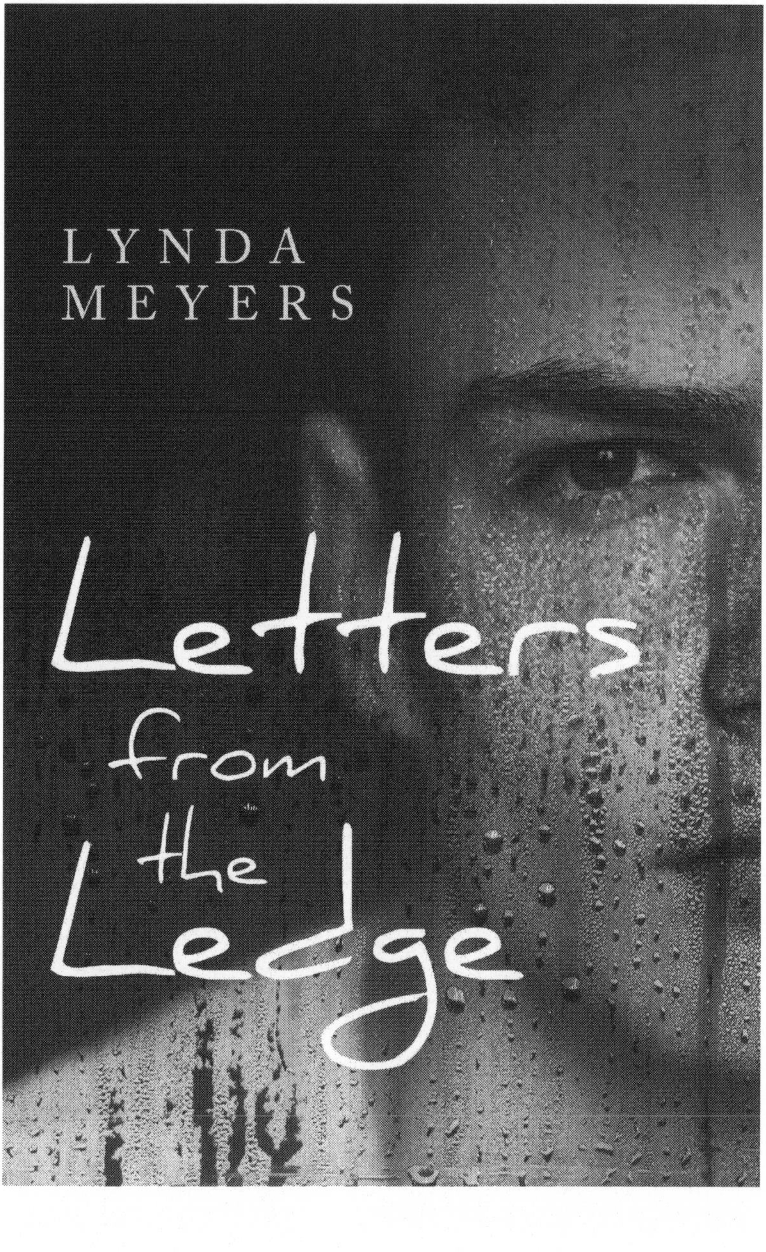
LYNDA
MEYERS
Letters
from
the
Ledge

LETTERS FROM THE LEDGE

Still reeling from the suicide of his best friend Tess, seventeen-year old
Brendan struggles to overcome addiction and identity issues. Walking the
ledge outside his Manhattan apartment has become its own sort of drug, as
he stands night after night with his arms outstretched, ready to fly away.

Sarah can see him from her window and begins journaling about a boy on a
ledge. Paige and Nate, a young couple in another building, can see both
teens from their fire escape.

None of them know the others are watching, but a strong desire for freedom
resides in each of them, and as their lives begin to intertwine, that desire
will be tested.

Three buildings. One city block. Three stories. One common thread.

Sharp, humorous, and deeply layered, this chronicle of a suicidal teen's
survival explores the reality of addiction and other tough issues, but does so
easily, through the use of multiple perspectives, intelligent dialogue and
authentic characters. Equal parts romance, contemporary drama, and
coming of age, this highly engaging and intensely beautiful novel
challenges our cultural perceptions in the battle for balance, deftly
uncovering the hopes, dreams and fears that keep us from falling, and
ultimately teach us how to fly.

Made in the USA
Middletown, DE
11 December 2019